Fat

Fatal Breach

Linda Rawlins

Riverbench Publishing LLC

Fatal Breach

by

Linda Rawlins

ISBN 13: 978-1482570779

ISBN 10: 1482570777

Discover other titles by Linda Rawlins at

www.lindarawlins.com

All quotes from the Bible are taken from the New International Version.

Riverbench Publishing, LLC
PO Box 1252
West Caldwell, NJ 07007

Dedicated to

My Mom – Joyce

For her faith and encouragement

My Husband – Joe

For his love and support – the true yin to my yang

Matthew, Krista, Ashley and Stephen

For being the most loving kids ever!

Acknowledgements

Writing a book is so much more than typing at a keyboard. It truly takes a whole team of people to help create, edit, publish and promote a book. I'd like to thank some of the special people who helped me with Fatal Breach.

Doug Whiteman – for taking time out of his busy publishing schedule to review and help with the development of this book.

Paul Marinaccio – Top Shot Season 3 – for helping with all things relating to weapons and police procedurals. All errors are my own.

Bonnie and Frank Leone – for all the information on Log Cabins and great hair.

Joyce – my greatest cheerleader – for initial editing, feedback, and reading the manuscript at least a thousand times.

Matthew Liotti – for his invaluable assistance in everything, but most of all – story development, cover art, marketing and product design.

Krista Liotti – for helping to develop my younger characters and her loving assistance at all public events.

My circle of first readers for their wonderful feedback – Carol M, Anita U, Lorraine R, Joe L, Ron and Zelda F, Sandi C and Jennifer M.

To Ray – for ethereal support.

William C Vantuono – for networking support.

Helen B – for being such a good sport.

To all the librarians and support groups – you've been so helpful on my journey.

Most importantly to my readers for being so patient and caring!

"I am the good shepherd; I know my sheep and my sheep know me"

John 10:14NIV

Happy Blessed Reading!

Chapter One

Turning the key, he locked the desk and stood up. Grabbing his suit jacket, he hesitated for just a second before putting it on, despite the overwhelming heat outside. He assured himself the flash drive was safely tucked inside his left breast pocket. It had to be, his life depended on it. The flash drive had been delivered by special messenger with instructions to use only that one. The download had taken exactly eighteen minutes. All that information copied in mere minutes. The flash drive was small, with a special design, the letters 'S' and 'F' surrounding a small crook, stamped in gold. They would know if he used a different one.

Turning off the desk monitor; he collected the rest of his papers and slipped them inside the briefcase. The Italian leather felt smooth and natural in his hand. The bag had been a gift from a former colleague who died in a most unfortunate circumstance, but he didn't want to think about that now. He needed to stay calm and finish what he'd started.

The day had been grueling and seemed to drag on forever. He couldn't stand being at work for another minute, especially now that the download was complete. Fishing his keys off the desk, he turned to leave the small office. He took one last look around, knowing he'd never be back to Burlington, VT, or his lousy job. The boss would make sure of that. Today was Friday; hopefully the company wouldn't find out about the download until Monday. Losing his job was the least of his worries. He'd be lucky if he wasn't in jail for the rest of his life, or dead. But he had no choice. Either comply or die. The message had been quite clear.

The rest of the employees of the Vandersen Group would stay until five o'clock, he was leaving now. With trembling hands, he turned to open the door, but stopped when he heard soft footsteps in the hall. It would've been a normal sound except they paused right outside, as if someone was waiting or listening. Heart pounding, he moved to the side of the file cabinet. Minutes went by. Hearing only his own pulse in his ears, he took a deep breath. He was being ridiculous. No one at work knew what he was doing or who had contacted him. His only directive was to complete the task today and return the flash drive as soon as possible. The download had just finished. It was too soon for his company to notice. Could someone else be watching him?

After a few moments, the footsteps continued down the corridor. Exhaling a deep breath, he relaxed and leaned back against the wall. Being paranoid was not going to help.

Leaving his office, he stepped into the corridor and locked the door. His pulse started to race as he made his way toward the elevator, or should he use the stairs? Both were death traps if he was being followed. Trying to be as quiet as possible, he opened the fire door to the stairs and stepped onto the concrete landing. Swiftly, he made his way down three flights, past fire hoses and equipment that was attached to the wall. Hanging on to the railing with his left hand, he turned the last landing and jumped down the remaining two steps. The sleeve of his jacket caught the edge of a metal box holding a fire extinguisher. Buttons went flying and the sleeve ripped straight up to his elbow. Catching himself, he noticed his left arm was scratched and bleeding. Why now? He dabbed at the blood while he steadied himself, readjusted the sleeve of his suit jacket and prepared to enter the lobby. As he stepped forward, he was startled by a coworker, who flung the door wide open in a rushed attempt to get to a meeting. Pausing once more to wipe sweat off his brow, he prayed for strength to finish this assignment. Adrenaline pumped through his body and his right hand felt wet where he was holding the briefcase. Finally, he opened the door and stepped into the marble lobby. His eyes darted around the area and found nothing alarming. With a smile plastered on his face, he crossed the vestibule in ten quick strides and prepared to exit the building. At that moment, Jimmy Griffin thought he had actually made it.

Chapter Two

Dr. Amy Daniels walked into the autopsy suite of the Rocky Meadow General Hospital and looked around. The first thing she noticed was the smell. Odors were so distinctive, especially the scent of antiseptic, which usually followed the pungency of death, gangrene or cancer. During her residency, she was taught to use a mentholated rub under her nose to camouflage the stench of a decomposed body. It had helped, but not enough.

In the center of the green tiled room, there was a fresh corpse lying on a hard steel table, waiting for a final exam. His skin was ashen and Amy knew it would be cold to touch. His eyes were closed as if he didn't want to see what was coming next and he was right because it wouldn't be pleasant for either of them.

Turning to the counter, Amy opened his chart and began to review the case. The recently deceased collapsed outside a local pastry shop, after clutching his chest. Someone had called 911. An ambulance and emergency help arrived almost immediately and after securing the patient, the ambulance reached Rocky Meadow General in record time.

"Are you our new medical examiner?"

Amy looked up at the sandy haired man standing in front of her. "Only until I can be replaced," she said, with a wry grin. He was in his twenties, clean cut with fresh scrubbed skin and a nice smile.

"Oh, well, hi anyway. I'm Alex Diggs, the morgue attendant."

"Nice to meet you, Alex," Amy said, with a slight nod.

"You too," he said, as he shifted his feet. "If it's okay with you, I'll start to prep the suite and you'll let me know when you're ready?"

"Thank you, that would be much appreciated," Amy said, as she looked back down at the chart. She'd been asked to fill the medical examiner's position for the next several weeks. The current pathologist had a personal emergency and was forced to leave immediately. There weren't a huge amount of replacements in the surrounding area of Rocky Meadow, VT, so Amy was chosen to cover the postmortem exams.

An experienced trauma surgeon, Amy was the only available physician who could perform the procedures necessary to check the dead. She'd worked in an autopsy suite early in her training to learn the anatomy, normal and otherwise, that she'd need to repair, throughout her surgical career. The dead patients didn't need anesthesia and they never bled out, but the anatomy was usually the same.

She didn't want to do autopsies, but was politely asked, and then practically begged, by the administration. Amy had no choice. She was under contract with the hospital and the verbiage didn't exclude working or performing exams in the morgue. Rocky Meadow rarely had a murder and the administration would remember the favor when it was time to reevaluate the progress of her clinic, which as luck would have it, was about two weeks away.

The poor guy on the table didn't know she was inexperienced with the dead. He didn't care either. According to his chart, he'd been fifty-six years old, overweight and smoked. The chest pains that grabbed him earlier in the day were the only warning he received that his heart was about to stop. He'd told himself the discomfort from eating donuts all these years was gas and not a symptom of clogged arteries. The fact that his sugar was high didn't matter either; it was a small bite or so he thought. He'd died despite robust resuscitative efforts in the emergency room.

"Are you left or right handed?" Alex asked from across the room.

"What?" Amy said, as she looked over at the morgue attendant.

"I wanted to know what side of the table you'd be working from, so I can set up properly," Alex said.

"I'm right handed. I stand at the patient's right side, alive or dead," Amy said.

"Okay, got it."

The last time Amy was in an autopsy suite was when she'd visited the dead body of the bastard who killed her sister and shot her niece. Before that, Amy's life had been sort of normal. She'd practiced as a trauma surgeon for a prestigious hospital in Boston and unknowingly saved the life of the man she later found out was responsible for her sister's death during a home invasion. Her niece had been shot in the head and was still in a coma.

The bastard died in the hospital, several days later, when he tried to escape from his police guard and failed. Amy visited the morgue to make sure he was dead, but the tragedy had already taken its toll on her ability to continue working in the hospital. After dealing with her sister's funeral and ensuring her niece was well cared for in a good neurological institute, Amy came close to having a nervous breakdown. Counseling and medications didn't help as much as she'd hoped, so she decided to move to a quiet place and sort things out. She left her position in Boston and transferred to a small community hospital in Rocky Meadow, Vermont where she could continue practicing medicine without the constant crisis of a trauma surgeon's schedule.

"Doctor, are you ready to start?" asked the morgue attendant, breaking into her thoughts.

"I need a few more minutes," Amy said. "I'm almost done with this chart."

"So, can I do the final prep?" He asked again.

"Yes, I have to go to the locker room and change. I'll be back in a few minutes." Amy put the chart down and hurried to the women's locker room to choose a new pair of surgical scrubs. After changing her clothes, she looked at herself closely in the bathroom mirror while she arranged her hair in a knot. An attractive woman in her thirties, with light brown hair, brown eyes and long legs, she was of medium build. She'd lost weight since moving to Vermont, probably from spending time outdoors, hiking and walking. Back in Boston, she would've been in the operating suite all day or down in the lounge waiting to be called. Here in Vermont, she'd found time to exercise. Even so, the stress of the last six months had left its mark with tiny lines around her face and eyes. The rewards of life experience.

Placing a clean, white coat over her new scrubs, Amy secured her locker and started walking toward the suite. Obviously, the morgue patients were not alive, but sterility had to be maintained; especially, for cases where forensic evidence needed to be collected. Nearing the table, she wondered who'd changed for her sister's post. What had they been thinking as they got ready to examine the dead? An autopsy was much easier when you weren't emotionally connected to the patient. Tragic circumstances yes, but life moves on. Amy realized that life hadn't moved on for her until she transferred to Vermont and met Father Michael Lauretta, a psychologist priest, who served as the pastor of the Rocky Meadow Retreat House and St. Francis Church. Father Michael spent the last several months helping Amy work through feelings that were suffocating her since the tragedy. She still needed to deal with the anger and guilt. Most of all, she had to allow herself to accept what happened and grieve. But Amy also wanted to know why it happened. Why her sister, her niece? Why had they been targeted? The violence was so pointless. Maybe that was the reason she'd been so fiercely protective about Willow.

Approaching the corpse, Amy noticed Alex had her gown, hood and gloves all ready. Cold air was necessary to delay the decay of the dead, and the suite was downright frigid. Donning the gown and gloves maintained sterility, but also helped Amy stay warm. She motioned to Alex she was ready, and together, they approached the table. After examining and photographing the dead body, Amy stepped back while the cadaver was rewashed. She made some notes and then repositioned herself at the side of the autopsy table. Using a scalpel, she made her first incision. Working methodically, she dissected, while dictating her findings toward a microphone suspended above the table. For the next two hours, they examined, measured, weighed and photographed various parts of his body. Using these findings, she'd generate a report and sign the death certificate.

Turning off the overhead microphone, she turned to Alex, and said, "That's it, and we're finished."

"Nice job, doctor," Alex said. "You were very thorough."

"Thanks, the findings and report will have to be reviewed before it's released, but I'm confident it'll be complete," Amy said, with a tired sigh.

"C'mon, you got it, Doc," he replied. "They say the first case is the hardest."

"Let's hope so," Amy joked, as she made her way back to the locker room, not realizing she would soon find out that wasn't true.

Chapter Three

FBI Agent Marcus Cain sat at his desk as he reviewed the information on the computer screen in front of him. He loved science and technology. As a young black man, growing up in Newark, NJ, he was captivated by computers and easily understood the software that made them work. Initially, his family couldn't afford their own, so Marcus worked after school to save money. In the interim, he spent his free time in the public library, surfing the web and gaining knowledge. Marcus studied hard and finished college with a master's degree in computer science. His teachers called him Marcus; the rest of Newark called him Cain.

Unfortunately, his brother wasn't so lucky. He got involved with a gang and one rainy day was shot and killed in a turf war on the streets of the city. Watching his mother cry for months, Marcus Cain silently vowed to help fight the war on crime, but he wanted to do it his way. Investigative work had always intrigued him, which is why he decided to become a cyber specialist for the FBI. Tracking down criminals was compelling, but using computers was fascinating.

Marcus Cain was a young, lean, well-muscled agent who loved fine clothes. He shouldered his side arm instead of using a traditional waistband holster, so he could wear nice suits. Newark, NJ was a tough town and none of his family or friends wore fancy clothes or had access to the types of technology or imaging equipment he worked with on a daily basis. He took his job seriously and loved every minute of it. He was lucky to have gotten out of a poor neighborhood and a rough life.

Several months ago, he was assigned to assist the supervisory senior resident agent at the Federal Building in Burlington, Vermont. Fourteen Vermont counties were technically overseen by the Albany, NY division, but Cain was happy to be in Burlington, as the scenery, especially Lake Champlain, was beautiful and a far cry from Newark, NJ.

His partner, Sam Oakes, was a well seasoned, gray haired, fifty-seven year old FBI agent, who learned to fight crime the old fashioned way. He'd been taught to pound the pavement and had a thick network of informants in places no one would suspect. Sam had little patience for the cyber stuff and was easily frustrated. Seeing Cain sitting in front of his computer, playing the keyboard like an instrument, he called out, "Hey, Cain, what are you doing?"

"Exactly what it looks like," Cain said. "I'm tracking something down."

"Yeah? Like what?" Sam asked, as he watched Cain's fingers fly over the equipment.

"I was analyzing computer data, from shipping manifests, for a local DEA investigation. I think I cracked their case and know where those prescription drugs are crossing over from Canada. Take a look at this," he said, as multiple images appeared on a large, glass, wall monitor. "See this boat?" He pointed to the touch screen. "I've been tracking the sailing pattern of this particular vessel over the last three months. It's always the same direction before a new drug shipment hits. Like the old saying goes, we need to see an agent about a boat. I think this route is the key to the whole damn investigation."

"Let's do it," Sam said, as he grabbed his jacket, stood up and stiffly left the desk. "I've got a guy I want to talk to about those drugs anyway."

"Right behind you," Cain said, as he logged off his computer, adjusted his suit jacket, Glock holster, and followed Sam out the door.

Chapter Four

Leaving his office building, Jimmy Griffin hit a wall of hot air, similar to a rush from a blast furnace. "Damn," he murmured, as he wiped his face with the ripped sleeve of his suit jacket. Rapidly walking down the street, he could taste sweat, as it dripped down his face. Jimmy entered Church Street and looked for the used bookstore. The brick lined street felt warm after absorbing a full day of heat from the sun.

He sat at one of the white, wire mesh tables and cursed as he replayed the memory of the day's work drama in his head. Placing his fancy briefcase on the table, he loosened his tie. He didn't know what to do next, except wait for instructions. How did he get into this mess to begin with? His mother told him not to gamble; he should've listened. Unfortunately, he didn't heed her advice and racked up some serious internet debts. That must be how they found him. At first, he was excited about the proposal. They promised to get rid of his debts and pay him a generous amount of money as well. The first thing he'd buy was a slammin new car. After that, he'd see the world. He wanted to get lost, in case they decided to track him. Jimmy hadn't picked out where he was going yet, but all the magazines were in his briefcase. The Pacific Islands looked beautiful. He was a plane ticket away from freedom and grateful he wouldn't have to work with computer nerds anymore.

It was a simple download. A bunch of sixteen digit numbers. That's how he had to think of it. Not credit card or bank accounts, just a pile of numbers. He was tired of this company anyway. Sick of the constant theatrics, sick of the cliques, and sick of the people that sucked up to the boss. Still, he'd always held his tongue. He needed his job. Jimmy kept thinking he'd make enough money to catch up and pay off the gambling debts, but that never happened. So when they called him, he agreed to do the download. Actually, he hadn't been given a choice but now that it was done, he'd finally have money to pay his markers and disappear. Why was he so anxious? He told himself to shake it off, finish the task and worry about it later.

Church Street was crowded, even for a Friday. The drink vendor was busy with a long line of thirsty patrons. Irritated families pushed strollers along, while summer students from the local colleges jostled to get into their favorite pizza place. Tourists stopped to take photos while they waited to order ice cream.

Jimmy continued to sweat. In front of him, a couple of young boys zipped down the street on bicycles. Swerving to miss a child, one of the boys sideswiped a man holding a large strawberry cooler. The cup flew out of his hand and showered Jimmy's face and chest with the syrupy, icy contents.

"Dammit," Jimmy yelled, as he jumped up from the shock of the icy liquid. The man in front of him was screaming at the boys, as they raced away on their bicycles, laughing as they looked behind them. Jimmy brushed the chunks of beverage off his jacket and wiped his face with sticky hands. The man walked toward him and stammered as he tried to apologize for something that wasn't his fault. He held up a bunch of napkins and started to wipe the front of Jimmy's jacket.

"Let me get that for you," the man said.

"No, get away, just friggin' get away from me," Jimmy shouted, as the pressure built in his head.

"Hey, it was an accident. Those stupid kids..," the man tried to explain.

"Get the hell off me," Jimmy spit again, as he brushed the man's hands off of his chest. Jimmy continued to wipe the front of his jacket with his handkerchief. He didn't know if the syrupy liquid had seeped through the material but the flash drive wasn't in a protected case. The whole damn thing could be ruined. He had to check.

Removing his jacket and tie, Jimmy opened the first two buttons of his white dress shirt. The armpits were soaked in sweat and damp material clung to his back. He couldn't believe it was so hot. The front of his shirt was wet, pink and sticky. Considering the heat, he was happy to have the jacket off. Vermont wasn't usually this uncomfortable in July, especially near the lake. The damned flash drive had better be dry.

As he fumbled with the coat, a ringing from the Italian leather briefcase made him jump. It was the throwaway phone; he knew it would be them. They had monitored the computer system and were now aware he had the download. Jimmy dropped the jacket on the table and quickly wiped his hands on his pants. Reaching into the briefcase, he grabbed the phone, clicked the green button and raised it to his ear.

"Hello?" Jimmy said nervously.

"Congratulations, Mr. Griffin," said the muted voice on the other side of the phone. "You have the flash drive?"

"Yea," Jimmy said, knowing he hadn't checked yet.

"Good, we want you to walk to the end of Church Street, toward the church. You'll see a fountain."

"Then what?"

"There'll be a man with dreadlocks wearing a bright, yellow shirt. He'll be sitting on the ground, playing guitar. His instrument case will be open for donations. Place the flash drive inside a bill and toss it into the guitar case. Then, just walk away."

"What about my money?"

"When we confirm the download, we'll send you an account number with a pin," the voice said.

"How do I know you're not gonna screw me?" Jimmy asked.

"You don't, but you have no choice. If we're satisfied, the sum of money will keep you comfortable for a long time. Use it to leave the country. Five minutes, Mr. Griffin. Oh, by the way, since you'll presumably be a rich man, I'd suggest you use a twenty dollar bill."

Jimmy grumbled. Taking a deep breath, he said, "Fine, let's do this."

"Then, I'd suggest you start walking, Mr. Griffin," the voice said, before the phone disconnected.

Dropping the phone into his pant pocket, Jimmy picked up the jacket and searched the inner left breast compartment. The flash drive wasn't there! He wanted to get this over with and move on, but now he couldn't find the friggin flash drive! Fumbling with the material, he checked again. Where was it? Becoming frantic, Jimmy went through the jacket and searched every pocket. He shook out the sleeves. Throwing it on the table, he felt the lining, in case the drive had slipped inside. Nothing! Thinking back, he was sure he'd put it in his left breast pocket. Now, he wasn't so sure. Feeling panicky and confused, he couldn't think. Maybe it fell out when he took the jacket off? The other man had used napkins, but he hadn't actually touched the material. Jimmy crouched to get a good look at the ground. He dropped to his knees, leaned forward and felt around the pavers. Combing the area, he found straws, gum, used napkins, but no drive. He turned around to look under the other tables. There was nothing except garbage. Shaking, he decided to check the jacket again. The flash drive had to be there and he missed it.

He stood up and turned toward the table but there was no jacket or briefcase in sight. Scouring the area, Jimmy realized, with a surge of anger and panic, that now, everything was gone. Someone had taken his belongings and more importantly, the flash drive. He couldn't believe it. They probably planned it this way. The guy on the phone distracted him while everything was stolen. They'd get the information and he'd be out of a job and the money. If it was them, they had everything. If not, he was in serious trouble. Either way, he was screwed.

Chapter Five

Sparkles of light danced reflectively off the waters of the Divide. The sun was hot and the river refreshing. Dr. Amy Daniels sat on a wooden bench, facing the water. Sitting beside her was Father Michael. Now good friends, they were enjoying their regular visit.

Amy continued to search for understanding and a quiet place in her soul. The bench, which had been placed in front of a river known as the Divide, was situated on the edge of property owned by the St. Francis Retreat Center. Amy would visit, as often as possible, to meditate. The powerful current always managed to center her thoughts and minimize her problems. Clearing her mind, she tried to find answers but often settled for calmness.

The day she met Michael, he'd injured himself, while running on a hiking trail. He'd limped down from the woods and asked to sit with her. It was a chance meeting that turned into an immediate friendship. Michael was a very handsome man. He was in his thirties with brilliant blue eyes that danced in a face covered by a crown of dark, wavy hair. At five foot ten, he had a trim, muscular physique that showed his love of exercise. A charming smile and relaxed demeanor helped to radiate his vitality. Unfortunately, Amy didn't realize he was a priest until they worked together to protect Willow.

Willow was a young, hospital volunteer Amy met after moving to Rocky Meadow. Abandoned at birth by her parents, Willow was raised by her wealthy grandmother, who had been murdered last year, leaving her a very rich, lonely girl, with an uncaring guardian.

Still sensitive from her own family tragedy, Amy was instantly overprotective. Willow was the same age as Amy's comatose niece. The difference was, Willow was wide awake and needed someone to touch her heart. Amy helped her reunite with her mother, Marty Davis, who was in rehab for alcoholism. Amy also kept Willow safe from her father, a murderer, who was only after money. He stalked Willow and almost killed Amy as well. Thank God, Michael was there to save her. Bonded by the near death experience, Amy and Michael became very close over the last three months. When they met, they usually laughed and enjoyed each other's company as he continued to help her deal with the harsh feelings that tormented her.

"How are things working out in the hospital?" Michael asked, in a soft-spoken voice.

"Right now, I hate it," Amy said, her face clouded, as she shifted on the bench and crossed her arms in front of her. "They're making me act as the temporary medical examiner. It's not a good place for me."

"Because it's difficult for you to confront death?" Michael asked kindly, trying to understand her feelings.

"Emotionally, yes," Amy said. "Medically, I can do a basic postmortem exam and record my findings, but I'm not an expert. They should be looking for someone else to do this job."

"Because you're not qualified or because you don't want to?" Michael prodded gently.

"I don't want to, that's why," Amy said, with exasperation. "Six months ago, I was in a Boston morgue identifying my sister's body and then the scum who killed her. Doing autopsies will be difficult for me."

"My poor friend," Michael said, with a sigh. "The autopsies may trigger bad memories, but time and faith will help you get through."

"We'll see about that," Amy said, as she shook her head.

"Perhaps, there's a reason you have to do this," Father Michael suggested. "This could be part of your journey."

"Therapy 101?" Amy asked sarcastically.

"Just a thought, friend, that's all," Michael said gently. "Even if it was, therapy is never easy. You have to work through crisis to purge your feelings. You can't ignore it and we know confrontation can be difficult."

Amy shifted and relaxed her arms. "Let's change the subject, shall we? Willow said something about going to Burlington with you?"

"Yes, that's right. I've asked her to help Father Victor, Katie and me at the soup kitchen tomorrow."

"I haven't heard you or Katie mention Burlington before. Is this something new?" Amy asked, a little too sharply.

Father Michael laughed softly. "Technically yes, but it's been in our bulletin and announcements for weeks. I know you're still a bit distracted when you come to mass."

"I get there as often as I can, but things are hectic lately," Amy said defensively. "Half the time, I'm working on the weekend. Other days, I'm just really angry. I don't know if it's at myself or God, but I'm just not in the mood to go to church."

"You need to renew your faith if you want to strengthen it," Michael suggested. "You once told me you were very spiritual, as a child."

"Yes, that was before my sister was killed."

"God didn't pull the trigger," Father Michael said.

"I know, but I want to know why he let it happen," Amy said, choking as her tears started to fall.

"You're not going to find out, friend, if you don't make your way back to him," Michael said, as he gently took her hand. "If you don't want to go to church, read your devotional at home. Just take a step, he'll lead you along."

"I'm trying," Amy said. "I'm trying for my niece and for Willow."

"Well, I'm glad you're bringing her to mass," Michael said, as he dried her face with his handkerchief. "Willow doesn't know why her parents left or her grandmother was murdered and now she has to deal with her father's death as well, but I'm pretty sure she doesn't blame God."

"How is it you always come back to this during a normal conversation?" Amy asked, as she looked at Michael.

"Occupational hazard," Michael said, with a grin and a shrug. He put his arm around Amy's shoulder and gave her a squeeze. "I'm sorry, no more therapy for today."

"Thank you," Amy said, managing a small grin.

"Want to come to Burlington with us tomorrow and help us feed the homeless?"

"I can't. I'm working in the clinic tomorrow. We've come pretty far since I convinced the hospital to give it another chance and I need to be there," Amy said apologetically.

"Well, maybe next time. The Archdiocese is asking all the local churches to help out, so we're taking turns. There'll be another opportunity," Michael said.

"Is Katie doing the cooking?" Amy asked, knowing Katie was an extraordinary cook. Katie Novak, a pleasant woman with dimples and brown curly hair, had been the resident cook and housekeeper for St. Francis and the Retreat house for several years. Father Michael offered her the position after her husband died and Katie readily agreed. She wanted the work and it allowed her to stay near her husband.

"Yes she is," Michael said, with a slight nod. "She has such a good reputation; we have to plan for double the guests."

"I'm already salivating and I'm not even going," Amy said. "Maybe this is good for Willow. Katie can teach her how to cook. I'm trying to guide her toward something that interests her instead of the volunteer work picked out by her guardian and lawyer."

"I'll mention it to Katie," Michael said. "We could always use the help around here."

"How is Father Victor?" Amy was referring to a priest that had come to St. Francis three months ago for counseling and decided to stay. "I haven't seen him in the hospital."

"He's fine, thank you. He started boxing with Tony at the gym on a regular basis."

"I'll bet they both enjoy that," Amy said, with a slight laugh. Tony Noce, an ex-cop from NYPD, was the owner of Hasco's Bar and Grill. He was also smitten with Willow's alcoholic mother and had been very instrumental in getting her off booze and into rehab.

"They do. I'm glad Father Victor stayed in Vermont. His presence has been a gift to me. He's helped tremendously in the last couple months," Father Michael said.

"How about Father Pat Doherty? How's he doing?" Amy asked, referring to an alcohol dependent priest that had been sent to Father Michael for counseling. As part of his treatment, he'd stopped drinking completely and decided to stay and help parishioners with similar problems.

"He's doing well. He hasn't gone back to drinking and I think he's really invested himself in the local meetings."

"I'm happy to hear that. By the way, I've heard from Willow's mother," Amy said.

"Oh? How is Marty?" Father Michael asked.

"She's good. She's almost done with the extended rehab and she's looking forward to coming back to Rocky Meadow. I know Father Doherty has been working with her. Marty's planning on going to local meetings for support. Maybe, the soup kitchen would be good for her too."

"We'll welcome her to the fold," Father Michael readily agreed. "We can always use another friend. Katie's been talking about opening her own soup kitchen at St. Francis. I know it's something she's wanted to do for awhile."

"I'm sure there are plenty of people who'll welcome it," Amy said thoughtfully. The economy is tough now. A lot of patients are coming to the clinic because they don't have health insurance. They've lost their jobs and can't keep up with bills. A soup kitchen would be a great help to some, but a lot of work for Katie. She's good with the community, but she'd need support. Willow would be a great help to her, if she wanted to do it."

"If they both work there, it may help her connect with her mother," Father Michael said gently. "When Marty gets back from rehab, they'll have a lot of feelings to process. Have faith. Things will work out. Why don't you just rest your mind and enjoy this beautiful Friday afternoon? After all, it's going to be a great weekend."

"We'll see," Amy said warily. "We'll see."

Chapter Six

Jimmy Griffin barely heard the throwaway phone when it started to ring. He hadn't found his things and was standing in the middle of Church Street, looking at tables.

"Where are you, Mr. Griffin?" The muted voice said, when Jimmy answered the phone. "What's going on?"

Jimmy had no reply. He didn't know if he was being set up or not.

"Remember, we're watching, Mr. Griffin. Whatever game you're playing won't end well, for you," the voice warned.

"I'm not playing any game," Jimmy replied, with an edge to his voice.

"You should have been down to the fountain by now. Where are you?"

"I'm still on Church Street, but I ah, have a little problem," Jimmy stammered nervously.

"Which is?" The voice asked sharply.

"Well, um, at the moment, I can't quite seem to find the flash drive," Jimmy said quietly.

After thirty seconds of total silence, the voice said, "I hope, for your sake, you're bluffing, Mr. Griffin."

"I know I have it somewhere," Jimmy said, in a hurry. "I need time to get my hands on it."

"I'm sure I don't have to tell you that download is worth hundreds of millions of dollars. You've interacted with several of our members. If you've lost that information, you're a very expendable loose end. Goodbye Mr. Griffin."

Jimmy yelled into the phone. "Wait! I didn't want to say, but I think someone took it from me. My coat and briefcase were stolen and I think I recognized the guy. Gimme a chance, maybe I can find him."

"Money is lost with every minute that passes, Mr. Griffin. This operation took months to set up," the angry voice said. "Anyone associated with you and the flash drive will now be a problem. We'll give you some time, but use it well; these may be your final days. Find it Mr. Griffin and find it quickly."

"I'll find it, 'cause I'm gonna find the bastard that took my things," Jimmy yelled into the phone, while taking deep breaths. "How do I get back to you?"

"Don't worry Mr. Griffin, we'll be watching you," the muted voice warned. "The download will become less useful as each day passes, but there's some vital information on it that may be worth sparing your life."

"Please," Jimmy whined. "Give me a chance."

“The game is on. We suggest you start now.” The line went dead in Jimmy’s shaking hand. His dizziness was replaced with nausea and a pounding heart. Jimmy sat for a full five minutes, taking deep breaths, before he started the most serious game of hide and seek he’d ever play.

Chapter Seven

Just after midnight, early Saturday morning, the Vandersen Group cyber-security guard picked up the private phone and called his superior.

"Yes?" A quiet voice answered the phone.

"Sorry to bother you sir, but I think we have a breach," the guard informed him.

"Are you sure?"

"The daily activity just turned over. Earlier today, there was a download that lasted eighteen minutes onto a portable plug and play storage device, most likely a flash drive."

"Where did it happen?"

"The Burlington Office, Vermont, computer ID 35028, sir. I'm trying to access the employee ID information."

"Call me immediately when you have it," the voice commanded. "We need to know what was downloaded."

"Of course," the guard hesitated. "Ah, sir?"

"Yes?"

"You should know there's a distinctive program signature," the guard said.

"What are you trying to tell me?"

"I'm not positive, but I think the download may have had something to do with Shepherd Force. You're familiar with them?"

After a long pause, the voice barked, "Of course I'm familiar with them. Find out exactly what happened and contact me immediately. If Shepherd Force is involved, I want you to call the Burlington FBI office as well. Let them know the breach happened to the Vandersen Group and get them in on this pronto."

"Yes sir," the guard replied crisply.

"One more thing," his superior barked again.

"Yes, sir?"

"Tell them I want Cain. I want FBI Agent Marcus Cain, got that? We've got a potential crisis on our hands."

"Yes, sir, of course, sir," the guard answered as the line went dead.

Chapter Eight

The ride was pleasant enough. The group from St. Francis Church was nestled in the minivan, on their way to the soup kitchen in Burlington, VT. It was a beautiful morning. Adjusting her IPod, Willow watched as the scenery passed by. She'd never been to a soup kitchen and had no idea what to expect. Katie and Father Michael asked her to join them and help out. Father Michael was driving. Father Victor, a big, tall priest, was sitting in the front passenger seat for the extra leg room. Katie was sitting in the middle row of seats with Willow beside her. Willow wasn't sure she'd like the soup kitchen, but everyone at St. Francis had been so kind to her since her father died, she'd do almost anything to help them and of course, Dr. Amy. Amy had almost been killed trying to protect her from her bastard father. Willow was glad he was dead. He never loved her. After being gone all these years, he actually came back thinking he'd get money. Grandmother's money, which was now, technically her money. Well, her trust fund anyway. Willow was sad that Amy couldn't make it today, but Amy said she'd come next time. She'd promised. In the meantime, Willow enjoyed working with Katie at the church and retreat house and with Amy at the Rocky Meadow General Clinic.

When they arrived in Burlington, they traveled down Main St. and turned right onto North Ave. After a short while, they made a left onto a small road that led toward a beautiful view of Lake Champlain. Slowing down, the van turned into a large parking lot that fronted a one story, yellow, brick building. A dumpster sat next to the building, littered with cardboard boxes and black garbage bags. Tucked next to the dumpster was a rusty shopping cart holding several pieces of dirty old luggage. Looking around, Willow watched a woman stationed at the front door of the building beckon several people inside. They were carrying trays of cooked food and boxes of baked goods, paper plates, cups, utensils as well as cases of water, juice and milk.

As Father Michael parked the van, Willow couldn't help but notice a small group of people standing near a tree. They weren't exactly dirty but didn't look well kept. Their clothes were wrinkled and ill-fitting. One woman had long, gray hair that was horribly tangled in several places. She was wearing an old, oversized, men's plaid jacket. Several members of the group were missing teeth and they kept watching the front of the building while shuffling in place.

"Who are these people?" Willow asked.

"What people, dear?" Katie responded, with a smile.

"Those people, standing near the tree." Willow said, as she pointed them out.

"Oh, they're waiting for the food to be ready," Katie responded.

"Why don't they wait inside?"

"Some do, some wait outside to smoke and some help us set up." Katie said, as Father Michael turned off the ignition and opened the doors of the van.

"That's the reason we're here, Willow," Father Michael said. "To feed all the fine people that need a little help getting back on their feet. Some have been homeless for a long time and others have just recently lost their jobs or home. When we help others, we actually bless ourselves. You can read that for yourself in the Bible. I'll show it to you when we get back. It says -

The generous will themselves be blessed, for they share their food with the poor. Proverbs 22:9 NIV

Of course, we have to make sure that Father Victor doesn't get to the food table first," Michael said, as they all laughed.

"I'm already hungry and I ate an hour ago," Father Victor complained, as he picked up several trays of food from the trunk of the van. "Do we get to eat the leftovers?"

Katie erupted with a hardy laugh. “Oh, Father Victor, your appetite has been one of my greatest joys and challenges.”

“C’mon now, I’m serious,” Father Victor said. “Can we have some lunch once everyone else is fed?”

“Don’t worry, Victor,” Father Michael responded. “I’m sure Katie would love an excuse to cook something special for you.”

“Thank God for small favors,” Father Victor said, with a large smile.

“Not so small from where I can see,” Katie murmured, with a shake of her head. “Let’s get this food inside, shall we? Willow, can you carry the bread?”

Chapter Nine

Jimmy Griffin paced near the edge of the woods, across the street from the soup kitchen. He felt grimy and needed a shave. His clothes were wrinkled, soiled and smelled. Taking a shower would seem like heaven right now. He'd been very shaken up after the last phone call and still not sure if they were playing games with him. It was possible they distracted him and took his things. Jimmy looked for his belongings through the night and walked up and down Church Street five times. He'd walked down alleys and driveways. He looked in all the dumpsters and for the first time, in many years, he prayed that God would help him find his jacket and briefcase. He was a computer nerd and believed in science, but Jimmy thought a prayer couldn't hurt. His mom always prayed to St. Anthony when she was looking for something, but he couldn't quite remember the tale. She'd told him why St. Anthony was the proper saint and it had something to do with salt. No, that wasn't right; it was a Psalter, a volume of the Book of Psalms. Jimmy started giggling to himself. Mother would smack him if he made that mistake in front of her. He remembered her saying, "St. Anthony, St Anthony, please come around. Something's been lost and can't be found." That's all he could remember, but maybe it would work.

Jimmy was tired and hungry and by early this morning, he'd been ready to collapse. Sitting in an alley to rest, he looked up and saw his jacket. It was definitely his coat, with the torn left sleeve, but it was being worn by a homeless man. Jimmy jumped up and ran after the man with the intent of punching his lights out, after he retrieved the flash drive. For a short time, Jimmy felt an actual glimmer of hope. Maybe, he'd still be alive by the end of the weekend.

Bursting out of the alley, Jimmy spotted the homeless man talking to a cop. He tried to act casual, but turned his face toward the shop windows as he passed them. He didn't know if the police were looking for him yet and he didn't want to be recognized. It hadn't been twenty four hours, but felt like an eternity.

Jimmy waited at the corner until the cop walked away. The homeless man walked across the street and Jimmy followed him, as fast as he could, without attracting attention. He wanted to wait for an inconspicuous place before he approached the guy. They wound up here, at the yellow, one story, brick building which was the local soup kitchen. Jimmy wanted the crowd in the parking lot to die down, and then he'd go find the guy. He'd bring him outside and kick the crap out of him for stealing his stuff and risking his life. Jimmy had no money, jacket or briefcase. His wallet, keys and personal cell phone were all gone. Thank God, he'd put the burn phone from Shepherd Force in his pant pocket.

Chapter Ten

Marcus Cain sat at his desk and booted up his computer. Saturday morning, 9:00 am, and already it was an active day. He picked up the phone on the third ring. “Cain.”

“They’re here,” said an officer stationed at the entrance of the Federal FBI building in Burlington, VT.

“Good, bring them in.” Cain got up from his desk and motioned to his partner, Sam Oakes. “The owners of the Vandersen Group are here.”

“Finally,” Sam said. “You take the lead since this involves computers and we both know, I don’t know much about that.”

As Cain put his suit jacket on, the door to the office opened. Two steely looking men, dressed in expensive suits, were escorted into the main room by an armed security officer. Cain walked over to the men and extended his hand. “Marcus Cain, good morning gentlemen.”

“Morning, Mr. Cain. I’m Stanley Harris and this is Steve Vandersen ,” one of the men said, while motioning to his partner. Both reached out and shook hands with Cain.

"Let's go talk inside," Cain said. "I'm sorry but we'll have to use one of the interrogation rooms for now. Things are a bit crowded these days."

"That's fine," Steve said, as they walked down a small corridor and entered a drab room with bare walls, except for a large mirror. They sat at a plain table, which was bolted to the floor, and tried to get comfortable in standard issue chairs.

Cain spoke first. "Okay, I understand you have a problem with your computers. How can the FBI be of help?"

"We're from a company called Vandersen Group," Stanley Harris said. "Perhaps you've seen our motto? Vandersen Group, providing the best resources and solutions for digital fiscal management."

"In other words, we help manage the companies that take care of your money and credit cards. We provide security, maintain identity records and monitor patterns of spending for unusual activity," Steve said. "Everything is computerized and scrutinized on a regular basis."

"Now you're entering my specialty, gentlemen," Cain said, as his interest picked up rapidly.

"We've heard of your expertise with computers," Steve said. "That's why we requested you."

"Oh really? So what happened?"

"Early this morning, I got a call from one of the cyber-security guards. Their job is to watch the monitors for irregularities in the system," Stanley said. "There was an alert that an unauthorized information download had taken place."

"Downloads are instant red flags and rarely allowed since this information is so sensitive," Steve explained. "Every computer in our company is monitored for irregularities during its daily run."

"I'm following," Cain said.

"So when the security guard called about a download, we put an instant trace on it. We've indentified the computer IP address and location."

"And the operator?" Cain asked expectantly.

"Yes. The computer is registered to an employee named Jimmy Griffin. We don't have individual offices under camera surveillance, so it's possible that someone else was at his desk," Stanley said. "The log shows that Jimmy personally signed in, but he didn't sign out. He basically just disappeared."

"Have you tried calling Mr. Griffin?" Cain asked.

"Of course," Steve answered. "We're not getting an answer on his cell phone or home phone. All we know is that an eighteen minute download was performed on his computer, presumably by him."

"You have cameras in the building?" Cain asked.

"Every hallway, elevator, stairwell and common area. The employees are made aware they're being recorded before they start working in the building."

"We'll need the footage surrounding the time of the download," Cain replied.

"We're in the process of pulling it now," Steve said.

"Your employees are bonded?" Cain asked.

"Every employee has an extensive criminal background check. They're photographed, fingerprinted and bonded before they're hired. We usually take graduates that specialize in computer programs and love crunching numbers," Stanley explained.

"How long has Mr. Griffin worked in your company?"

"Approximately three years," Steve said. "Employees are recertified on a yearly basis and we're notified of any arrests or criminal activity. Again, that's a mandatory condition of their employment with the Vandersen Group."

"What if they have problems, but don't get arrested?" Cain asked.

"I'm sorry? What do you mean?" Stanley asked.

"What if an employee has a family member that needs expensive chemotherapy or some sort of personal financial crisis? Do you monitor for personal activity?"

"As much as is allowable, without invading their privacy," Steve said. "The supervisors are hired to interact with the employees on a regular basis. We generally know when there's a family crisis that may affect their work."

"Our concern is for the employee, but naturally, we have to make sure our surveillance is pristine as well. If an employee can't handle the job, we have to make other arrangements," Stanley explained.

"Has Griffin ever have trouble at work? Maybe with coworkers?" Cain asked.

"Not that we're aware of, but we're contacting his supervisor now."

"Excellent. Let's start from the beginning. You said there was a download from Jimmy Griffin's computer that occurred when?"

"Yesterday, at approximately 2:30pm, it lasted for eighteen minutes," Stanley said.

"How much information can be obtained in an eighteen minute download from your company?"

"Huge amounts," Steve said. "Millions of dollars worth depending on whether the information is for personal use or being sold."

"In other words, an employee could potentially steal a credit card number and use it personally or download thousands of them and sell the information."

"Yes, but not just credit card numbers. We also monitor bank accounts, securities, holding companies and financial property of all kinds. That's why this type of breach can be enormous and the reason the computers are monitored so closely."

“So what’s the company protocol with this type of situation?” Cain asked.

“Every account that goes through a breached computer is immediately flagged. We start double checking all transactions. We contact the banks and it’s up to them what they do with their clients. We can’t shut anything down since we only monitor the activity. Besides, we represent half the banks in the nation. A shutdown would cause sheer pandemonium.”

“So the stolen information could be valuable weeks later?”

“Absolutely, depending on the banks’ policy in this circumstance. Usually, they notify their customers to change passwords and watch for unusual activity. The credit card companies handle it a little differently. The customers that don’t have computers are usually notified by phone or mail. Their purchases are held or questioned but the customer doesn’t know why until they get a notice in the mail or told to call their financial institution,” Steve explained.

“That makes sense,” Cain said.

“Of course, our internal monitors start securing information instantaneously as to the details of the breach. All this, while simultaneously making contact with the FBI,” Steve explained.

"We'll need to see that information, immediately gentlemen, as well as the employee files on Jimmy Griffin," Cain said, while writing his thoughts in his notebook. "We'll put out an immediate BOLO. He won't be able to access any airports without being picked up. What about his family?"

"According to his file, he doesn't have any family," Stanley said. "There's no mention of a wife or children. I don't think his parents are alive either. For all we know, he may have been working with them all along."

"What do you mean?" Cain's partner, Sam asked.

"Well, besides monitoring the breach itself, we're able to pick up specialized computer language in our system," Steve explained.

"Program signatures?" Cain asked, while nodding his head and keeping his facial expression blank. "I'm familiar with them. What aren't you telling me?"

"Well, we're not sure, but we think Jimmy may have been working with Shepherd Force."

Marcus Cain's interest rose immediately. "Are you serious?"

"As a heart attack," Steve said, with a nod of his head.

After a few seconds watching Steve's face, Cain turned to Sam and said, "We need to get some data warrants and call the Director. We may have a major cyber attack on our hands."

Chapter Eleven

Amy stretched her arms above her head, took a deep breath and leaned back. She was sitting in a rolling chair at the front desk of the clinic. They had been busy this morning. Amy was glad to see an increased amount of patients coming in for services. Evidently, the word was spreading the clinic had improved and was available to patients with little insurance and low income. The Rocky Meadow Hospital Administration had agreed to keep the clinic open, despite lack of funds. They'd given her three months to prove the hospital would save money by eliminating routine care in the emergency room. Amy used a few ideas from her former hospital in Boston and so far, they seemed to be working. But now, the clinic was up for review, so she couldn't refuse their request to stand in as the medical examiner.

"Hey, no breaks here. Get back to work," Dr. Lou Applebaum teased, as he walked up to the desk. Amy stood up and grinned at Lou. "What's an important cardiologist like you doing in the clinic?" Amy and Lou Applebaum had become good friends several months ago when she helped to keep his patient, Ben Lawrence, from being murdered by Willow's father.

"I wanted to see what this clinic looked like," Lou said.

"I'm still waiting for you to offer cardiology services here, one day a month," Amy countered. "I'll show you whatever room you want to see. Technically speaking, it's not that exciting, but business does seem to be picking up."

"I noticed. The only doc I see in the ER lately is Ernie. As a matter of fact, I told him I was coming to visit you. He sent a message and said you'd understand. Helen is back?"

"Really, with what?" Amy asked.

"That's all he said," Lou answered. "Is this the infamous Helen I hear about all the time?"

"The one and only, you know like hell on wheels, Helen."

"Well, Ernie thought you might want to visit her when you have a break," Lou said, while leaning forward and placing his hands on the counter. "By the way, I'm still waiting for that rain check for dinner."

Amy immediately blushed. "I, ah, don't know my schedule."

"Well, why don't we set a date and schedule life around that?" Lou asked, with a mischievous smile. "We're both supposed to go to the regional medical staff meeting next Thursday night. You'll have to report, especially since you're the medical examiner now. I know a great little restaurant in Diamond Point, NY. It's not that far of a drive, besides it would be nice to get away from the hospital for awhile." Lou wanted to get to know Amy better since the day she'd started working at Rocky Meadow General. Finding a killer had interrupted their first attempt at socializing. "How about it? Thursday night? We'll go to the meeting and then run over to NY for dinner."

"That sounds nice," Amy said, a bit flustered. She couldn't believe she was nervous. She was a trauma surgeon who hadn't been on a date since medical school. Who had time?

"Great," Lou said, with a big smile. "I'll call and make a reservation. It's a gorgeous place, right on Lake George. You'll love it."

"Sounds beautiful," Amy said, wishing she could call her sister to tell her.

"It is, believe me. I'll finish rounds early so we can leave around 4:00 pm. I'll call you Wednesday night for your address and by the way, dress is nice casual."

"Okay, great, see you then," Amy said, with a silly grin and high pitched voice. She couldn't feel any more awkward. How chic was that?

"Looking forward to it. Bye Amy," Lou said, with a wink, as he reached over the desk and gently placed his hand over hers.

"Bye," Amy squeaked out, as her stomach broke into a fit of flutters.

Chapter Twelve

Willow walked into the brick building holding a paper bag full of warm loaves of bread. The smell of onions, chicken and rosemary made her mouth water instantly. For once, she was in agreement with Father Victor. She hoped they got to eat the leftovers. Looking around the room, she noticed many different tables set up. Some were scarred, some were new, but all were covered with bright tablecloths and had small decorations in the center. She followed Katie into the kitchen and placed the bread on the counter. There were volunteers slicing meat, mashing potatoes and taking heated aluminum pans out of the oven. Willow spied the largest pot of chicken soup she'd ever seen, bubbling on the corner of the stove.

"Katie," one of the women cried out as she gave Katie a large hug. "I can't believe you're finally here. To what do we owe this honor?"

"Oh go on, Sue," Katie brushed off the compliment. "Father Michael got a call from the archdiocese to come help and here we are."

"Our guests are very lucky today," Sue said. "We'd have another two-hundred mouths to feed if they knew you were doing the cooking."

"Don't be ridiculous," Katie said, with a laugh. Looking at Father Victor, she said, "You can put that box on the table." Katie beamed as she began to pull trays of food from the box.

"From the looks of your priest friend, I think you're use to cooking larger portions." They both laughed like schoolgirls while Katie picked up her serving spoons. After a second, Sue turned to Willow and said "So, who do we have here?"

"This is Willow," Katie said, as she placed her hand on Willow's arm. "She helps us at the retreat house and was kind enough to volunteer for the soup kitchen today."

"That's wonderful," Sue said. "Do you like to cook?"

"I don't really know how," Willow said defensively.

"Now, you leave her be," Katie said, as she came to her rescue. "She's come a long way and does a great job in the kitchen. She's learning. Someday, she'll be a wonderful cook."

"Maybe," Willow said, shrugging her shoulders and looking clearly uncomfortable. "What do you want me to do now?"

Katie handed her a stack of small plates. "Why don't you start with the salad, dear? Use these salad tongs and put a small portion of greens on each one of these plates. You can set up on that long table in the corner and spread the plates out when you're done. When our guests line up for food, they can take a salad plate and move on to the next station."

"Okay, I can do that." Placing her IPod in her pocket, she balanced the plates, tongs, and a large bowl of salad as she made her way to the table.

"She seems like a sweet girl," Sue whispered to Katie. "What's the story?"

"Oh the poor dear, her parents aren't around, so we're doing the best we can to help her have a family," Katie said, with a sad smile on her face. "But enough of that, let's get to work."

Katie turned and bumped into Father Michael as he carried another set of trays from the car. "Katie, I think I got everything you wanted, but you'd better check," Father Michael said, as he placed the pans on the counter.

"I'll look it over to be sure. Father, I'd like to introduce you to Sue Callahan. She's been one of the driving forces behind this soup kitchen for years."

"Nice to meet you, Sue," Father Michael said, as he shook hands with her. "I'm sure you're one of the beloved shepherds in our world today."

"Well, I don't know about that," Sue said. "But I do like to watch over the flock that visits my soup kitchen."

"And I'm sure they're all very hungry, so let's get this food out there," Katie said, as she shooed everyone back to work.

"Did you bring any of your famous apple pie?" Sue asked, looking over the desserts.

"Of course I did. Eight of them to be exact, but I don't see them here," Katie said, as she looked around the kitchen counters. "Perhaps, they're still in the van." Seeing Father Victor walk by, she asked him to go to the car and check. Returning to the dessert table, Katie said to Sue, "I put them all in a box and watched as Father Victor put them in the car. He'll find them. You watch, he'll bring them in."

Sue smiled. "You better count them when they get here to make sure he didn't eat one on the way."

Still laughing like two school girls, they continued to prepare for the meal.

Chapter Thirteen

Jimmy watched the crowd of people filter into the brick building. The clang of a bell had announced the food was ready and everyone lined up to go inside and eat. Clearly, they all knew one another and were use to the ritual. Jimmy watched the man wearing his jacket stand in line. He seemed to know everyone and smiled when he spoke with his friends or shook their hands. Once everyone was inside, Jimmy planned on going to the door and looking around. He'd make sure there was no way for the homeless guy to sneak out back. As soon as he could, he'd get the jacket and hopefully this nightmare would be over. He didn't want to attract attention or the police. What he did want was to find a bathroom. After one night on the street, Jimmy was tired of peeing on trees and sleeping on the ground. He couldn't imagine how the homeless lived like this all the time, especially in the winter. Now dirty, sweaty, and hungry, his stomach was growling as he smelled the divine aroma of the food.

As he watched the soup kitchen, the back of Jimmy's head began to tingle. Moving his shoulders, he shrugged when he felt the hairs on the back of his neck stand on end. Jimmy looked around but didn't see anyone or anything out of place. Still, he was unnerved. His mother used to say that someone was walking over her grave when that happened. Except, he wasn't dead at the moment and he hoped he wouldn't be anytime soon. Jimmy sensed, rather than saw, the man standing in the woods behind him, holding the Beretta U22 Neos. Jimmy was told he'd be watched but didn't know they'd sent a professional "closer" to follow him with one set of instructions. Get the flash drive, no loose ends. They didn't care whether it was Jimmy or the people he associated with, they wanted the flash drive as soon as possible. Feeling uneasy, Jimmy crossed the street to get to the soup kitchen.

Chapter Fourteen

Sam looked at Cain and said, “Explain this to me. What’s Shepherd Force?”

“A ghost organization,” Cain said.

“What?”

“It’s a ghost organization. Shepherd Force is a name used by an internet activist group that’s been the cause of major computer crimes and crashes for the last two years. No one’s been able to touch them.” Cain said, as he shook his head.

“How are we defining an internet activist group?” Sam asked.

Steve Vandersen answered his question. “As an unknown group of computer specialists that perform cyber attacks, cyber theft or cybercrimes, under the guise of protecting the average citizen.”

“A computer vigilante group?” Sam said.

“Exactly,” Cain said, with a nod. “Now you’re getting it. These specialists only hack computers of organizations or even countries that supposedly harm the rights of the average citizen. They call themselves, 'hactivists' and they use computers or computer networks to promote political gain or as a means of protest, but there are a lot of copycats that do the same thing for criminal reasons.

Sam turned to Steve, "So then, who did you piss off?"

As Steve shrugged, Cain said to Sam, "Actually, they must respect the Vandersen Group. All they did was get a download of information. If they really thought they were compromising citizen's rights, they would've hacked their company and crashed their systems. With a company like Vandersen, that would've caused some serious panic."

"As global as we are, we're still small potatoes compared to the sophistication of Shepherd Force," Stanley said. "We're just the fish food, so to speak."

"Hey fellas," Sam said. "I must be getting old because I don't fully understand what the hell you're talking about."

"In other words, Shepherd Force only attacks corporations or countries with large computer systems that are somehow controlling human rights," Sam patiently explained. "But they still need to be financed. Assuming it's Shepherd Force, they'll get their operating money from credit cards or bank accounts in order to cause huge headaches for the corporate or financial world. Potentially, everyone makes a small donation for the greater good, unwillingly of course."

"For instance?" Sam asked.

"Well, as an example," Cain answered, "let's suppose they felt a pharmaceutical company was charging astronomical amounts of money for a particular drug. Shepherd Force may take over their computer systems for a day. The usual shipments would go out to the various hospitals and patients to avoid any delay in healthcare, but all the invoices would be changed to read a zero balance."

"I see," Sam said, as he nodded his head.

"Or perhaps a certain credit card company has too high of an interest rate," Steve explained. "Shepherd Force would change the interest rates for a day. Just one day, would cost the credit card company a ton of money in lost revenue."

"So how does Vandersen Group play into this?" Sam asked.

"Well, every organization needs funds to operate," Stanley said. "By hacking into our computers, they have access to half the national banks and finance organizations. With just eighteen minutes of downloads, they could access enough accounts to siphon off the funds they need to continue their operation for a long time. Most of the finance companies have policies that don't hold the customer responsible, so the parent company not only takes the loss, but actually winds up funding Shepherd Force for their next target."

"That's actually pretty ingenious," Sam said, mostly to himself.

"That's why we're fish food for the next big project," Steve said. "In their own defense, they feel they're helping the average citizen by perpetuating crimes against larger organizations, to expose them if nothing else. They're shepherding their flock, get it?"

"Now, I get it," Sam said. "A cyber vigilante group, interesting."

"Yes, we actually call it an internet activist group," Cain pointed out, "but they're no different than anyone else in this world. I know they want to help people on one level, but when you resort to an illegal method, you're just as guilty as the criminals. It's better to let the proper authorities take care of things."

"These groups usually feel the proper channels are too corrupt or slow," Steve explained.

"Not to mention the problems you have if there are multiple activist groups with different goals in mind," Cain said, with a nod. "Or one group that decides to take over the whole computer world for their own purpose. Seriously, this kind of activity can lead to major international problems."

"Okay," Sam asked, "so what's this program signature stuff all about?"

"Computer code is distinguishable. Every computer programmer has their own touch," Steve said. "When the information was downloaded to the flash drive, we think it left a signature in our system that can identify the original programmer. If we can trace it, we can confirm Shepherd Force is behind this. If we recover the flash drive, we might be able to locate them. Of course, that's assuming Shepherd Force hasn't gotten hold of it already."

"Maybe Griffin hasn't handed it off yet," Vandersen said. "We need to get out there and find him."

"Or Griffin could be lying dead in the basement of your building and Shepherd Force is long gone," Cain said. "We need to confirm he actually left the building, so pull all the video you have and start checking. Meanwhile, let's get some officers over there to do a visual search."

"Wow," Sam said. "What happened to the old days when you chased a guy out of a bank and down the alley? It's a good thing I'm close to retirement." Sam shook his head as the rest of the men at the table chuckled.

"Yes, Sam, it's a whole new digital world out there," Cain said. "Let's go to work!"

Chapter Fifteen

Jimmy reached the parking lot and walked up to the large window at the front of the yellow, brick building. He glanced inside, but years of grime made it hard to see. Leaning forward, he placed his hands to the side of his face and rested his forehead against the window. He watched as hungry people politely lined up and took a tray. Starting at the front table, they helped themselves to salad and made their way down the line to pick up bowls of soup, as well as plates containing pasta, chicken, mashed potatoes and ham. There were fruits, vegetables and buttered bread. A side table held large coffee urns with stacks of paper cups and a third urn with hot water. Nearby were packets of sugar, creamer and tea bags. Plates with cake, pie and cookies were there to finish the meal.

Looking over the crowd, Jimmy saw the homeless man, wearing his jacket, standing in the middle of the line, helping himself to a nice meal. Jimmy's stomach growled and reminded him he hadn't had anything to eat or drink in the last twenty four hours. He'd been too nervous to eat yesterday and hadn't been able to buy anything since his jacket, wallet, money and keys were stolen.

"Don't be shy son, just go on in and grab a plate," Father Victor's voice boomed in Jimmy's ear. "And while you're at it, maybe you can hold that door open for me."

Startled, Jimmy visibly jumped about a foot off the ground and almost knocked the boxes containing the eight apple pies out of Father Victor's hands. Shaking, he turned around to see the priest had walked up to the front door and was standing directly behind him. Jimmy tried to speak but his dry throat prevented any words from coming out as he stared wide-eyed at the priest. He was so intent on the food and indoor activity; he'd been completely oblivious to his surroundings. Thank God, the priest wasn't part of Shepherd Force.

"Sorry, didn't mean to scare you," Father Victor said, with a smile. "I was hoping you'd open that door for me. You look like you could use a bit of food as well. It's free, no strings attached. Just walk right in there and get on line." Shifting his weight, Victor rebalanced the two boxes in his hands as he watched Jimmy turn and fumble with the door handle. He held the door wide open as Father Victor crossed the threshold and went inside the building. Jimmy quickly followed him, thinking he'd be safer inside and realizing he was indeed very hungry, tired and weak.

"Thanks my friend, now you go get in line," Father Victor said, as he continued walking toward the kitchen with the pies. "You've got one of the best cooks in the state out here today; you'd best take advantage of it."

Taking a deep breath, Jimmy glanced around the room and spotted his jacket. The homeless man had filled his plate and chosen a table near the side door. As he sat and prepared to eat, another priest stopped to speak with him. Jimmy realized he'd have to wait a few minutes before he could get the guy alone and he was hungry. Not wanting to be obvious to anyone else, Jimmy looked around and found the bathroom. He used the facilities, washed his hands and face, and joined the food line.

Slowly Jimmy inched forward. He started by collecting a tray. Shifting his weight, he added plastic utensils and napkins. Continuing to watch the man in his jacket, he moved forward and picked up a small plate of salad. "What can I get you dear?" Katie asked him, when he reached the main serving table. Standing with serving spoons at the ready, she stood smiling at him.

"What?" Jimmy asked, turning his head back toward the food.

"Just tell me what you'd like and I'll make a nice plate for you," Katie explained. "You can have some of everything if you want, just say the word."

"Oh, ah, well I guess I'll have the chicken," Jimmy said, in a flustered tone.

"Fine, how about a nice piece of ham to go with it?"

"Sure," Jimmy said, nervously balancing his tray.

"You like potatoes?" Katie asked, while she filled a large plate with food. "Will you be wantin' gravy on all this?"

"Yeah, that would be good," Jimmy answered, while looking back toward the homeless man.

"Looking for a friend, dear?" Katie asked him, while she swiftly filled the plate with food and placed it on his tray.

Turning back to Katie, he said, "I thought I saw someone I knew, but I'm wrong."

"Well, I'm sorry to hear that. You'd best be on your way so you can eat while the food is warm. There's a basket of bread at the end of the table. Make sure you get a drink, too."

"Thanks, I appreciate it," Jimmy said, as he continued on. He couldn't help feeling nervous. He was tired and hungry and would've liked nothing more than to have a good meal and a long nap. He couldn't risk losing sight of the guy in his jacket. Balancing his tray at the edge of the beverage table, he gladly poured himself a hot, steaming cup of coffee and added several packets of sugar. That should wake him up. He placed the coffee on the tray and made his way toward the side door. Spying an open seat at the table right next to his target, Jimmy sat down and greedily started eating his food and drinking his coffee. The food tasted better than anything he'd recently ordered in a restaurant. Jimmy chuckled to himself. Yesterday, he was reading brochures of all the exotic places he planned to visit with his ill-gotten money. Today, he was eating in a soup kitchen and glad to be alive.

Chapter Sixteen

Amy stared at the clinic computer. Fingers moving over the keyboard, she added a few more words to her electronic chart notes. Satisfied she'd answered all the mandatory questions, she hit save and waited. If all the "fields" were answered correctly, she'd be rewarded with a message that said her submission was successful. Had she left a required line blank, she'd receive a message telling her more input was needed. Switching from paper charts to electronic medical records was frustrating and time consuming. The hospital had placed new computers in every room of the building over the past several months, trained the physicians and staff to use them and started the mandatory conversion from paper to digital records. The theory was all records would be more accessible to personnel. Treatment would be streamlined and fewer mistakes would be made as all health professionals, including pharmacy technicians, would be able to keep track of daily notes, testing, drugs ordered and any reactions or progress that occurred. For privacy sake, sensitive information was only available with a special password. Unfortunately, it took time to learn the software, especially when boiler plate computer programs required screen after screen of specific data, as well as the confidential code of the medical license identifying the doctor filling out the information. To add insult to injury, the computer program started a timer from the second the program was opened to the time the program was complete or closed. Once a note was started, it had to be completed. There were times when all the data wasn't available or there were too many patients to spend twenty minutes trying to figure out how to work the confusing software. Notes were being scribbled on paper and then transferred to the computer at the end of the work shift which added several hours to an already busy day. Of course, things were more complicated when the system was down or the programs weren't working properly.

Pushing her chair away from the counter, Amy got up and found her purse. "Thank goodness, I'm finally finished. I'm going over to the ER to see a patient and then home to relax for the rest of the weekend," Amy said to Kathy, as she ran her fingers through her hair. "My charting is all done, and I put the lab requests in through the computer. Just make sure the blood vials get picked up by the lab, please?"

Kathy smiled up at Amy from where she was completing her nursing notes on another computer. "You got it doc. Listen, thanks for all you've done for this clinic. If you hadn't helped us three months ago, it would've been closed by now. Since we've gotten some support, it's really started to pick up and I know there are a lot of happy patients out there."

"No problem Kathy, I'm glad to see people get the help they need. Being open on Saturday mornings helps too, since patients don't have to take off from work. We finish early enough to enjoy most of the weekend. The ER flow is better and we've actually managed to break even on our supplies," Amy said. "By the way, could you put together some information I can take to administration when I go for that meeting next week. Not only do I want to show the clinic is growing and saving resources for the hospital, I'd love to add some specialty clinics."

"Anything particular in mind?" Kathy asked, with a sly look on her face.

"If I can get some volunteers, I'd start with the basics. Cardiology, Endocrine for diabetics, Gynecology and then grow from there. I'd get a specialist to see patients one day a month and we'd charge them on a sliding scale. Something like that, I'll have to think about it before the meeting," Amy said. "We've made a good start."

"Well, you go have yourself a good weekend," Kathy said, as she rested her hands on her computer keyboard. "I'll talk to you Monday."

“Thanks Kathy, take care,” Amy said, as she threw her purse on her shoulder and walked away from the desk. Amy left the clinic through the back door which opened into the main hall of the hospital. Turning to the left, she made her way to the ER to check on her patient, Helen.

Chapter Seventeen

"Can I get you more coffee?" Willow asked, as Jimmy looked up from his plate. "Would you like me to bring you some pie?"

"No, no thanks," Jimmy said, as he finished the food on his tray. He didn't want to have anything else in case he had to leave.

"Okay, have it your way," Willow said, as she walked away.

Jimmy glanced back at the homeless guy sitting near him. He'd finished his dinner and then some apple pie. He was leaning back in his chair and looked very sated at the moment. Jimmy tried to take the opportunity to talk to him, when Father Michael walked up holding a black plastic garbage bag.

"Hey, can I take your plates?" Father Michael asked, as he first offered the bag toward the homeless guy. "How about you, Ray? You done eating for today?"

"That I am, but I wish I could fit more. That's some of the best damn food I've had in a long time," Ray said, rubbing his stomach. Father Michael waited as Ray collected his plates, napkins, cups and utensils and threw them in the bag.

"You can leave the tray, we'll have someone go round and pick them up."

"Thanks," Ray said, as he nodded his head.

"Why don't you help yourself to another cup of coffee?" Father Michael offered.

Jimmy watched the exchange between the two men. Now, he knew the homeless guy's name was Ray. He looked tired; his jeans were faded and dirty. His hair was uncombed, but clean and he'd taken the time to wash his face. Ray actually preened as he straightened the lapels of his newfound suit jacket, which obviously didn't match the plaid shirt he wore underneath. Jimmy's stomach turned as he watched Ray fumble in the inner pocket of the jacket. After a few seconds, the only thing Ray pulled out was an old, partially bent, used cigarette. It had probably been smoked halfway down by someone else and thrown to the ground. Ray must have picked it up and saved it for after dinner.

Standing up, Ray headed for the side door of the building. On his way out, he bent and lit the cigarette on one of the flames keeping an empty chafing dish warm. Puffing enough to make sure the cigarette was lit, he opened the side door and left. Jimmy jumped up instantly, almost knocking his tray to the ground and followed Ray out the side door. Finally, he had his chance.

Outside the door, Jimmy noticed a path that led toward Lake Champlain. The ground was covered with pine needles, small rocks and broken sticks. Had he not been chasing Ray, he would've enjoyed this beautiful day. It was warm, the lake sparkled and a cool breeze spread the scent of refreshing pine. Jimmy spotted Ray, standing near a large rock approximately five feet down the path, staring at the lake. Ray took a puff on his cigarette and slowly blew out smoke rings over his head. Jimmy sauntered up to him and said, "Hey, great day isn't it?"

Jumping at the unexpected voice, Ray turned around. "Sure, it's beautiful."

"Where did you get that jacket?" Jimmy asked, with a mean look on his face.

"Hey calm down, Buddy. I found it," Ray said nervously.

"You expect me to believe that?" Jimmy asked.

"You can believe whatever you want," Ray said, with an edge. "What's it to ya, anyway? It's mine, get lost."

"As of yesterday, it was mine and I want it back," Jimmy hissed through his teeth.

"Whoa, little keyed up, aren't ya? It's a nice jacket, but it's ripped. You're probably not gonna wear it again."

"I had all my stuff with that jacket," Jimmy said, not wanting to specifically say flash drive. "You must be the bastard that stole my briefcase, my phone, and my keys. I don't want any trouble; just give me my stuff back."

"Hey, hold on there. The only thing I found was this jacket next to the dumpster last night," Ray said, as he gestured with his hand, the cigarette stuck between the first two fingers. "I don't know nothing about anything else."

"Listen, I had something important in there. Give me the jacket," Jimmy said in a testy voice. "I might even give it back, but I have to check for something." He was hoping Ray hadn't searched the pockets.

"Alright jerk face, wait a minute," Ray yelled back. He flicked the small cigarette butt to the ground and rubbed it out with his shoe. As Ray started taking off the jacket, he looked up to see Father Michael walking toward them.

"So what's going on here?" Father Michael asked, with a soft soothing voice. "I was taking the garbage out and could hear the two of you from the top of the path."

"This guy has my jacket and I want it back," Jimmy said through clenched teeth, as he started to circle round Ray.

"Ray, is that true?" Father Michael asked nicely, stepping closer to Jimmy to make sure he didn't throw a punch at Ray.

"I found this jacket near a dumpster on Church Street last night," Ray explained. "It was rolled into a ball on the ground. I was chilly, so I took it. I figured someone threw it out cause the sleeve is all ripped. See?" Ray said, as he held up his arm to show Father Michael the torn sleeve.

"Chilly? In this freaking heat? Yesterday, I was on Church Street and someone stole my stuff. I need that jacket; I have something important in it. Just give it to me, please," Jimmy said.

"Okay boys," Father Michael said, while holding his hands up in front of the two of them. Turning to Jimmy, he said, "I'm sure Ray wouldn't mind giving you the jacket. If your things aren't there, he can show us where he found it so we can go take a further look. Now, just calm down."

Ray, standing with his back toward the building, took off the jacket and threw it at Jimmy. "Here take your stupid jacket, piece of garbage."

Jimmy lunged at the jacket and started going through the inner pockets but didn't find the flash drive. He put the jacket on; just to make sure he examined the inner pocket exactly as it was when he wore it. "It's not here," Jimmy said, his breath becoming labored as anxiety grew in his gut. He looked at Ray, "It's not here. Did you take it?"

"Take what? Buddy, I don't know what the hell you're talking about, you..," Ray started to say, but was cut off mid-sentence. He stared wide-eyed for a second and then, as if in slow-motion, he fell straight forward while blood trickled from his mouth. When his face hit the ground, Father Michael and Jimmy noticed the bloody hole in the back of his head. They were frozen for a few seconds, disbelief written over their faces. Seconds later, they heard a muted gunshot and a branch split in two near Jimmy's head.

"Holy crap, we're gonna die," Jimmy screamed, as his chest started heaving.

Chapter Eighteen

Father Michael stared at the dead body of Ray Fuller for a mere millisecond before he grabbed Jimmy's arm and screamed, "Run." He pulled him toward the lake. Together, they ran down the wooded path. More gunshots sounded behind them. Branches continued to fly as they tore down the path, tripping on occasional roots and dead leaves. Dirt and small rocks went flying each time their feet hit the soft ground. With ragged breaths, they reached the edge of Lake Champlain and stopped for a second on a small cliff. In the distance, sirens wailed as a flock of birds flew up in the air around them.

"What the hell do we do now?" Jimmy yelled.

Looking down, Father Michael saw a dock next to a boat house at the base of the cliff. The water splashed up against the rocks and he hoped it was deep enough. Father Michael crossed himself, touched his closed hand to his lips for a kiss and then said, "We jump."

"What?"

Pushing Jimmy to the edge, Father Michael yelled out,

Though he may stumble, he will not fall, for the Lord upholds him with his hand. Psalm 37:24 NIV

With his arm around Jimmy's waist, Michael hurtled them both off the cliff and into the lake.

Both men plunged into the depths of the water and the cold temperature was shocking at first. Bubbles rose to the surface as their bodies thrust downward. Time seemed to crawl as they slowly floated back up. Bullets sliced through the water in slow motion. Jimmy stared at him wide-eyed with cheeks puffed out. His hair, floating above him, looked like a windblown field of tall grass. Only Michael noticed the dark cloud surrounding Jimmy's body. Lungs burning, their heads broke above the water. Michael quickly pulled Jimmy under the dock. Gasping for air, they pressed themselves as close to the boathouse wall as possible.

"Crap," Jimmy said, while spraying water from his mouth and trying to catch his breath. All was unearthly quiet except for the lapping of cold water against the structure. The dock creaked as it moved with the small waves. Father Michael took deep breaths as he floated in the water and strained to hear noise from above. Looking down, Jimmy saw the blood oozing from his left upper chest, staining the wet fabric of his beloved jacket. Panic seared up in his throat as he said, "I've been shot." Father Michael looked toward him and watched helplessly, as Jimmy's face turned ghostly white and his limp body disappeared under the surface.

Chapter Nineteen

Walking into the emergency room, Amy headed toward the central desk and spied Ernie clicking away at the computer. “Hi Ernie,” she said, drawing his attention as she approached the counter.

Looking up from the keyboard, he said, “Hi Amy, you got my message?”

“Loud and clear, thank you,” Amy said, turning red.

“Well, I was going to page you, but Lou was looking for an excuse to see you anyway.”

“Ernie, really,” Amy said, as she continued to flush.

“I’m not kidding. I barely ever saw the guy before you started working here. Now he’s in the ER all the time, just checking to see who’s here,” Ernie said. “The person that’s not here is you, so I sent him over to the clinic. He can visit you over there now,” Ernie said, with a smile.

“I don’t know him that well,” Amy said, while making a face.

"Well, he obviously wants to get to know you," Ernie replied, with a smirk. "Talk to him, make his day."

"Alright, enough of that already. So what's up with Helen?" Amy asked.

"Ah yes, your good friend Helen is back," Ernie said, picking up her chart.

"Is she okay?" Amy asked.

"Yea, she'll be okay. Just some cuts and bruises. At the tender age of ninety-one, she's very lucky. She apparently fell while trying to feed the birds." Ernie started laughing as he gave her his notes. "She'll tell you all about it. Room two," he said, as he held up two fingers.

"Okay, you don't have to make it sound so creepy," Amy laughed. "I'll go see her." Amy started reading the ER notes as she made her way to the exam room. The report probably wasn't in the system and there wasn't a full paper chart as the ER was switching to digital records as well. All she had were some scribbled notes and Amy couldn't read them any better than anyone else.

Reaching the exam room, she knocked on the door and peeked inside. "Hello? Anyone in there? It's Dr. Amy," she said, as she walked into the exam room. Amy spied Helen in the ER bed, the sheet pulled up to her chest. A head of blue-white hair rested on the hospital pillow. She had a big smile on her face, as if Amy had just arrived to have high tea with her.

There was a nasty bruise on Helen's nose and a cut over her left eyebrow, but her grin was ear to ear.

"Hello, how are you?" Helen asked, with a fragile voice.

"I'm fine, Helen. The question is how are you?" Amy asked, as she pointedly looked at her nose. "You've got quite a bruise there. Do you want to tell me about it?"

"Well, I was trying to feed the birds and I fell over," Helen said, with a laugh that shook her shoulders.

"I'm so sorry to hear that. Did you pass out?" Amy asked, with a concerned voice.

"No, not really," Helen answered her.

"Did you get dizzy?"

"No, I just fell over," Helen said.

"Maybe you tripped?" Amy tried again to understand what had happened.

"Nooo," Helen said, as she drew out the word.

"Helen, I'm sorry to keep asking questions, but I'm trying to picture exactly what happened so I know what tests to order. When a person falls for no reason, there could be a medical problem."

"Oh, there was a reason, honey," Helen said, with an impish look on her face. "The stool slipped."

"The stool? I thought you were standing in the backyard feeding your birds. I'm guessing there's more to this story?"

"Why, yes you could say that. I'll tell you, but you'll say I've been a naughty girl," Helen said, in her own defense.

"Oh boy, you had your clothes on this time, right?" Amy asked, referring to an incident in the spring when Helen ran out of her house naked to get rid of a mouse she'd found in her underwear drawer. Her elderly neighbor, Harold, had been standing there, trimming the shrubs, which scared Helen. Trying to run back inside, she tripped over a bra and broke her ankle. Both Helen and Harold were brought to the emergency room for evaluation.

"Of course I did," Helen said, with a grin. "But ever since I broke my ankle and Harold saw me naked, he won't come over and help me with my garden anymore."

Amy coughed very loud to cover the deep laugh that erupted from her. "Well, poor Harold didn't know what to do when he saw you like that. You frightened him," Amy tried to explain.

"I frightened him? He scared me," Helen said, with a laugh.

"Okay, out with it," Amy said. "Tell me what happened today."

"Well, okay but don't get mad."

"Helen," Amy said, with a warning look.

"My bird feeder has been empty for a month now. I have a nice big bird feeder and Harold used to fill it up for me, but now he won't come over," Helen said petulantly. "It hangs from one of the trees in my backyard."

"Go on," Amy encouraged.

"Well, I felt bad for the birds so I decided to fill it myself, but I can't reach it from the ground," Helen explained.

"This doesn't sound like it's going to be good," Amy mused to herself. "So what did you do?"

"Well, I brought out my step-stool. It's the one I keep in my kitchen."

"Not a good idea," Amy said, shaking her head. "No one was there to hold it for you?" Amy asked.

"Like who? I live alone. Anyway, I got on the top step and I lifted the bag of bird seed. You know, the bag that was on sale at the food store this week," Helen said.

"You mean the twenty pound bag?" Amy asked, remembering the circular that had been left in the waiting room.

"Yes, I believe that's what it was," Helen said. "That's how much fits in the birdfeeder."

"You lifted a twenty pound bag of bird seed, at the age of ninety one, standing on a step stool?" Amy asked incredulously.

"Of course, honey. Who else is gonna lift it? I carried it home from the market too," Helen said defiantly.

"You must be very strong," Amy said, with a surprised look.

"Now wait, I want to tell you," Helen rushed on. "Do you have time?"

"Yes, Helen," Amy said with a smile. "I'm all ears. So what happened?"

"Well, I took the top off the feeder and lifted the bag, but I had to lean forward to pour it in," Helen explained.

"Yes?" Amy waited.

"And the darn step stool fell over and I went face down in the mud." Helen said.

"Ouch, that's how you hit your head?" Amy asked. "Did you pass out?"

"Oh no, I felt myself going so I simply floated to the ground," Helen said sweetly.

"You floated to the ground?" Amy asked, as she tilted her head to the side. "Really?"

"Yes, that's what happened. I simply let myself go limp and floated to the ground," Helen said.

"That must have hurt," Amy said, as she glanced at Helen's nose.

"It sure as hell did," Helen complained. "I got up and went inside. I thought it was broken for sure, so I drove to the emergency room."

"You drove here yourself?"

"Yes, why is that a problem?"

"No, but you could have had a serious head injury or a concussion," Amy said. "What if you got dizzy on the way over?"

"Well no one was around," Helen complained. "As it is, my bird seed went flying. It's all over the ground now," Helen said, with disgust in her voice for the first time. "The birds will have to eat it that way."

"Helen, you're lucky you didn't break your neck," Amy lightly scolded.

"Well, in the old days I didn't have a problem," Helen said, her voice sad.

"I'm sure, but you're ninety one years old, now," Amy said softly.

"Oh, so I have to act my age?" Helen asked. "I don't feel ninety one, but my body won't do what I want it to do anymore."

Amy blew out a big breath. "I know and I'm sorry about that. Do you have a headache of any kind? Does your neck hurt?"

"No, I'm fine," Helen said with a grin. "I'm just waiting for that cute little fella to come back in and check on me."

Amy burst out laughing this time. "I'm sorry, Helen. I didn't mean to be rude. You're just too cute, that's all." Helen sat in the bed with a big smile on her face. Amy performed a neurologic exam and rechecked the results on the chart. "I think that cute little fella is getting ready to send you home soon," Amy said mischievously. "But you have to promise to come to the clinic in two days, so I can check you again. Promise?"

"Ok, I'll be there," Helen said, with the small, fragile voice. Amy was beginning to realize the fragile tone of voice was used as more of a show than anything else. Helen was apparently very good at the little ol' lady routine when she wanted to be.

"Can you get a ride?" Amy asked.

"I have my car," Helen said. "I'll drive myself."

"I'd really like someone to pick you up. You shouldn't be driving. You can leave your car for now and someone will get it home for you. You need to be careful and if you have any dizziness or headache, call me and I'll come to you, okay? Promise me?" Amy asked again with sincerity.

"Okay, I promise," Helen replied, looking at her with big eyes.

"You may feel very achy and sore tomorrow or have a bad headache."

"I'll be alright," Helen said.

Amy knew that Helen was a fighter. She had to be strong to be this functional at the age of ninety one. "Let me go talk to Ernie and hopefully, you'll be on your way home soon," Amy said.

"Okay, I'm not going anywhere yet." Helen focused on smoothing the sheet that surrounded her.

Amy waved as she backed out of the room. Laughing, she made her way to Ernie who was still pecking at the computer keyboard at the desk. "You're right; she looks like she'll be fine. Did you get a CT Scan by chance?"

"CT of the head, all normal," Ernie said, as he handed her the report. "At her age, the fall could start a bleed three months from now, but for today, all is normal."

"Well, she's waiting for the cute little fella to come back in and let her know when she can go home," Amy said, with a straight face. "Hey, maybe if you're lucky, you and Helen can double with me and Lou." Ernie made a wry face and was about to comment when Amy's emergency beeper went off at the same time she was paged overhead by the hospital operator for an outside call.

"That can't be good," Ernie said, glancing at her face.

"No, I'm sure it's not," Amy agreed, as she picked up the phone at the central desk. "Dr. Amy Daniels."

"Dr. Daniels, you have an emergency call from the Burlington Police Department. May I put it through?" The efficient operator asked politely.

"Yes, of course," Amy said, with a sigh.

After a series of beeps and clicks, an authoritative male voice came on the line. "Hello?"

"Dr. Amy Daniels. Can I help you?"

"This is Burlington PD. You're the acting medical examiner?"

"Currently, yes I am," Amy replied, with a knot in her gut.

"We caught a homicide in Burlington. Male, gunshot to the head," the dispatcher reported.

"Oh, what's the address?" Amy asked, with her most official voice.

The officer recited the address and helped her with directions. "You'll see a lot of people there. Everyone knows it as the soup kitchen."

"Excuse me? Did you say soup kitchen?"

"That's correct ma'am. They were serving a meal today so there are a lot of people there."

"Is anyone else hurt?" Amy asked. Ice chilled her veins as she realized that Willow and the rest of the gang from St. Francis were probably there.

"We believe there's another gunshot victim, but he's alive, at the moment."

"Do you have a name?" Amy asked, as her throat constricted.

"No, ma'am. The only name that's mentioned here is a Father Michael Lauretta, but I don't know why. He could be the victim or a contact. Not enough information."

"Thank you," Amy said dryly, as her head swam. "I'm on my way." Damn. Her hands shaking, she threw the chart over to Ernie and said, "I've gotta go."

Chapter Twenty

"Michael? Michael, where are you?" The booming voice echoed over the lake. Father Victor was standing at the top of the cliff with his hands outstretched, calling for him. Michael wasn't sure if he was seeing things or not, but for a second, it looked like Father Victor was calling the Archangel Michael to come guide the way. Either way, Victor was there at the top of the cliff, ready to help.

Michael peeked out from under the dock and tried to call back. "Victor, down here." When Father Victor looked down, he tried to call again. Michael couldn't wave as he was holding the languid body of Jimmy Griffin. "We need help. Victor, please come down."

Searching the lake, Victor finally located the source of Michael's voice. "I'm coming, hang on." The big priest turned around and yelled to someone behind him, "I see them, they're in the lake." Immediately, he started scrambling down the dirt laden, steep slope of the precipice. Rocks dislodged as he half slid, half clambered down the cliff. Reaching the bottom, his foot slipped a little too far and landed in the water, but Father

Victor reached out and grabbed a branch from a nearby tree. Using the tree branches as a guide, he worked his way over to the boathouse and made a small leap to the pier. Running to the end, he got on his belly and reached under the dock. “Michael, give me your hand. I’ll pull you up.” Shouts were heard coming down the cliff as other police and rescue workers made their way toward the dock.

“Victor, here try to lift him,” Michael said, as he floated Jimmy from the underside of the dock. Victor was able to pull Jimmy from the water like a small child and lay him on the wet wood.

“Is he dead?” Victor asked, as he looked at the limp form.

“I don’t know, he was shot,” Michael answered, his teeth chattering as he started to shiver in the water. Victor turned and lifted Michael out of the water with ease as rescue workers ran onto the dock and immediately started checking vitals.

“He’s got a pulse, he’s alive,” shouted an officer. “Get an ambulance here, pronto.” The officer opened his bag and pulled out a silver thermal blanket. He placed it over Jimmy Griffin’s body and began to examine the gunshot wound in his left upper chest.

Father Victor took off his jacket and wrapped it around Father Michael who sat cross-legged and shivering. “Are you okay? Did you get hurt?”

“No, but I’m freezing and a little lightheaded at the moment,” Father Michael said softly.

Within minutes, a boat driven by a Burlington police officer arrived at the dock with paramedics on board. Jimmy, Father Michael and Father Victor were loaded into the boat before it turned around and sped away to a waiting ambulance on a nearby shore.

Chapter Twenty One

Amy's hands gripped the wheel of her Audi as she drove at breakneck speed to reach the soup kitchen in Burlington, VT. She couldn't do this again. She couldn't lose another friend to violence. Looking for a parking space between the police cars and rescue vehicles, she spotted an open area across the street. She jammed on the emergency brake, turned the key and jumped out of the car. To her relief, the first person she saw standing in the parking lot was Willow. Hugging herself tightly, Willow was clearly upset and when Amy called out to her, she looked up and waved. Without hesitation, she ran toward Amy and threw herself in her arms. Amy held her for a few seconds, hard enough to leave little room for hurt or fear.

"Are you okay?" Amy asked, looking down at Willow's scared face.

"Yes, but I don't know what's going on," Willow answered, as her eyes started to tear up. "Father Victor went running off and someone said Father Michael was hurt."

Amy's stomach clenched. "Listen, we don't know anything yet; let's just wait until we have more information. Like Father Michael always says, we have to have faith," Amy said, with a tight smile.

"Thank God, you're here. I was so scared, but I feel better already," Willow said, hugging her again. Amy's heart broke to think this poor girl had no other family to cling to.

"Where's Katie?" Amy asked, looking around the parking lot.

"She's inside. The police chief asked her to make coffee because we're supposed to stay indoors. They don't want anyone wandering toward the path. Plus, he said something about taking everyone's name and address for statements."

"Well, I'm sure they're hoping someone witnessed something," Amy said gently. "Why don't you go inside and help Katie? Tell her I'm here, but I have a few things to do with the police, okay?"

"Okay," Willow said, throwing her arms around Amy one last time. "Please, be careful."

"Wouldn't have it any other way, now go inside," Amy smiled.

When Willow was safely inside the building, Amy looked around the parking lot. She saw police cars, ambulances, water rescue trucks and a hearse, but no priests. Lights were flashing and yellow crime scene tape was everywhere. Where to start? She really didn't want to do this.

Amy grabbed a young officer's attention. "Pardon me," she said.

"Please ma'am, everyone has to stay inside the building," he said, in an irritated tone.

"Excuse me, officer. Who's in charge here?" Amy tried again, getting annoyed.

"That would be Chief Watson, ma'am. But you'll have to wait until later. Please go inside the building."

"Listen, officer ..," Amy hesitated while she looked at his name plate. "...Kent, you'll all be waiting a long time if you don't get me to the Police Chief, right now. I'm the medical examiner."

Officer Kent paused for a second and looked at Amy without saying a word. "Yes ma'am, right away." He walked away and spoke into a shoulder microphone, fastened to the left upper part of his uniform. After receiving a response, he walked back to Amy, pointed to the right and said, "Police Chief Watson is down that path, ma'am, with the vic."

Amy managed to mutter a tight "thank you," and headed toward her first homicide as a medical examiner.

Chapter Twenty Two

Chief Watson walked up the path and greeted Amy with a nod before she got to the body. "Dr. Daniels I presume?"

"That's right," Amy said, as she shook his hand. "I'm the official medical examiner for now and I want you to know, this is my first homicide."

"How did that happen?" Chief Watson asked, with a lopsided grin.

"Well, someone had to fill the position until Dr. Frey gets back from his emergency leave. They chose me," Amy said, as she shrugged.

"Have you ever seen a dead body or a bullet wound?" Watson asked, as he raised his eyebrows questioningly?

"Of course, I'm a doctor. As a matter of fact, I was a busy trauma surgeon in Boston for many years so I've probably removed more bullets and treated more gunshot wounds than most of your officers," Amy said, bristling a little.

Holding his hands up, Watson chuckled a little and said, "Whoa, I just wanted to see what experience you had. In this case, the TOD, you know, time of death," he explained slowly, as if she were a child, "is pretty straight forward since we have witnesses. The COD, cause of death, is pretty obvious too," Watson said, with a grin. "Manner of death is a typical GSW, gunshot wound to the back of the head. Looks like a .22 caliber. We found a stray bullet in a nearby tree. You'll have to dig around a little to find the one in the vic's head though, to confirm."

"Thank you, I'll do just that," Amy said, making a face. "Can I see my patient or body now, whatever?"

"All yours, doc," the Chief said, as he escorted her down the forest path. Amy signed into the crime scene, put on gloves and booties and walked over to the body of Ray Fulton.

"Has anybody moved him?" Amy asked the Chief, as they both examined the corpse.

"Not that I'm aware of and certainly not since we got here," Watson said.

Ray Fulton was laying prone, face down, his head stuck in a pool of pine needles and blood. A sickening coppery smell filled the air and it didn't mix well with the scent of clean mountain pine. Amy paused a few moments to take in the surroundings. When she first arrived at the parking lot, there had been a litany of screeching birds. Here, the path was eerily quiet, as if the birds and animals had scattered when death and violence moved in and refused to come back.

There were several crime scene techs moving around, taking photographs, measuring bullet holes in trees and gathering samples that were placed in special evidence bags. Amy spent some time looking over the body and the bullet hole in his skull. Afterwards, she pointed to the cigarette butt on the ground.

"I assume someone is going to bag that, just on the off chance it came from our shooter."

"They know their job, doctor," Chief Watson said, with an exasperated tone.

"Sorry, just trying to be complete," Amy said sheepishly.

"We've all read the forensics books," Chief Watson said.

"Fine, when they're done taking their photos, I'd like to turn him so I can get a look at his face," Amy said, now getting annoyed.

Nodding his head, Chief Watson called out, "Hey Phil, you guys done with this side?" When the technician gave him thumbs up, he yelled out, "Then come over here and let's get him turned." Two crime scene techs walked up to the body, placed a tarp on the ground and rolled him over so there wasn't any loss of trace evidence. They immediately started shooting photos of his face, which was now covered with dirt, pine needles and dry crusted blood. His nose was flattened from lying face down.

"I don't see an obvious exit wound," Amy said, staring at his face, ears and neck. She knew that bullets had been known to travel within the body and come out strange places. She'd have a closer look, once he was back in the morgue and his body washed. "I don't see any other gunshot wounds."

"Me neither, but technically, one in the back of the head would be enough," said the Chief.

"Do we know if this was the intended victim?" Amy asked.

"No idea, we're just getting statements now," Chief Watson said.

"Okay, once they're done, they can bag his hands and take him to Rocky Meadow General," Amy said, with conviction. Back at the morgue, she'd have time for a long, close look at the wounds. The chief was right of course; the cause of death was pretty obvious with an open gunshot wound to the head.

"You got it, doc," the Chief said, with a small smirk.

"Do you have any other info on what happened here?" Amy asked, her frustration starting to mount.

"Well, according to a Mrs. Katie Novak, our vic here, Ray Fulton, was having dinner at the soup kitchen and stepped outside to grab a smoke. Seems that another gentleman, nervous guy, went out right after him and the two started having an argument. One of the priests, a Father Michael," Chief Watson said, looking at his note pad, "followed them to see what the problem was. Several minutes later, gunshots were heard and a Father Victor ran out. Mrs. Novak then called the police. No one returned to the soup kitchen, so another gentleman looked out and saw the vic lying on the ground." Chief Watson flipped a couple of pages and went on. "Let's see, there was no one in sight when police arrived on the scene. Everyone was sent back inside the soup kitchen and the crime scene contained until CSI got here. Several officers followed the path." Chief Watson closed his book and looked up at Amy. "They found the rest of them down at the lake. "One of them caught a bullet, but the shooter was gone."

Amy took a deep breath as her stomach clenched. As if rehearsed and timed perfectly, the Chief's radio receiver started to crackle. He turned away to take the report but Amy could still hear a disembodied voice providing coded details. After a brief conversation, the Chief was informed that an ambulance was en-route up the hill and Rocky Meadow General had been put on alert to notify their trauma surgeon, Dr. Amy Daniels. Chief Watson turned to Amy, "Aren't you Dr. Amy Daniels?" He asked, now clearly confused.

"Why, yes I am," Amy said, relishing her turn to provide the sarcastic smile while removing her gloves.

"Double duty, interesting," Chief Watson said, as he turned back to his radio receiver. "Dr. Daniels is here with me now. Stop at the parking lot on your way up. We'll be right out."

Chapter Twenty Three

The ambulance made its way up the boat launch and stopped when it reached the parking lot of the soup kitchen. The back doors were opened by an EMT who then returned to his position, near the patient. Jimmy Griffin was lying on a stretcher, shivering despite the heavy blanket covering most of his body. His face was pale but there was a fine sheen of sweat covering his forehead. A blood pressure cuff was wrapped around his right arm and an IV flowed into his right wrist. His left shoulder was sporting a large white pressure bandage and he had an ugly scratch on his left forearm. His clothes were on the floor of the ambulance, along with a cell phone.

Sitting on the ambulance bench, Father Michael was wrapped in a heavy blanket. Occasionally leaning forward, he talked to Jimmy with a soothing voice, trying to calm him as the EMT's worked. Father Victor hopped out of the ambulance to get out of the way.

“I’m going inside and check on Katie and Willow,” he said to Father Michael. “I’ll see you when you’re done here.”

“Victor, thanks for everything,” Michael answered, with genuine feeling.

“I live to serve,” Father Victor said, as he nodded to Father Michael and then walked off.

On the far side of the parking lot, Chief Watson and Dr. Amy reached the top of the wooded path and walked toward the ambulance. She still didn’t know who’d been shot. Her heart and her mind raced. Trying to heal after losing her sister and dealing with the aftermath of her niece’s injuries, she moved to Vermont to get away from violence and now found herself in the thick of guns and death once again. Being a trauma surgeon, working all hours, she was never able to have strong relationships. It was hard for her to rely on someone who may not be there for her when she needed them, simply offering comfort after a bad day in the hospital. When her family was victimized, she swore she’d never get close to anyone again. She couldn’t face being hurt like that. She hated the feeling of no control, panic taking over her brain, while the rest of her body stood by helplessly. In the hospital, her surgical world was a tightly controlled environment and she called the shots. She was safe there. But not out here, not now.

Amy continued walking toward the ambulance, not knowing if the one person she started to trust, to relax with, and care about was wounded. He was a priest; she shouldn't feel this emotional about him. She was still so raw from her own recent brush with death. He'd saved her life and she'd do whatever she needed to save his.

As they reached the ambulance doors, she looked inside and saw Jimmy lying on the stretcher and Michael sitting on the bench. He had the blanket up to his chin since he was cold, but he broke into a large smile when he spotted her. Dark, wet hair plastered his face. His hand came up in a half wave as he leaned toward her to squeeze her hand. Amy stood on the ground and felt a wave of relief as she realized he was okay. He looked cute with wet hair on his forehead and she yearned to push it back for him. Amy didn't know who was on the stretcher but Michael was healthy. Her throat tightened as she fought back tears that wanted to spring to her eyes, knowing he was safe.

"Doc, you okay?" Chief Watson asked, looking at her as if she were a newbie to a wound.

"I'm absolutely fine," Amy said, as she lifted herself inside the ambulance. Sitting next to the EMT examining Jimmy, she asked, "What do we have here?"

The EMT gave a rundown. "Looks like a thirty-five year old male, with a GSW to the left chest and shoulder. He apparently jumped off a cliff, along with his priest friend here, to avoid getting shot and landed in the lake." Amy looked at

Michael with an expression that said, 'really?' as the EMT kept talking. "The cold water probably slowed the bleeding a little. We think the bullet went straight through, but not sure about that. Bleeding is controlled for now. His vitals are stable, but a bit thready. We want to get him down to Rocky Meadow General as soon as possible.

"Did you put anything in the IV?" Amy asked, as her comfort zone kicked back into place.

"Not yet, doc," the EMT said, as he analyzed her to assess her skill.

Amy expertly drew on a new pair of vinyl gloves, after using an alcohol based hand sanitizer on her hands and gingerly picked up the bandage to get a look at the wound. The bullet hole looked fairly clean having been washed by the lake, but it was still seeping blood. "Okay, call it in and get him down there. We'll be able to take films and have him prepped for the OR pretty quickly. Take as much medical history as you can on the way and make sure you keep that IV line open."

"You got it, doc," the EMT said. "Are you riding with us?"

"No, I'll meet you at the hospital," Amy said, thinking she wanted to touch base with Willow and Katie before she left. "I've got to check someone else first."

"Ok, we'll see you there," the EMT said with a nod.

"No one's going anywhere yet. Apparently, we need a minute," Chief Watson said.

Chapter Twenty Four

All heads turned at once and looked toward the open doors of the ambulance. Standing there was Chief Watson with another officer.

After a few seconds of silence, Amy said, “What’s wrong?”

“Doctor, would you mind stepping out of the ambulance?” Chief Watson said.

“Can I ask why?” Amy gave a questioning look.

“You can, when you step out of the ambulance,” Chief Watson replied.

Amy glanced back at Michael, confusion written on her face. She took off her vinyl gloves and placed them in the receptacle pointed out by the emergency medical technician. Jumping down from the ambulance, Chief Watson pulled her aside to speak privately.

“I got a call from headquarters. It seems Burlington PD was just contacted by an Agent Marcus Cain of the FBI. He wanted to know if we had any local information on a man by the name of Jimmy Griffin. It seems he's a person of interest for a federal crime that was committed within the last twenty four hours."

"You're kidding me," Amy said, hearing the shock in her own voice.

"No doctor, I'm not," Watson said. "I confirmed he was in our ambulance and would be on the way to the hospital to have surgery for a gunshot wound. Since you haven't left yet, the FBI requested an officer stay with the patient from this point on."

"Okay, if we must," Amy said. "But he needs to go now."

"That's fine, doctor," Watson said. "I told Agent Cain the bullet wound didn't seem to be life threatening. That's correct, isn't it?"

"I don't know, Chief. He may have a collapsed lung; it depends on where the bullet went. I won't know for certain until we examine him and get some x-rays, but he's conscious, breathing and seems stable at the moment."

"Okay, our officer needs to stay with him for now. If something happens in the ambulance and this fellow admits to anything, we need to be there."

"Oh," Amy said, clearly at a loss for words. "Is there any special reason for that?"

"There's something called a dying declaration. If a prisoner utters something on his deathbed, it can be admissible in court. Also, I want you to know the FBI is already en route to the hospital and plan to meet you there."

"That sounds rather ominous," Amy said to the Chief.

"If you haven't had the pleasure of working with the FBI, it'll be an interesting introduction," Chief Watson said, with a sarcastic smile on his face.

"Thanks for the warning, I think," Amy said, as she nodded. "We have to let the ambulance leave. The patient is bleeding and needs to get to the OR stat.

"You got it, doc," Chief Watson said, as the officer climbed into the ambulance and took a seat near the head of Jimmy Griffin's stretcher.

"Hey, watch my IV line," Amy said, as she pointed to the rolled up, trapped, tubing coming from under Jimmy's arm. "The fluids are pinched off."

"I'll fix it," the EMT said, as he pulled the line free.

Amy nodded and backed away from the ambulance as she continued to survey the scene inside. As they jostled seats, Amy called out to Father Michael. "I've got my own car. Get checked in the ER and I'll meet you at the hospital as soon as I can."

"See you there, friend, drive safe," he said, as he nodded and offered a serene smile. She watched as an officer slammed the doors and slapped the back of the ambulance twice, with his open hand, to signal the driver to leave.

Chapter Twenty Five

Walking toward the soup kitchen, Amy stopped Chief Watson. "Do you know what this is all about?"

"I have no idea," Watson said. "They didn't share any information with me, but I'm sure someone will call looking for crime scene photos and reports."

"Okay, I guess I'll find out later, since the FBI will be at the hospital with the patient," Amy said, as she shrugged.

"We can keep in touch. You can get me at Burlington PD. If I'm not there, just tell them who you are and they'll patch you through," Watson said. "In the meantime, there's nothing else to do for the vic. The team is done, baggin' and taggin' so to speak. Everything is in a van on its way to Rocky Meadow General."

"Then I guess I'll take it from here, unless the FBI wants to yank the body," Amy said, not caring if they did. She didn't know the local protocol and couldn't wait for the regular medical examiner to get back to work.

Looking down, Chief Watson cleared his throat and said, “Uh, I hope you realize it was nothing personal back there. I’m sure you’re trained better than most. We’re used to the same people being involved in our cases and lately, a lot of strangers are coming out of the woodwork.”

“No offense taken. I had a set routine in my trauma suite back in Boston. It’s not easy when someone changes routine,” Amy said.

“We should stay in touch. I’m curious to see what happens,” Chief Watson said.

“Call me anytime, you can come watch the post if you want to,” Amy offered with a smile.

“That’s okay, the report will do just fine,” he said, with a laugh. “I’ll let you know if we get anything else on our end. I doubt we will with this FBI business but it’s been nice meetin ya,” he said, as he extended his hand and shook hers.

“Thanks, Chief. Same here,” Amy said, as she watched him walk away. With his back to her, he raised his right arm and waved.

Amy turned and headed toward the building again. She took in the grime covered windows and the peeling door, as she crossed the threshold. Inside the big single room, were a number of people sitting at tables, playing cards, talking, drinking coffee and eating cookies. Several officers were holding discreet conversations with individuals in the corner, taking notes as they spoke. A female officer, posted near the door, asked for her name, contact info and the nature of her business. After explaining who she was and what she wanted to do, the officer waved her forward.

Amy found Katie, Sue and Willow near the kitchen. They were washing dishes, cleaning counters and refilling coffee pots. The food was either all gone or put away. The remaining dessert was on the table and rapidly disappearing. Father Victor was dragging large trash bags to the back door, but for now the door remained closed.

Katie rushed over to Amy when she saw her standing near the kitchen door. "Dr. Amy, what's going on, dear? Where's Father Michael? Is he okay?" Katie asked, as she looked behind Amy hoping to get a glimpse of the priest.

"He's fine, Katie. He stayed with the ambulance which is on its way to Rocky Meadow," Amy said. "I wanted to check on everyone before I left."

"We're alright," Katie said, as Willow walked up to the group with a tray of dirty, dessert dishes.

"Are they going to let us go?" Willow asked worriedly.

"Of course they will," Amy said, trying to reassure the girl. "You're not under arrest. They're just gathering information in case they think of any other questions."

"They won't let me take the garbage out," Father Victor said. "I think they're planning on going through it for something."

“I’m sure they have to collect all the evidence they can,” Amy said. “Maybe they’re afraid you’ll walk into the crime scene.”

“Is that poor man, Ray, really dead?” Katie asked.

“I’m afraid so,” Amy told her, as she smoothed Willow’s hair.

“Do they know who did it?” Sue asked. “Is it safe around here?”

“They seem to be looking at everything,” Amy said. “As far as I know, they don’t have anyone in custody, but I’m sure whoever shot him, is long gone.”

“I thought I may have seen a man, for a second, when I was running down the path,” Father Victor said. “Everything happened so fast, I’m not sure what I saw.”

“Maybe you scared him off,” Amy said. “Did you tell the police about that?”

“I told the officer in the dining room,” Father Victor said. “He put it in his notes.”

“Good, that’s all you can do,” Amy said. “I’m glad everyone is okay, but I have to get back to the hospital. I’ll try to see Father Michael in the ER before I go up to surgery. Will you be able to get back to Rocky Meadow by yourselves?”

“We’ll be fine,” Katie said. “I have an extra set of keys to the minivan. Father Victor can drive us back.” Turning to him she said, “You do have a license, don’t ya father?”

“Sure do,” Victor said. “I learned to drive in Chicago.”

"Lord, have mercy," Katie said, as she blessed herself. "We'll go to the hospital and check on Father Michael."

"Good, I'll probably see you there. Take your time and drive safe," Amy said, as she gave Willow a little hug. Grabbing her keys from her purse, she turned and hurried out of the building.

Chapter Twenty Six

Walking away from the operating table, Amy stopped at the bio-hazard receptacle, near the door of the surgical suite, to dispose of her vinyl gloves. The container was strictly reserved for bloody medical waste. Taking off her mask and green surgical gown, she threw them in the bin with the gloves. The new pair of blue surgical scrubs was still clean. Next, she yanked off her cap and shook out her light brown hair.

She was tired, shaky and couldn't remember the last time she'd stopped to eat. The surgery had gone well. By the time she'd arrived at the hospital, Ernie had examined Jimmy Griffin and ordered the appropriate testing. The x-rays showed the bullet had passed cleanly through his body. His clavicle was fractured, but the bullet missed the lung and the chest x-ray was normal. Jimmy was cleared for general anesthesia, since his lung hadn't collapsed. His blood count was low from the blood he lost, but Amy was able to take him into surgery immediately, explore the wound and repair the vessels. After being bandaged, he was sent to the recovery room for observation and a transfusion.

She never got a chance to speak to Father Michael as he was being questioned by the FBI when she arrived at the ER.

Pulling her knee-length white doctor's coat over her scrubs, she left the surgical suite. Standing in the hall, with his arms crossed in front of his chest, was a handsome black man, wearing an expensive suit.

"Can I help you?" Amy asked. "The waiting room for family is around the corner. You really shouldn't be in this area."

He extended his hand. "Cain, Marcus Cain, FBI."

"Oh, Chief Watson said you called the Burlington Police Department about this patient." Amy said.

"Jimmy Griffin," Cain said. "We have an interest in a patient by that name."

"Jimmy Griffin is now in recovery," Amy said. "You'll have to confirm his birth date and social security numbers to make sure it's the same man."

"You can bet we'll do that and match his fingerprints as well," Cain said. His grey suit jacket was slightly open on the side, revealing his Glock in a shoulder holster. Looking straight at her, he asked, "Well, did he survive?"

"Of course, he survived. I told you he was in recovery. The bullet went right through his body. Technically, we just cleaned up the wound."

"Did he say anything in there?" Cain asked, watching for her reaction.

"Like what?" Amy asked. "He moaned until we put him under."

"Did he talk about what happened in the woods?"

"Why no, he didn't," Amy said, looking at the FBI agent. "He was anesthetized and asleep for a majority of the time. Before that, he'd been given narcotics for pain in the emergency room and he'll be given more pain medicine in the recovery room. Since a patient has to be fully coherent to be accountable for any decision or information they offer, I don't think it matters much anyway, does it?" Amy shot back.

"True, let's try to remember he's the criminal, not me," Cain said. "I'm just doing my job."

"I appreciate that, but he didn't say anything to me," Amy said, her fatigue kicking in. I have no idea what happened out there."

"There's more to it than that," Cain said quietly. "I wanted to know if he said anything."

"Listen, Agent Cain," Amy said.

"Cain, just Cain," he returned.

"Ok, Cain," Amy said, emphasizing the name. "I have no idea what's going on, so I don't think I can help you."

"I understand you're also doing the post on the homicide victim. I'd like to go over that case with you, but you look a little overwhelmed right now," Cain said.

"Quite frankly, I'm exhausted," Amy admitted. "It's Saturday night and I've been working all day. I'll do the autopsy in the morning, if you want to come back and observe."

"You got it doc. I'll check in with you tomorrow, about Jimmy Griffin and the vic."

"That makes sense. Griffin will be out of it for most of the night," Amy said.

"That's okay, I'll wait until tomorrow. If he's medicated, the officer assigned to watch him tonight will have it easy. Unless, of course, whoever killed our friend in the morgue decides to come back and try it again," Cain said, with a straight face.

That threat hadn't even occurred to Amy until Cain verbalized it so casually. Just the thought of another killer in the hospital chilled Amy to her core. She'd really been mistaken to think Rocky Meadow would be a nice quiet place to live. At this rate, Boston seemed safer.

"I assume you've put security on alert?" Amy asked.

"Of course," Cain said, with a patronizing tone. "We've got local police posted in several places around the hospital."

"That's good, as long as they don't upset the other patients," Amy said petulantly. "I can't help you tonight, Cain. I'm going down to the ER to check on Father Michael and then I'm going home. I'll do the post on the victim in the morning.

As the medical examiner, I'm supposed to investigate why this man was killed. If you want to talk to me tomorrow, you'll find me in the morgue."

"Fine," Cain said, with a nod. "I'll look forward to seeing you in the morning, doctor."

Amy was still shaking her head in disgust as she banged through the stairwell door on her way to the emergency room.

Chapter Twenty Seven

Ernie lifted his head when Amy walked up to the central nursing desk in the emergency room. "Hey, you look really tired," he said, looking at the bags starting to form under her eyes.

"I could die standing up and I don't think they'd notice for an hour," Amy said, while yawning. "What a day, I'm exhausted. You've been here forever, too. How long has it been?"

"Going on fifteen hours," Ernie said. "At least I got to take a nap in the lounge. You've been running from clinic to crime scene to surgery."

"I thought I left all this, in Boston," Amy said, with a tired laugh.

"Seriously, how are you holding up?" Ernie asked, with a worried look on his face.

"With what?" Amy asked, shrugging her shoulders.

"C'mon, it can't be easy being forced into the medical examiner's position. I know you're familiar with trauma and all, but you were just a victim yourself three months ago. That's got to be hard on you."

"I guess it is," Amy said, playing with a pen on the desk. "I'm not real happy with it."

"Well, we can certainly use you back in the ER. The schedule's been tight since you've been running the clinic and being the medical examiner. Plus, Artie's on vacation," Ernie said. "I'm pulling extra shifts all over the place."

"I'm sorry, Ernie," Amy said. "The clinic is really starting to take off and I'm trying to keep a lot of routine stuff out of the ER. You shouldn't get bogged down with simple ear infections and strep throats."

"That's true and none of this is your fault. It's been crazy here today and having a murder in Burlington didn't help. It was crowded before the ambulance got here with your patient."

"You did a great job getting him ready for surgery. I appreciate that," Amy said.

"Yeah, despite the FBI team. When they first got here, they used every room they could. I'm trying to send the patient up to OR and they're grabbing fingerprints. I think they followed the other body to the morgue."

"They better not have touched him. I have to do that autopsy in the morning," Amy said. "I'm not looking forward to it."

"You might as well sleep in. He's not going anywhere," Ernie said, with a grin. "By the way, Lou Applebaum came in and cleared your prisoner for surgery. I think he was hoping he'd see you."

"Ernie, what am I going to do about him?" Amy asked.

"What are you asking me for? Hell, go out with him already so he leaves me alone," Ernie chided her. "And, your priest friend was sent to room three, but he had to get in line with all the sick tourists, once the FBI finished grilling him."

"Is he still here? That's why I came down," Amy said, looking around the room.

"No, he was discharged a little while ago. He was fine, really. He just got an unexpected start to his new cliff-jumping hobby."

Amy shook her head. "He's lucky he didn't break something."

"By the time he left, I think he wished he had," Ernie said. "He had his housekeeper, Katie, fussing after him. Willow was here as well. After a while, Father Victor took them all home. He said they had some interesting stories to write for their homilies in the morning."

"Wow," Amy said. "What a day."

“It sure was and don’t think you escaped their attention either. Katie brought some food for us working stiffs. Bless her little heart, she can fuss over me all she wants,” Ernie said, with a big smile.

“She’s a great cook,” Amy agreed, her stomach growling.

“I’ll drink to that,” Ernie said. “Your plate is in the lounge. You have to warm it up. I’ll admit if you didn’t show up, I was going for seconds.”

“Not tonight, my friend,” Amy said laughing. “Thanks Ernie, for holding down the fort.”

“No problem, go get some grub,” Ernie said, as he turned back to the computer.

Smiling to herself, Amy walked to the doctors’ lounge and found her plate of food. Relaxing for the first time that day, she ate the best chicken and rice she’d ever tasted. Leaning back in her chair, she thought, “God Bless you, Katie Novak.”

Chapter Twenty Eight

Amy stood in front of the autopsy table, staring at the corpse of Ray Fuller. He lay on the table; his body a grayish white from loss of blood, the pallor of death. For some reason, she and the autopsy table were on a platform, raised from the rest of the room by three feet. Normally it was cold, but now it was icy. Frost seemed to cover the dead man's eyes and the room was very quiet. Usually, she heard the exhaust fan or running water but today there was total silence. Something was very wrong. Hearing a noise, she turned toward the door and saw water start flowing into the room. It ran across the floor, filling the autopsy suite. Waves crashed against equipment and walls as a cold wind blew through the room. The water was getting deeper and passage from the platform was blocked. If she wanted to leave, she'd have to jump into the dangerous current. Dread filled her chest as she realized she was trapped. Amy turned toward Ray Fuller, her only companion on Cadaver Island. Slowly, as if he knew something she didn't, the corpse began to smile. Just a hint at first, then his death grin grew wide. His head lolled toward her side of the table, still smirking. Amy couldn't tear her eyes away. She was scared, cold and trapped. The water continued to surround the platform and now lapped at her ankles and feet, but she couldn't move and she couldn't take her eyes off the dead man. His frozen lids suddenly snapped open and black, dead eyes stared right at her. Her scream caught in her throat as she fell backward toward the water, she was falling……

Amy jumped up. Her whole body twitched as she grabbed the bed for support. Heart racing, she felt short of breath, gasping for air. Beads of sweat poured off her forehead, down her back and in between her breasts. The room was dark, too dark. She reached over with shaky hands and snapped on the bedside table lamp. 2:00 am. The damn dreams again. Taking a deep breath, she fell against her pillow and calmed herself. Her pulse was slower, but her heart was banging in her chest. Her feet were sweaty and she needed to use the toilet. Feeling anxious, she slowly got out of bed, took a deep breath and put on her robe and slippers. When she got to the bathroom, she used a warm cloth on her face to wash away the sweat and the fear. Every time she was overwhelmed, she'd have the damn nightmares. After relieving herself, she washed her hands and made her way back to the bed. Feeling cold, she changed pajamas and slipped under the covers to warm up. Her mind raced over the previous day's events. First the morning clinic, then the crime scene and eventually surgery. Amy had been exhausted when she went to bed. She was used to days like that when she lived in Boston. She'd been one of the first responders for trauma surgery and would go through days of craziness before she'd get a break and then have to start all over. She wasn't used to being in crisis mode anymore. Maybe she'd been looking for an excuse to leave her old job. Things were not as calm in Vermont as she had hoped, but they weren't as bad as Boston. She knew she didn't want to go back.

Lying in bed, she was now warm but wide awake and a little frightened. She hated to do it, but she picked up the phone and dialed. Her head was on the pillow, eyes closed, waiting for the call to be answered. On the fourth ring, she finally heard a voice.

"Dr. Amanda Chase," a sleepy voice said.

"Amanda, it's Amy," she said, gripping the phone.

"Amy, hey how are you honey? Is everything okay?"

"Yes, just a little shaky. I needed to hear a familiar voice," Amy said.

"Are you having those dreams again?" Amanda asked knowingly. Dr. Amanda Chase had been a housemate of Amy's during medical school in New Jersey. She knew that Amy had dreams when she was emotionally and mentally fatigued. Amanda remembered hearing her scream in her sleep when they over studied for exams or took thirty-six hour shifts. The two women had become close friends and were always there for each other, during medical school and after graduation. Amy had chosen to specialize in trauma surgery, to save as many broken and bleeding patients in the grip of acute violence or tragedy as she could. Amanda had chosen to specialize in hospice care and was an extraordinarily compassionate physician dedicated to making the inevitable sting of death as pain free and spiritual as possible for both patients and their families.

At their graduation, the two women swore they would stay close friends and support each other while dealing with violence, death and dying. They had stayed close, through their residencies and practice. They'd made a promise to visit each other, at least once a year. Unfortunately, the last visit was during Amy's sister's funeral and Amanda made Amy promise to call her whenever she needed her, night or day. They'd joked they'd probably be awake anyway, since their schedules were never routine.

"Yes, and I just had a beauty of a nightmare," Amy said quietly.

"Bad day in the office yesterday?" Amanda asked.

"You could say that, I felt like I was back on a thirty-six hour shift," Amy said. "But I'm starting to relax a little. How are things by you?"

"Same as always, we never run out of hospice patients. By the way, Father Juan is doing really well," Amanda happily reported, referring to a priest that Amy met through Father Michael in Vermont. He had been diagnosed with cancer and wanted to return to his New Jersey home. Amy called Amanda for help and she was able to start him in an experimental treatment program and fulfill his wish.

"I'm so glad to hear that," Amy said. "He's such a nice priest, but he was so anxious, I felt bad for him."

"Well, don't feel bad, because he's very stable," Amanda said. "The best thing you did was to refer him to the experimental treatment program."

"Is he improving?" Amy asked.

"He just had a PET scan and it's completely negative," Amanda announced proudly.

"That's wonderful," Amy said excitedly. "I can't wait to tell Michael."

"Michael? Is there something I don't know about?" Amanda asked coyly.

"You know, Father Michael. The pastor that Father Juan was visiting when I met him," Amy defended herself.

"Oh, you threw me off without the "Father" in there," Amanda said.

"Well, I don't call you Doctor every time I talk to you, even though I know you are one," Amy said.

"Okay, calm down, just asking is all," Amanda laughed.

"Is he gaining weight?" Amy asked.

"Who?" Amanda asked.

"Father Juan, is he gaining weight with the new treatment?" Amy asked. She was happy to hear the good news. Amy knew that Amanda always calmed her down by distracting her long enough to have the dream details fade away from her thoughts. Giving her good news about a former patient was a great way to accomplish that.

"He's gained eight pounds and he's back to playing basketball," Amanda answered. "Only for short periods at a time, but just watching and coaching his kids is a healthy tonic for him. His immune system is stronger."

Amy laughed as they recited the motto of their old Immunology teacher, "A happy person has a happy immune system."

"Have you been happy, Amy?" Amanda asked.

"Well, I'm better than I was," Amy said. "I got off to a rough start in Rocky Meadow, but for the most part, I can see having a serene life here."

"You haven't gone through the winter yet. Let's wait and see what that brings," Amanda teased her.

"Well, the leaves will be changing in another month or so. Think of all the tourists that flock up here to see that," Amy said.

"Point taken," Amanda agreed. "I want to be one of those tourists some day. I've always wanted to hike and look at the beautiful leaves in Vermont. Maybe I can arrange a weekend up there this fall."

"That would be great," Amy quickly agreed. "I'd love to have you at my cabin."

"My, that does sound rustic and cold for some reason," Amanda said.

"It's actually very beautiful, all granite and marble with beautiful cedar wood. I'm renting it for a short time with an option to buy. I didn't want to commit to anything for now. You know, until I sorted things out," Amy said honestly.

"Well, don't wait too long. Those thoughts will be with you on some level for the rest of your life. Live your life in the meantime. Do fun things and go meet a guy," Amanda laughed.

"Look who's talking," Amy chided. It'd been hard for either one of them to have a relationship with the hours they worked.

"Well, neither one of us is getting any younger. I'm gonna start looking one of these days," Amanda said.

"That's fine, just don't talk about your work when you go out," Amy said. "Not everyone wants to hear about death and dying."

"What else is there?" Amanda asked.

“You have a serious problem, my friend. First of all, there’s sleep and I better let you get back to yours,” Amy said. “Thanks for being there, Amanda. I’m serious; you don’t know how much that means to me.”

“No problem, honey. Read a good book and get some sleep yourself.”

“I will, goodnight,” Amy said, as she hung up the phone. She felt a hundred percent better, but definitely needed more rest before getting up in the morning to complete the real autopsy of Raymond Fuller.

Chapter Twenty Nine

Amy rolled over in bed when she heard the birds singing outside her window. Tiredly, she opened one eye to see daylight had broken. After speaking to Amanda, she'd finished a novel that was growing roots on her bedside table and fallen into a deep, dreamless sleep. Stretching, she pulled back the covers and got out of bed. She put on her robe and slippers and padded into the kitchen to make a pot of hot, strong coffee. She'd need it to get through the day. Her only priority was finishing the post on Raymond Fuller, especially since the FBI was breathing down her neck. She wasn't quite sure what was going on, but she'd get to the bottom of it at some point.

Amy dressed in a comfortable set of scrubs and put on her favorite rubber soled shoes. She'd learned early in her career that wearing the right shoes saved her from a lot of back pain, especially if she had to stand at the side of an operating table all day. Tying her hair in a pretty French knot, she went back to the kitchen and poured a cup of coffee for the road.

The rest of the pot went into her travel thermos for later. The coffee at the hospital was acceptable, but not always enjoyable.

Jumping into her Audi, she drove down the small lane and made a left onto the main road. The weather was beautiful and not as hot as the last two days. Unfortunately, she wouldn't see much of it. The autopsy would take a while. If she worked steadily, she'd be able to visit her favorite bench before returning home for the day. Traveling to the hospital, she was still in awe of the beautiful scenery around her. There were times when the open view of the mountains and lakes was breathtaking. She told herself to concentrate on the road and not drive off the side of a cliff because she was staring at the landscape. Driving down the last of the hill that lead from her house, she saw The Divide. After following the river for a short way, she saw her favorite bench and St. Francis Church in the background. The parking lot was crowded as Sunday mass was getting ready to start. Cars hurried over the wooden covered bridge so churchgoers wouldn't be late for mass.

Amy hadn't been able to see Michael at the emergency room and didn't want to call the rectory late last night. He'd probably been asleep after his narrow escape and she didn't want to wake him. Perhaps, she'd be able to see him at the bench today.

Amy passed the turn to the covered bridge and made her way to Rocky Meadow General Hospital. Pulling into the empty doctors' lot, she parked near the back entrance and entered the building. She took the elevator to the basement and walked through the main doors to the morgue. Amy noticed that Mr. Fuller's body had already been pulled out of the refrigerator. He was lying face down on a stainless steel table in the center of the sterile, green tiled, well-lit autopsy suite. His body had been washed and Alex was photographing various angles of the gunshot wound.

Amy stopped long enough to let Alex know she'd be ready in a few minutes. In the locker room, she changed into sterile scrubs. She'd been happy to see that there was no platform or abnormal water on the floor of the autopsy suite. Using the hospital phone, she called the nursing desk on the VIP floor to get a report on Jimmy Griffin. Assuring them she'd be upstairs to check him after the autopsy, she hung up and finished dressing. Securing her things, she started back to the autopsy suite. Once again, her gown, gloves and hood were all laid out, ready for her to start. Before putting on the rest of her medical garb, she paused long enough to look over the slim chart that had hastily been compiled for her dead patient.

Raymond Fuller had been a sixty-five year old, Roman Catholic, homeless veteran, living on the streets of Burlington, VT. As a child, he'd grown up on his family's farm and at age nineteen, was drafted by the United States Army. He went to boot camp, and then transferred to active duty. Ready to proudly serve his country, he was sent to Vietnam, where he stayed until 1970. He fought for the USA and survived, but not without seeing his fellow soldiers tortured, maimed and killed. Some didn't die right away. Some went home and later committed suicide. Others were addicted to drugs, but not Ray. He made it through and returned to Vermont. Just being back in the USA seemed like a dream come true. He thought he'd survived. Ray was happy to be home and tried to work on the farm that was owned by his relatives. Not long after, his nightmares started. He would awaken in the middle of the night, shaking and sweaty after revisiting Vietnam in his dreams. He started having panic attacks during the day and stopped working because he couldn't focus. Feeling lost, he asked his family to take him to the local VA, where he was diagnosed with Post Traumatic Stress Disorder or PTSD. The medications made him feel better at first, but he still couldn't hold a job or a relationship. With time, his family members drifted away or died which left Raymond Fuller homeless and broke. He survived by living in shelters and soup kitchens, until yesterday. There was no record of criminal activity or altercations and no apparent reason to be a target of an assassination. Victims were murdered for pennies in the city, but not with a professional weapon, such as the one that was used on Raymond. Amy would have to investigate a little more deeply for this case.

Gently placing the chart on the counter, Amy turned to get ready for the autopsy. Reflecting on his life, she felt bad for him as she slowly donned her surgical gown and gloves. Motioning to her technician, they walked over to the stainless steel table and looked down at his body. After a moment, she reached up and switched on the overhead microphone.

"This is Dr. Amy Daniels, dictating the external exam for Mr. Raymond Fuller. He is a Caucasian male, sixty five years of age, approximately 142 lbs, with a gunshot wound to the occipital region of his skull. No other signs of blunt force trauma are noted. There does not appear to be an exit wound in the cranium." Amy went on to methodically describe the condition of Ray Fuller's body. She went into detail with the wound and all other external markings. Scars and tattoos were noted as well as the photographs Alex had taken.

Once they flipped the body and the external exam was completed, Amy and Alex took a short break to stretch and set up for the next phase of the autopsy. Resettled near the table, she reached up and switched the microphone back on. Alex handed her the first instrument she would use to open Ray's chest. Her technique was precise and smooth from the experience she'd had in the operating room. Not having to worry about anesthesia, the procedure was quicker than live surgery, but she still worked methodically to avoid destroying any potential evidence they might find.

Opening the chest cavity, they removed the heart, lungs and other organs. After being weighed, each organ was further dissected and checked for disease. Following an established routine, they worked until the entire body had been examined for evidence, disease or trauma. The cranium was saved for last. After measuring the entry wound from the bullet, they removed the top of the skull using a special saw. The brain was removed and dissected, as they documented the damage caused by the bullet. Once the bullet was found, it was placed in a sterile evidence container. Later, it would be cleaned and tested for DNA, fingerprints and other important forensics.

"Okay," said Amy, with a sigh. "I think we've done everything we need to do here. I feel sorry for Raymond."

"I read his chart. It seems like he was a nice guy," Alex said, as he shrugged his shoulders and stretched his neck.

"Yes, it does," Amy agreed. "Alex, you can put everything back and close him, okay?"

"You got it, Doc," Alex readily agreed.

"You have experience with that, right?" Amy asked, just to be sure he was qualified.

"Hey, I've done a lot of closures," Alex said, with a hurt look on his face.

"I'm sorry I asked. I don't know if Ray has any family or where he's going next, but I want it done right," Amy said, offering a small apology. "No offense, Alex."

"No offense taken, Dr. Daniels," Alex replied.

"What's your deal anyway?" Amy asked.

"Whadda you mean?"

“Why are you here? How’d you get this job?”

“I saw it in the paper,” Alex said. “Forensics interests me, so I applied for the position. At first, I wasn’t sure if I was gonna be grossed out, but it’s been pretty cool so far. I’m going to school part-time, so I can do more after I graduate.”

“Like what?” Amy asked.

“I don’t know yet, maybe FBI forensics or become a pathologist. I’ll figure it out,” Alex said, with a smile.

“I’m sure you will,” Amy replied. “Do a good job with Ray, okay?”

“You got it, Doc,” Alex said, as he started putting all the organs in a large plastic bag to be placed back in the chest cavity.

Chapter Thirty

Removing her gown and gloves, Amy looked up when she heard her name. Marcus Cain was standing at the door of the autopsy suite, wearing an expensive brown suit and a very shiny gold badge. Walking into the room, he nodded his head.

"Nice job, doctor," Cain said.

"Thank you. You're a little late," Amy said, sarcasm obvious in her voice.

"Got here as early as I could," Cain said, as he held his hands out to the side.

"How can I help you?" Amy asked. "You know you're not supposed to be in here."

"Truce, okay?" Cain said. "I'm really not a bad guy. I want to get whoever did this as much as you do."

"Okay," Amy said tersely. "If you want to work together, then we'll do that. Otherwise, please stay out of my morgue."

"I apologize if I offended you."

"Good, because there's a nice young man here who thinks he may want to be an FBI agent one day. I'd hate to have him see a bad example of one."

"Okay, it's all good," Cain said. "Now, if we're working together as a team, what can you tell me about the vic?"

"Nothing more than we already know. I pulled a .22 caliber bullet from his brain. It's in an evidence container. You can take it for DNA, fingerprints and ballistics."

"My team will take care of it," Cain said, as he nodded his head. "Anything else?"

"I'm thinking you shouldn't wear a suit like that to an autopsy. You never know what can spill on it," Amy said, as she suppressed a grin.

"Hey, it's Sunday. I always like to look nice on Sunday. I told you, I'm staying back, not crossing the threshold," Cain assured her. "Now, what about Mr. Fuller?"

"Well, I'm thinking poor Mr. Fuller must have been exposed to some Agent Orange in Nam," Amy said.

"Why's that?" Cain asked.

"His bladder had a tumor in it and he had emphysema," she replied. "I have to see if there are medical records at the VA. It may not be from Agent Orange. Maybe his smoking just caused the bladder cancer and lung disease. Either way, it's not what killed him yesterday."

"But it would have," Cain asked.

"Eventually," Amy said, as she shook out her hair. "I'm not sure he knew about it. If the bladder cancer was from Agent Orange, then the government may have paid for treatment and he might have gotten some compensation. It's sad really."

As she spoke, the sound of a phone interrupted the quiet whispery noise of the autopsy suite. Amy turned back to the center of the well-lit room, and said, "Alex, is that your phone? You know we don't allow phones in here, right?"

"Not mine, doc. I left my phone in my locker," Alex yelled back over his shoulder, as he continued to close the body.

"I know it's not yours," Amy said to Cain. "I'm standing right next to you and mine's in my locker as well."

"Then where's it coming from?" Cain asked, as he looked around.

"It sounds like your office," Alex said.

"That's odd, it's a Sunday," Amy said, as they started walking toward her office. Amy followed the ringing sound and realized the phone was the landline on her desk. She reached over and lifted the handset, "Hello?"

"Do you have it?" A muted voice said over the phone.

"What? Excuse me?" Amy said.

"The flash drive, do you have the flash drive?" The voice said again.

"Flash drive? You must have a wrong number. I have no idea what you're talking about," Amy replied, while making a face at Marcus Cain.

"Keep him talking," Cain whispered in her other ear, while making circles with his hand. Pulling out his cell phone, he walked away and started to dial someone.

"I'm sorry, who am I speaking with?" Amy asked.

"That's not important," said the voice. "I want to know if you have it now. Was it with his belongings?"

"What things? Are you related to Raymond Fuller?" Amy tried again.

"I'm not concerned about Raymond Fuller, he was just collateral damage. I'm calling about Jimmy Griffin. You do have his belongings, don't you?"

"I don't know what you're talking about. Collateral damage? What's that supposed to mean?" Amy said, as she started to get upset. "Who is this?"

Cain was standing on the other side of the room. He had his cell phone to his ear, speaking in a hurried, hushed tone. Amy noticed that Alex was paying close attention as well.

"No one you know," the voice said.

"This is Dr. Amy Daniels. I'd like to give you the information you're looking for, but I need a little help here."

"I already have plenty of information," the voice said. "I know where you are. Jimmy Griffin has something of mine and I want it back. Find it, Dr. Amy Daniels," the voice said menacingly. "I'll give you further instructions when I call back. If you don't, there will be consequences."

"Are you threatening me?" Amy asked, but the phone had clicked off. She looked at the phone, then Cain, and forced a laugh. "Can you believe this guy? What the hell was that all about?"

Cain was over to her in a few quick strides. "What exactly did he say?"

"Well, first I don't know that it's a he, because the voice was muted somehow," Amy started. "But I was basically just threatened."

"How did it leave off?" Cain asked eagerly.

"He told me to talk to Jimmy Griffin about a flash drive," Amy said. "Apparently, he's going to call me back at some point. He said if I don't have the flash drive when he does, there'll be consequences."

"I was trying to trace the call, but you weren't on long enough. It's probably a burn phone anyway," Cain said.

"Then obviously, you know something I don't," Amy said. "Alex, do you know anything about this?"

"No, but your phone rang earlier today," Alex said, while walking over toward them.

Cain's head snapped up. "Did you answer it?"

"Not me," Alex said. "I'm not allowed to touch anything on the medical examiner's desk."

Amy turned to Cain. “The voice said he didn’t care about Raymond Fuller. He said he was calling for Jimmy Griffin. How did he know he was at Rocky Meadow General? Who else saw Griffin in the emergency room, beside my medical staff?”

“We had an agent fingerprint him, process him,” Cain said, his voice quiet. “The ambulance drivers and anyone else at the scene yesterday knew he was transported to Rocky Meadow General.”

“Did the FBI take Griffin’s things?” Amy asked Cain directly.

“I’m sure we did. It’s an active investigation and all personal belongings would be taken for evidence, but I was waiting near recovery to talk to you,” Cain pointed out, as he reached for his cell phone.

“Well the voice was very insistent about a flash drive,” Amy said. He said it was his, he wanted it back and if I don’t have it when he calls, there will be consequences. I still don’t understand how he knew to call me directly or the morgue.”

“Maybe he was watching all the commotion yesterday,” Alex suggested.

“Or talked to someone else who told him about the hospital,” Amy said, trying to solve the puzzle.

“Or the third choice,” Cain said, as he slowly shook his head and looked around.

"Is what?" Amy asked.

"The third choice is he's watching us right now, somehow," Cain pointed out.

"What? You can't be serious," Amy said, clearly upset with the idea.

"Do you have a computer camera or a laptop in the lab?" Cain asked.

"Just what are you suggesting?" Amy asked.

"These organizations have experts working for them," Cain pointed out. "Activating a remote camera on a laptop or computer would be simple for them. As long as we're in view of the camera, they could see everything."

"What organization are we talking about?" Amy asked.

Struggling to make a decision, Cain looked at the both of them and finally said, "This is strictly confidential but we think this is the work of an organization called Shepherd Force."

"What exactly is Shepherd Force?" Amy asked again.

"They're all over the place, if you know where to look," Alex said excitedly. "They're a well-known activist group that uses the internet to hack into computer systems."

"He's right," Cain said. "They're responsible for a lot of cyber-crime and we've been trying to get a lead on them for a long time now."

"They're like cyber legends," Alex said. "Bad dudes."

"Mr. Fuller is sure dead enough to prove that," Amy said.

"Or it could be a copycat," Cain pointed out. "We don't have enough to go on right now."

Walking out into the autopsy suite, Amy turned and surveyed the room. "Alex, do we have any type of cameras in here?"

"There aren't any cameras or computers that I know of," Alex said, as the two men joined her. "We usually don't keep a laptop in here because they get covered with all sorts of body fluids and stuff. Then they have to get tossed."

"We have the overhead microphone," Amy mused aloud. "The recording is digital and usually retrieved from a different room. Any reports that are generated are printed or signed in the office, not here. It's my second autopsy so I don't know if this room looks different from normal."

"Alex, do you see anything that looks out of place or moved?" Cain asked. "Just in case someone came in here and hid a camera. It could be small, the size of a dime and still work."

Alex slowly moved around the room, looking at countertops, equipment and cabinet doors. "No, it all looks the same to me."

"Well, we still have to assume that we're being watched or recorded somehow, until we can prove otherwise. I'll get a team in here to do a sweep," Cain said, as he picked up his cell phone and started dialing.

"You'll let me know if you find a flash drive." Amy said.

Cain finished his conversation and turned to Amy. "Strictly need to know, Doc. It's for your own protection."

Amy was furious and rounded on Cain with hands on her hips. "You've got a lot of nerve, you know that? You come in here and ask a lot of questions and then shut me out?"

"Alex, it might be a good time to get a cup of coffee," Cain said, with a harsh look on his face.

"Got it, I'm outta here," Alex said, as he hurried from the suite.

Cain turned back to Amy. "This is an FBI case. We've got jurisdiction and we'll handle it."

"Then you should have taken the body back to the FBI lab before I started," Amy said, as she stared at Cain's face.

"We weren't aware of the homicide until we got to the crime scene," Cain said. "Our resources are stretched here, so Rocky Meadow gets the initial work. Beyond that, it's FBI business."

"That's fine, but don't forget, as the medical examiner, I've got a few responsibilities of my own."

"You already know the vic wasn't the intended target, so just finish your report and move on."

"I can't move on yet. I'm still the trauma surgeon assigned to Jimmy Griffin, unless the FBI has someone to join the staff and take over for that as well."

"Look Doc, we need to work as a team, but information is strictly need to know. I need to know everything you do. Beyond that, no promises."

"Cain, stay out of my way. I haven't released the body yet, so make sure your team doesn't touch the deceased or anything else on that table. I'm sending Alex back in to finish the body. Do your sweep and get out." Picking up the patient file, Amy turned and banged out the door.

Chapter Thirty One

“I’m so glad you’re okay,” Florence said, as she grabbed Father Michael’s arm on the way out of church. “I heard such horrid rumors I couldn’t wait to come to mass to check on you.”

“Yes, Florence,” Michael said, as he patted the hand now latched onto the crook of his arm. “I’m fine, really.” Florence was one of the parishioners, most taken with the good looks and charming personality of Father Michael. She was in charge of the annual church carnival but also made it her business to keep up on the gossip and drama of the church, so she’d be well informed when speaking to the other ladies.

“What would we ever do if we lost you?” Florence asked, almost tearfully. “You are the heart of St. Francis.”

“Actually, the Lord is the heart of St. Francis,” Michael said, as he stopped at the outside stairs and turned to face her. “I am just his humble servant.”

“You look tired, Father,” she replied, as she looked up at him. “I hope you rest today and take care of yourself.”

"My plan exactly, Florence," Michael said, as he tilted his head and offered a large, warm smile. "After all, today is Sunday. God rested on the seventh day. But first, I have to finish saying goodbye to my other parishioners. Please say hi to Ted for me, will you?"

"Of course, Father," Florence gushed, as she realized she was being dismissed. Looking around for her husband, she hurried down the stairs and headed for the car.

"I think she's a bit infatuated with you," Father Victor said, as he reached the top of the church steps and stood by Father Michael's side.

"She means well," Michael defended her, as he concentrated on shaking hands or wishing a pleasant day to each of the parishioners that left the church. Father Michael enjoyed knowing his parishioners and when time allowed, he looked forward to hearing about their families. There were times when he eagerly awaited to hear the outcome of a promising circumstance he'd been asked to pray for. He also took time to personally visit the families that were struggling or in crisis.

"But, she's right. You do look tired today," Father Victor said, as the last of the parishioners drove off in their cars. Walking back to the altar, they blew out the candles and hung up their vestments.

"Well, it was a late night for all of us," Michael admitted. "Sitting in the emergency room for hours, didn't help."

"At least you didn't have to go to surgery. Have you had any word on Mr. Griffin?" Victor asked, as they walked toward the rectory.

"No, I really couldn't get much information. I was planning on trying to see him at the hospital today," Michael said, with a quiet voice.

"I hope he realizes you saved his life," Victor said, as they reached the front door. "If you hadn't pulled him toward the lake, he'd be on the same table as that poor other guy this morning."

Father Michael looked up with a sad smile on his face. "Victor, he did get shot, remember?"

"You forget, I'm from Chicago," Victor said. "Being shot in the shoulder is a long cry from being shot in the head. I've seen enough of it to know."

"I suppose that's true," Michael said quietly.

"You know it's true and you kept him from drowning as well," Victor pointed out.

"Yes, but he was only in the water because I pushed him off that cliff," Michael said. "Otherwise he wouldn't have been in danger of drowning."

"No, he'd just be dead," Victor said, as the front door of the rectory was suddenly pulled open.

"Why don't you two stop standing there and come in for some breakfast?" Katie asked, as she stepped back to let the door open further.

"Thanks, Katie," Michael said.

"I have a nice buffet set out for both of you," Katie said. "I've been so nervous since we got back; all I can do is cook to keep my mind off yesterday."

"I think that's excellent therapy, Katie," Victor said gleefully. "And probably something you should keep up with for awhile."

"Okay, Father," Katie said with feigned annoyance. "You're not gonna starve, that's for sure. By the way, you'll let Father Michael fill his plate first, won't you?"

"As long as he doesn't eat too much," Victor said, with a laugh.

"Well, if you don't mind, we're eating in the kitchen this morning," Katie said. "There's nothing like a close brush with death to make you want to break bread together. Plus, Willow's here too. Father Michael, I hope you don't mind?"

"Of course not, Katie. I'd rather enjoy the company myself," Father Michael said, as they reached the kitchen.

Katie grabbed Father Michael's arm and held him back a step while Father Victor went into the kitchen. "Before we go in there, I was wondering if you've had any word from Dr.

Amy?" Katie asked. "I don't want to ask in front of Willow, I can tell she's worried sick about her."

Michael's face sobered immediately. "No, I haven't. I've been worried about her myself. I was hoping we'd see her in the emergency room last night, but they said she was still in the operating room when we left."

"She was looking a little pale about the whole thing," Katie said. "I could tell she was upset."

"I'm sure she is, considering what she's gone through these last six months," Michael said softly. "After breakfast, I'm going to the hospital to try and see this Griffin fellow. Hopefully, Amy will be there and I'll get to talk to her."

"Will you give her my best wishes?" Katie asked.

"Of course I will. I just hope I don't miss her," Michael said.

"Well if you do, come back and take a stroll down by that bench you two tend to meet at, by the Divide," Katie said, with a knowing glance and a nod.

"Katie," Michael paused as his face flushed to his ears. "We're just friends and she's very vulnerable right now. She needs the support. Her sister was murdered and then she was attacked herself. She won't even talk about her niece in that coma."

"Uh-huh, I got it. Good friends, I'd say," Katie answered, with a smile. "Just watch yourself, Father. It's all in the eyes."

"Hey," Father Victor's voice boomed into the hallway. "Are you two coming to eat or not? I'm ready for thirds."

"You just hold on there, Father Victor," Katie said, as she bustled into the kitchen. "I swear you must have a tapeworm."

Michael paused by the doorway before he went into the kitchen. He took a deep breath and for a second, tried to imagine Amy's sad, brown eyes.

Chapter Thirty Two

Walking back to her office, Amy tossed Ray's chart on the desk and dropped into the chair. She put her head in her hands and gently massaged her temples. This was her second case and she was being pushed by the FBI for answers. Amy already hated this job. As the acting medical examiner, she had a responsibility to look for deeper answers about Mr. Fuller's death. Perhaps he was in the wrong place at the wrong time. She didn't know. She knew very little about him beyond what was recorded in his chart. She didn't know much about Jimmy Griffin either and it seemed that she wasn't going to if Marcus Cain had his way. At minimum, she needed to ask some questions about the shooting at the soup kitchen. She shouldn't assume Raymond Fuller was an innocent bystander until she checked a few facts. Regardless, she realized she'd have to list manner of death as a homicide. If there was no further information, the FBI or police could finish the investigation.

Picking up the chart, she found Chief Watson's phone number listed inside. Knowing what she was about to do was probably wrong, she dialed the phone anyway. After three rings, he picked up.

"Watson here," The Chief's voice boomed over the receiver.

"Hi, this is Dr. Amy Daniels," Amy said, her voice hiding any nervousness she felt.

"Yes," he drew out the word. "The trauma surgeon and medical examiner. How are you?"

"Fine, Chief," Amy said. "I'm following up from yesterday. I wanted to know if there were any more details about the shooting. Anything I should know about Mr. Fuller?"

"Not really. We interviewed everyone and of course no one saw a damned thing. It seems Ray was a respected, well liked guy. No record of criminal activity or association. Most likely, this had to do with Griffin."

"I see," Amy said.

"What's the situation down there? How is Griffin?"

"He made it through surgery," Amy said quietly. "I don't know much about him beyond that."

Chief Watson's voice boomed over the phone as he erupted with a hearty laugh. "FBI stonewalling you too? These guys can be real jerks sometimes."

"Well, let's just say I've been shown my place," Amy said sarcastically. "Before I sign the death certificate, I wanted to make sure there weren't any important details that had surfaced.

"Sorry, Doc. Not much I can add to yesterday," Chief Watson said. "Keep my number, in case anything turns up on your end."

"Will do, thanks Chief," Amy said, before she hung up. Placing the chart in her desk, she left the office and made her way back to the autopsy suite. There were several technicians and an officer in the room. Not knowing what else to do, Alex made his way over to her.

"Are you okay with Mr. Fuller?" Amy asked.

"Got him closed up and back in the frig before the army got here," Alex said, pleased with himself.

"Good job," Amy said, with a smile. "I'm going to the locker room to change and then upstairs to see Griffin. Keep an eye on things. If they try to take anything they shouldn't, call me right away."

"Sure thing, Doc," Alex said, with a smile. "Go do what you gotta do."

"You have my cell phone number. Call me if anything strange happens, got that? I mean anything," Amy said.

"You betcha," Alex said, turning to watch the ruckus with wide eyes.

Chapter Thirty Three

After finishing the delicious brunch made by Katie, everyone went their separate ways. Michael disappeared into his study and sat at his desk for a few minutes. Everything had moved so fast since yesterday, he wanted some time to think things over and get a fresh perspective. Michael wasn't sure exactly what had happened. He'd stepped outside with the garbage, went to stop an argument and witnessed a man get shot in the head. He ran for his life with Jimmy Griffin and was now realizing the full horror of seeing Mr. Fuller lying on the ground with a large hole in the back of his head, oozing gore and bright red blood. Only a few seconds had gone by after the shooting, but it seemed like hours. At the time, everything had been in slow motion. Amy would know why the FBI was involved. Michael was worried about her and needed to talk to her. He felt unsettled after witnessing one man being murdered. He could only begin to imagine what Amy had seen throughout her career. Hundreds of patients with gunshot wounds, knife wounds, and limbs torn off had passed her table. Michael knew she'd treated patients mutilated by violence, car accidents, stupidity and occasional acts of nature. Some of her patients had died, but most lived, saved by her hand. The emotional impact from constant exposure to that kind of carnage must be very stressful in itself, but then to add the emotional impact of her sister's violent death would be too much. Amy was just starting to open up. She wouldn't talk about her own brush with death but was mentioning her sister more often. No wonder she wanted to rest on the bench and watch the river.

Then there was Katie's comment. Michael let it wiggle around his brain for awhile. It was true he was very fond of Amy, but they hadn't crossed a line of impropriety and Michael was very aware the line could get blurry. Opening his center desk drawer, he withdrew the letter from Father Lomack. It had been three months and Michael still hadn't heard from him. Father Lomack was supposed to attend the same counseling retreat as Father Victor, Father Doherty and Father Juan three months ago, but hadn't shown up. He sent a letter instead, outlining how confused he was about trying to love the Lord while falling in love with a woman in his parish. Father Lomack wanted more time to contemplate his feelings and intentions for this woman. Father Michael turned the letter over in his hand. His situation wasn't quite as delicate as that, but was he heading there?

In order for Amy to move on, he knew she needed to trust that someone special would always be there for her.

Michael wanted to be that friend who would support her, pick her up when she fell and provide unquestioning loyalty, encouragement and love, but he had to give some serious thought to potential consequences. As he replaced the letter and closed the desk drawer, he stood up and knew he was going to the hospital to see Jimmy Griffin, but mostly to find Amy. He needed to talk to her and make sure she was okay.

Walking into the front hall of the rectory, Michael picked up the keys to the church minivan. He was about to leave when he heard a voice behind him.

"Father Michael. Michael, wait a minute," Father Victor called out, as he made his way down the hall. "I'm so glad I didn't miss you. Are you on your way to the hospital?"

"Yes, as a matter of fact, I am," Father Michael said, as he held up the keys.

"Wonderful, would you mind if I went with you?" Father Victor asked, as he reached the front door. "I just got a call from Father Doherty. He was supposed to give communion at the hospital today. He and Marty were going to run a counseling session for the patients in detox, but the session was cancelled and they're not going to the hospital, so he asked if I could help and offer Holy Communion to the patients who want it."

"Of course," Michael said. "I have a few things to do, but I could help you when I'm finished."

"That's even better," Father Victor said. "As soon as I'm done, I have a date with Tony at Hasco's Bar and Grill."

"Really?" Father Michael laughed.

"Yes, we're both walking over to Mickey's Gym. I promised him a chance of redemption in the ring, but I'm not going easy on him this time," Father Victor said excitedly.

"Okay Victor. Don't hurt the man," Michael said, with a chuckle and light warning. "Don't forget, Tony was a cop with the NYPD. He may have skills you haven't encountered yet."

"Do you think I should wear my collar in the ring?" Victor asked, kiddingly. "You know, to throw him off."

"Of course not, and don't make assumptions, that's all I'm saying," Michael said, more to himself than Victor. "Have you ever heard the saying, 'Strive to be humble in victory and gracious in defeat?"

"You're right, Michael, I'll remember that," Victor said, with a laugh. "I'll meet you at the van in a few minutes; I have to collect my things."

As Victor hurried back to his room, Michael shook his head and walked toward the car.

Chapter Thirty Four

After changing in the locker room, Amy emerged wearing a clean, white coat. A stethoscope was draped around her neck, accenting her outfit as if it was a special form of medical jewelry. Walking over to the elevator, she pressed the call button. Within a few minutes, the doors opened and Amy stepped inside. As she punched the button to bring her to the fourth floor, Marcus Cain entered the elevator. Nodding to her, Cain turned and faced the doors as they closed. Within seconds, they were on their way up. Jimmy Griffin had been given a room in the VIP section of the hospital. Patients, who were famous or worked in highly sensitive political positions, were sequestered in the VIP section for their own safety, as well as the safety of everyone else in the hospital. Having had a recent experience with a murderer lurking in the building, the administration of Rocky Meadow General thought it more prudent to hide a federal criminal, as well as the agents in charge of his protection, in the VIP wing.

"Is it an annoying coincidence you're in this elevator or are you following me?" Amy asked.

"Strictly coincidence," Cain said, with his mouth tight. He offered nothing more and continued to stare at the doors as they made their way up to the fourth floor.

Amy and Cain exited the elevator and walked toward Jimmy Griffin's hospital room. There were two large muscled men standing in the hall, blocking the entrance to the door. Each agent wore a bullet-proof vest and carried a standard issue Glock in a holster. "Wow," Amy said, "Isn't this a bit of overkill for one post-op patient?"

"It's all protection," Cain answered. "We have one dead in the morgue, another in a hospital bed and we're not sure what happened or why. He's not healthy enough for a safe house. We'll watch him here until he can leave."

"It's a good thing we're in a special wing," Amy said. "These agents scare me. I can only imagine what other patients and their families would think."

"We'll be gone as soon as we have a proper place to take him," Cain said tightly.

"I heard that he's a computer specialist. What did he do?" Amy asked, frustration showing in her voice.

Cain ignored her question as he nodded to the agents in the hall. "Gentlemen."

"Do you have to be in here, right now?" Amy asked Cain, as he followed her into the room.

"I want to be with you when you talk to the patient," Cain said stiffly.

"That's fine, but I'm going to examine him first. I need to be sure he's not having a problem after surgery. He's lost a lot of blood. Hopefully, he won't need another transfusion," Amy said, slipping into clinical mode.

"You're the doctor," Cain answered.

"Thank you for that," Amy answered, with a nod. She turned and walked over to Jimmy's bed. He was lying on his back, with his head on the pillow and eyes closed. He looked weak, pale and uncomfortable as he shifted his body.

"Mr. Griffin?" Amy asked, as she approached the side of the bed. Cain was standing right behind her. Jimmy opened his eyes and jumped when he saw them standing close by.

"Damn, you scared me," he said, as his face turned ashen.

"I'm sorry Mr. Griffin," Amy said, in a soothing tone. He seemed so meek and mild mannered, Amy guessed any one of these agents could stop him without difficulty. She then reminded herself the major threat was an unknown gunman coming into the hospital to finish what had been started. She still hadn't figured out why. "I'm Dr. Amy Daniels. Perhaps, you remember me from yesterday?"

"Well, it's all pretty blurry. I think I remember you from the ambulance," Jimmy said.

"That's right," Amy replied. "I'm the surgeon who operated on you last night as well."

"Oh, how did that go?" Jimmy asked, with a worried look on his face.

"I'll explain everything in a minute," Amy told him. "I know you were still out of it from the anesthesia when I left the hospital, so you didn't quite understand everything."

"And no one will talk to me," Jimmy said. "The nurses have been in and out, but keep telling me to wait for the doctor."

"That would be me," Amy said. "I'll tell you all that I know, but before we start, there is something I want to point out. The man standing over there is an FBI Agent named Marcus Cain. He'll have some questions for you when I'm done. If you don't want him in the room while we talk, I can make him leave."

"What?" Cain asked, as he looked up sharply at Amy.

"Sorry, confidentiality rules," Amy said to Cain. "It's his choice."

"Do I have some kind of disease or something?" Jimmy asked, with a worried look on his face.

"No, we're just going to talk about your shoulder," Amy said. "But I have to ask you about some of the details from yesterday."

"Well, unless he's blind, he already knows I got shot," Jimmy said, as he made a face toward Cain.

"That, I do," Cain said, with a wry smile. "Before you start going over what happened yesterday, I want to make sure of one thing. Did one of the agents read you your rights?"

"Is that the 'You have the right to remain silent' thing?" Jimmy asked.

"Yea," Cain said. "That's it. Along with, 'anything you say may be used against you in a court of law'."

"They did that before," Jimmy answered, as he shifted in the bed and winced when he moved his shoulder.

"As long as I know you understand, we're good then," Cain answered. "You can proceed, Doc."

"Thanks," Amy answered, frowning back at Cain. Turning back to Jimmy, she said, "How are you feeling today?"

"Not that great," Jimmy replied.

"Are you in a lot of pain," Amy asked.

"Only when I move," he answered.

"Do you have any shortness of breath or chest pain," Amy asked, as she picked up a vitals sheet from the nightstand next to his bed. His blood pressure and pulse were stable. There was no sign of a fever and his oxygen saturation last measured his oxygen at 94%.

"Well, it hurts when I take a deep breath," Jimmy explained.

"That's okay, as long as you can get that breath," Amy said. "That's why we have that little white clip on your finger.

To make sure there's enough oxygen in your lungs. You'll have pain each time you take a breath. That's from expanding the ribcage and surrounding muscles. It'll hurt for awhile."

"What did you do in the surgery?" Jimmy asked.

"You were shot in the left shoulder," Amy explained. "The bullet went straight through your body, but it glanced off your clavicle or collar bone and damaged it. We repaired it last night, as well as making sure the bleeding was stopped. You had a chest x-ray to confirm your lung wasn't collapsed from the bullet."

"It's alright now?" Jimmy asked, as he looked at her.

"Yes, but now we watch for things like an infection or possibly worse, a blood clot in your lung. Your shoulder and upper chest will be painful for awhile and you might need physical therapy on that shoulder too."

"Is that all?" Jimmy asked, as he raised his eyebrows.

"That's most of it," Amy said, as she took her stethoscope from around her neck. "I need to listen to your heart and lungs." Amy leaned down and put the stethoscope on his chest. She moved it to a few places to better hear the different chambers and valves.

Jimmy's stomach clenched as he noticed that Cain leaned forward as well and had his hand placed over his gun, just in case he needed it.

"Can you roll toward me?" Amy asked him.

As he tried to comply and endure the pain, Amy walked to the other side of the bed and listened to his breathing through his back. She then put on a pair of gloves, removed his bandages and checked the wound. She poked and prodded the area and seemed satisfied that all was in order. Once she was done with the exam, she changed the original bandage with antiseptic gel and sterile gauze. The entire dressing was secured with clean tape and Jimmy was allowed to roll back to his original position. "That freaking hurts," he said, as he grimaced. A few beads of sweat popped out on his forehead.

"I'm sorry, I'll tell the nurse to give you something for pain," Amy said, as she surveyed her handiwork. She then cleaned and redressed the laceration on his left forearm as well.

"I have a few questions to ask him," Cain jumped in. "Before he takes the pain med and goes off to the Land of Nod."

"That's pretty interesting, coming from you," Amy said, with a chuckle as she took off her gloves and threw them in the biohazard bag.

"Why's that, doc?" Cain asked, with a puzzled expression on his face.

"As I recall from the Bible, I think it's Genesis, that's where Cain went after he murdered his brother, Abel." Amy said.

“From what I remember of Sunday school, I believe you’re right,” Cain replied with a smile. “But I don’t remember Abel getting into trouble over a computer.”

“I’ll be at the nurse’s desk if you need me,” Amy said to Jimmy. “And the nurse will be in with your pain medication. Please feel better.” Amy turned and left the room, but not before shooting a reproving glance at Cain.

Chapter Thirty Five

Michael directed the minivan to the parking space designated 'clergy only', located in the front circle of the hospital. Turning off the ignition, the two priests emerged from the car and headed toward the glass automated doors.

"I'm starting on the fifth floor," Father Victor said, as they crossed the lobby of the hospital. "Then, I'll work my way down to the second floor."

"Okay, I'll try to meet up with you as soon as I can," Michael said, as he looked around the lobby.

"If we don't connect, I'll page you?" Father Victor asked, as he tried to follow the direction of Michael's attention.

Turning back to Victor, Michael said, "That'd be great. I don't think I'll be too long. First, I have to find out where Mr. Griffin is. After I visit him, I want to find Amy and see if she's okay."

"You do what you have to do," Victor said affably. "I know you worry about her."

"Thanks for understanding," Michael said, with a smile.

"Just remember, when we're done here, you'll drop me off at Hasco's?" Victor asked, with a grin.

"Without a doubt, go in peace," Michael said, as he reached out and patted the large priest's upper arm. After watching Victor stride to the bank of elevators, Michael made his way to the visitor registration desk. A friendly, gray haired volunteer, wearing a pink smock, waited with a smile.

"How can I help you today, Father?" She asked, looking up at him.

"I'm here to see a patient by the name of Jimmy Griffin. I don't know what room he's in, but he was brought in yesterday," Michael said quietly.

"Of course, Father," the volunteer said, while looking through an index box of visitors' passes that were arranged in alphabetical order. "I'm sure he would welcome a visit." She continued to rifle through the box for a few seconds. Unable to find a pass with his name, she looked up at Michael and said, "Can you please spell that name for me?"

"G-r-i-f-f-i-n," Father Michael repeated, with a reassuring smile. "I think he just had surgery last night, in case that makes a difference."

"Why can't I find it? It should be in here," the volunteer half muttered to herself, as she reviewed the contents of the box again. "I don't see a Griffin listed, using an 'I' or an 'E'. I looked under 'J' for Jimmy, but I don't see anything listed there either," she said, as she looked up at Michael with a questioning glance. Adjusting her bifocals, she said, “I could call Admitting to find him, if you’d like to wait a minute, Father.”

“Yes, that would be very kind of you,” Michael answered, with a smile. “I’d appreciate that.”

Chapter Thirty Six

Cain pulled a chair to the side of the hospital bed. He sat down, a terse look on his face and said, “Mr. Griffin, I’d like to introduce myself. My name is Agent Marcus Cain, FBI.”

“Am I under arrest?” Griffin asked, with a panicked look on his face.

“Not at this point, you are a person of interest to the FBI for a federal crime. I can’t question you while you’re in the hospital or under medical care, but you’ll be hearing from us shortly.”

“About what?” Jimmy asked.

“We received a call from Vanderson Group about some difficulty with your computer. We’ll want to know if you have any knowledge about that.”

“What if I don’t?” Jimmy asked.

“Like I said, you’re a person of interest to the FBI. We’ve obtained warrants to search your office and the computers at work and home. Once we have that information, we’ll talk again. Goodbye, Mr. Griffin.”

Cain smoothed his tie and got up from the chair.

"Wait. What if I do know something? Can I make a deal?" Jimmy asked.

"I don't know for sure," Cain answered. "I guess it depends on what you know, but I don't want to bother you in the hospital."

"What if I want to talk? How about protective custody?"

"Why would you need that, Mr. Griffin?"

"Because they'll kill me," Jimmy answered nervously. "If I tell you, they're going to kill me," Jimmy whined.

"Looks to me like they're trying to kill you now, so I don't think it's going to matter either way," Cain pointed out.

"You have to promise to protect me," Jimmy shouted. "You can't let them get to me."

"I'm sure we'll do the best we can, Mr. Griffin," Cain said, to pacify him. Jimmy remained quiet.

"Alright, I'll go for now. Perhaps we'll talk again once you're released," Cain said, as he started to walk toward the door.

"No wait. I want to confess. I'll tell you what I did if you put me into protective custody."

Cain stopped and came back to the chair. "I'll certainly discuss it with my superiors. You understand I can't formally question you while you're under medical care, but you're free to tell me anything you'd like."

"Like what?" Jimmy asked.

"Why don't you start with why you have a bullet hole in your chest," Cain said, as he shifted in the chair. "We have a dead man downstairs and half of the Vermont FBI task force working on this case. What I'd like to find out is why?"

Swallowing hard, Jimmy said, "I don't know."

"I find that hard to believe, Mr. Griffin," Cain said, as he stared at Jimmy's face. "Let's start with this. Why were you arguing with Mr. Fuller?"

"Who?" Jimmy asked. "I don't know anyone named Fuller."

"Let me refresh your memory," Cain said. "He's the dead man from the soup kitchen. Now you know who he is?"

"Oh, him. He had something of mine and I wanted it back," Jimmy said sheepishly.

"Like what?" Cain asked, while staring hard at Jimmy. After a few seconds, Cain set his jaw and said, "Look, before I came to your little party in the woods, I had a long talk with the owners of Vandersen Group. Let me be quite clear about the situation. You're going to be a guest of the United States Government for a very long time. You can stay with us, in a federal lockup, until you grow old and die, or you can cooperate and perhaps be back on your own before you turn seventy. It's your choice."

"I wasn't sure how long it would take them to find out," Jimmy said, swallowing hard.

"Who are you talking about now?" Cain asked.

"Vandersen Group," Jimmy said quietly.

"Why don't you settle back and start from the beginning," Cain said, with a stony face.

Jimmy licked his dry lips and started talking. "I've always been good on computers. Working with numbers and software came easy to me. I had a few crappy jobs, but then I landed a position at Vandersen Group. It's hard to get hired there; they're a pretty decent company." Jimmy paused for a few seconds. Cain purposely didn't ask questions so Jimmy would feel obligated to keep talking. "I did pretty good for awhile. I got a new car and a nice apartment, but I had a little problem with making some, ah, online bets. It's easy to do, 'cause it's just typing, right? At first, I won a few bucks, but then I started losing. I made larger bets to cover the money I owed and screwed up pretty bad. I got deep in the hole."

"Go on," Cain said quietly.

"Well, I was getting squeezed pretty hard. I had to sell my new car to cover my losses, but I still couldn't catch up," Jimmy said, as he looked at Cain.

"So?" Cain said, encouraging him to continue.

"My, ah, internet bookie, I guess I could call him that, basically let on if I didn't come up with the money, real fast like, they were looking at taking body parts," Jimmy said, as he swallowed. "I think they were setting me up, to be honest with you."

"Setting you up how?" Cain asked sharply.

"Well, they waited until I was into them really deep. One day, I got a call. They wanted to make a deal," Jimmy explained.

"What deal and who's they?" Cain asked impatiently.

"They said they'd forgive all my gambling debts, plus give me a lot of money if I would get one download for them," Jimmy said, with a lopsided grin, as he shrugged his shoulders. "They had it all planned out too."

"Who planned it?" Cain was getting aggravated.

"My bookie and some of his friends that wanted information. That's what he said. It was just information."

"How'd it go down?" Cain asked.

"They sent me an envelope with a special flash drive in it. All I had to do was plug it in and let it run. There was a throw away phone in the envelope too. I was told to hang onto it and they'd get in touch with me after the download was completed."

"How did they know when it happened?" Cain asked.

"I don't know," Jimmy said. "I assume there was some tracking code imbedded on the flash drive."

"Then what?" Cain asked.

"Then, I went out to Church Street. I was supposed to wait until they contacted me. Meanwhile, some jerkwad spilt his drink on me so I took off my jacket to make sure the flash drive was ok," Jimmy explained.

"And?" Cain asked, while encouraging him to continue.

"They finally called the phone, but while I was talking with the bastard, someone stole all my stuff," Jimmy said.

"Right from under your nose?" Cain asked. "What'd they do? Pull a gun?"

"No, I put the jacket on the table to check the ground. I'd walked about five steps away 'cause I was looking for the flash drive," Jimmy said. "When I looked back, all my stuff was gone."

"So you didn't see anyone take it?" Cain asked, disbelief written across his face.

"I didn't see anything, my back was turned," Jimmy said. "I thought it was them, messing with me, ya know?"

"I assume it wasn't?" Cain asked.

"They said it wasn't. The voice called me back to see why I didn't make the drop off, so I guess he wasn't in on it."

"What then?"

"They told me I'd better get the flash drive back and fast. So I spent the whole night walking up and down Church St, looking for my stuff. I finally saw that homeless guy wearing my friggin' jacket."

"That homeless guy was Raymond Fuller," Cain said.

"I didn't stop and ask his name. All I know is he had my jacket and I needed to see if the flash drive was still in the pocket."

"How did you know it was your jacket?" Cain asked.

"Like I said, it was my jacket 'cause the sleeve was ripped," Jimmy said, with a sullen look on his face. "It got ripped on the way out of my building. Anyway, I couldn't talk to him 'cause there was a cop nearby. I didn't want to attract attention, so I just followed him."

"To where?" Cain asked

"To that soup kitchen," Jimmy answered. "He gets there and goes to talk to everybody like he's the friggin mayor of the homeless people."

"He was a war veteran from Vietnam," Cain said.

Jimmy looked down at his hands. "I just wanted my friggin jacket."

"Why didn't you ask him for it?" Cain asked.

"Well, that's basically what happened. He got in line to get food and I couldn't get near him. By that time, I was starving so I figured I had time to grab something. I made sure I sat real close, so I could watch him."

"And?" Cain asked.

"Well, when he finished his plate, the priest came by for the garbage."

"Father Michael?" Cain asked.

"I guess so, I don't know," Jimmy said. "Anyway, the guy gets up to go out the back door for a smoke, so I followed him."

"What happened next?"

"He wouldn't give me the jacket, so we were arguing about it," Jimmy said, as he started talking faster. "Then the priest came out the back door and was trying to calm us down and, you know, straighten things out. Next thing I knew, the homeless guy has a bullet in the back of his head and the priest is pulling me down some path. When we reached the end, he pushes me off the cliff, but I managed to catch a bullet in my shoulder anyway."

"Better than the head if you ask me," Cain said tersely.

"We went into the water and that's all I remember," Jimmy said. "Till I woke up in that ambulance, by the lake. My shoulder was hurtin' like a son of a bitch."

"Did you ever find the flash drive?" Cain asked.

"Nope. I put the jacket on to check the pockets, but then all hell broke loose," Jimmy said.

"So where's this flash drive?" Cain asked.

"Damned if I know," Jimmy said, with a shrug.

"What was on it?" Cain asked, raising his voice.

"Numbers, accounts, passwords, pin numbers," Jimmy said. "You name it. It could be anything like that. But it probably had some special coding too, because they insisted I use that flash drive and get it back to them, immediately."

"Did it have any special markings on it?"

"Yeah, there was a symbol in the middle. It looked like a staff, you know the kind of thing Bo-Peep walked around with," Jimmy said.

"A crook?" Cain asked.

"What?" Jimmy asked.

"A crook, a shepherd's crook," Cain answered. "Kind of like a question mark but with a really long bottom."

"Yeah, that sounds right. It had the letters 'S' on one side and an 'F' on the other."

"Shepherd Force, so it is them," Cain muttered to himself.

"I've heard about them," Jimmy said. "A real hactivist group."

"Then you would've been smarter to call the FBI," Cain said, as he stood up, his body tensing. "As it is, your gambling debts got at least one person killed and who knows what else."

"What now?" Jimmy asked, shifting nervously in the bed.

"I don't know, yet," Cain said. "It depends on when we can get you out of here. I'll need some time to talk to my superiors. When you leave the hospital, you'll have to give us a formal statement," Cain said. "Or we could just cut you loose and let them hunt you down. You know, use you as bait. We'll see." Cain got up from his chair. On the way out the door, he couldn't help notice Jimmy's face, white with fear. Feeling guilty for a millisecond, he quickly excused himself thinking the bastard deserved it.

Chapter Thirty Seven

Back in the minivan, Father Michael and Father Victor left the hospital parking lot. Michael spent most of his time trying to get the information he needed to visit Jimmy Griffin and find Amy. The hospital had no record of Jimmy Griffin, which he found impossible to believe. They apparently couldn't find Amy either. The volunteer had finally connected Michael with the operator who paged Amy several times. Not receiving a response, he asked her to call the morgue directly, thinking she may be in autopsy. Michael was told the post was done and Amy had gone upstairs to visit patients. After several more attempts, the operator told him there was nothing more she could do except try to place a call to her pager, but there were areas in the hospital where the pagers didn't receive the messages well, like the morgue. Besides, it was a Sunday, so the doctor may have already left the building.

Disappointed, Father Michael took the elevator and met with Father Victor. Together, they finished offering Holy Communion to those that requested it. They also provided last rites to the dying and prayed with some patients as well.

When they were finished, they went to the lobby and tried to overhead page Amy one last time, without success.

"Well, you tried," Father Victor said, attempting to console Michael. "Perhaps you'll hear from her later."

"I hope so," Michael said. "I know this is pretty hard on her emotionally."

"I'm sure it is, but that's where faith comes in, doesn't it?" Victor said softly.

"I guess so, we all get tested," Michael said very quietly.

"So, let's head over to Hasco's," Victor said eagerly. "I promised Tony we'd be there and I'm ready for a burger by now anyway."

"Don't let Katie catch you," Michael teased, as he turned the car toward the center of town. Within a few minutes they'd reached the driveway that led to a back parking lot for Hasco's Bar and Grill. Hasco's had been in the community for a long time and was one of the oldest bars in Rocky Meadow. The previous owner, Mr. Hasco, died and left the bar to Tony Noce. Tony was a cop for the NYPD and partners with Mr. Hasco's son, who was killed during a drug bust. When Tony traveled to Vermont to offer his personal condolences to the senior Hasco, the two of them became close friends. When Mr. Hasco died, he left the bar to Tony in his will, since there was no other family.

As Michael pulled into the driveway, he heard music through the open car windows. The front door of Hasco's was propped open with an old chair and there were several patrons standing on the sidewalk smoking cigarettes. Tony was very serious about no smoking in the bar since Marty, Willow's mother, finally agreed to go to detox for alcohol addiction. She was in her third month of a rehab program that involved telling her personal story to others in similar situations. Father Patrick Doherty stayed in Vermont after attending a mandatory counseling session with Father Michael for the same problem. Through Marty's hospitalization, as well as helping another patron of the bar named Larry Kalosy, Father Doherty was able to treat his alcoholism as well. Tony wanted to help them as much as possible so he started by having all smokers take it outside. The cleaner air made it easier for former drinkers to resist the craving when they came by the bar to visit. Granted, they shouldn't be in the bar at all considering the rules for people, places and things once an addiction is tackled, but Tony and Marty still saw each other whenever they could. Marty hadn't realized Tony was diluting her vodka with water, before she agreed to go to detox. Not for monetary reasons, since Marty never paid for her drinks, but he was trying to slowly wean her off the bottle until she made the connection on her own. Tony even offered his back room as an available meeting place whenever the detox group wanted it, but ultimately, the smell of alcohol and tobacco smoke that permeated the walls of the bar over the last fifty years was too sharp of a reminder for former drinkers of their ritualistic cravings. Coming to the rescue, Father Michael offered a room at St. Francis for their continued use. Katie always provided plenty of hot, strong coffee and delicious baked goods as well.

Bringing the car to a stop, Father Michael turned to Victor and said, "Well, here you are."

"Why are you stopping? Park the car and come inside with me," Victor said.

"I don't know," Michael said. "I was thinking about going back to the rectory to see if Amy called."

"You have a cell phone, don't you?" Victor asked, a little too sharply.

"Yes," Michael said. "Why?"

"Call Katie and ask if Amy called. If she didn't, you can relax and come inside for a break."

"That makes sense," Michael agreed. "You go inside. I'll call Katie and let you know what I'm doing."

"You don't have to tell me twice," Victor said, as he scrambled out of the car and made his way around the building to the front door of the bar.

Michael picked up his cell phone and dialed the rectory. After several rings, the phone was answered by Katie. "St. Francis, can I help you?"

"Katie, it's Father Michael," he said into the phone.

"Oh, hi," Katie replied in a friendly voice and then became concerned. "Is everything okay?"

"Yes, everything's fine. I just wanted to let you know I'm dropping Father Victor off at Hasco's. Apparently, he and Tony are planning to go a few rounds at Mickey's gym this afternoon."

"That's great," Katie said, with a laugh. "All that man needs is to work up more of an appetite."

"Katie, you love all the cooking you're doing lately," Michael teased her.

"Well it's nice to see someone who really appreciates a good meal," Katie responded.

"I'll be back soon," Michael hesitated, as he blushed. "I just wanted to check my messages. You know, in case anyone called for me."

Katie paused a moment before she said, "No Father, she didn't call. I haven't seen her on her bench this afternoon either. Whatever's going on must have her all tied up for now."

"Katie, don't say that," Father Michael said, remembering how she was bound and almost killed several months earlier.

"I'm sorry, dear, that was a stupid choice of words. I'm sure if the FBI is involved, something important is happening and she's just not able to talk to us right now. We'll hear from her soon, stop worrying," Katie gently soothed him, trying to lighten his mood.

"I can't help it," Michael said. "I have this feeling something bad is going to happen."

"Well, watching someone die and running for your life can do that to you," Katie said, as she clucked into the phone. "It's called anxiety, Father."

"If you hear anything, please call me," Michael instructed her.

"I have your cell phone," Katie told him. "Why don't you go into Hasco's and have a nice glass of wine to settle down?"

"I was supposed to run today," Michael said.

"Well, it's getting late and I already have dinner started. You can skip a day," Katie said. "Go relax, Father. I'll call you if I hear anything."

"Okay, see you later then," Michael said. He paused for a few seconds before he said, "Thanks, Katie."

"That's what I'm here for, Father. To take care of you boys," Katie said. "Now, go inside."

"Bye," Michael said, as he pressed end on his cell. He then parked the car and went inside the bar.

Chapter Thirty Eight

Cain finished talking with Jimmy and found Amy completing her chart at the nurse's desk.

"Find out anything interesting?" Amy asked him, as he approached the desk.

"Nothing I care to discuss," Cain said, with a blank face.

"Well did he say anything that would help me with Mr. Fuller's autopsy report?"

"I can't say specifically, but I believe Mr. Fuller was in the wrong place at the wrong time," Cain answered.

"Homicide, by bad luck?" Amy said. "I'll have to find a better way to write that up."

"That's your jurisdiction," Cain said. "Whatever you think would be appropriate."

"You're impossible Cain, you know that?" When she didn't receive an answer, she said, "I'm going down to the morgue and I hope I don't find your FBI boys tearing the place apart."

"I'll go with you," Cain said. He waited for Amy to log out of the computer and walked her to the elevator. After several minutes, they stepped in the empty car and went to the basement.

A couple of technicians were still in the morgue, performing various tasks. Watching them, from the door, was a hospital security guard. Amy was glad Alex had finished closing Mr. Fuller's body and placed him back into the refrigerator until more final arrangements could be made. Amy would sign the death certificate after she reviewed the final test results. There was no doubt the death would be listed as a homicide by gunshot.

"Will they be done soon? Amy asked, as they watched the technicians work the room.

"I'm not sure, but they need to be complete," Cain replied.

"What exactly, are they doing?"

"Looking for cameras, scanning for listening devices, sweeping the place," Cain said. "If we're lucky, we'll get a lead."

"What about my office phone?" Amy asked.

"One of our computer techs will process it. It's a long shot, but if they call back, we may come up with a number we can trace," Cain explained. "It helps that you gave permission. Getting data warrants can take forever."

"What if our 'friend' calls again?" Amy asked.

"The FBI will take care of it. We'll do our job," Cain said. "We're still not sure what's going on." One of the agents called Cain over and spoke to him in hushed tones. When they were done, Cain returned to Amy and said, "I'm told they didn't find any cameras in here, but it seems like he's got eyes on us somehow."

"That's comforting Cain, really," Amy said, as a nervous twitch hit her stomach.

"Just go about your normal routine," Cain said. "If you see anything unusual, call me."

"Maybe tomorrow, but for now, I'm out of here," Amy said, as she looked at her watch. "I can't believe it's 6:00 pm already. I was hoping to leave here early enough to ...," Amy said, then hesitated.

"To what?" Cain asked.

"To relax, that's what. It's Sunday, you know. I thought I'd relax by the church," Amy said in a snappish tone, as she forlornly thought about her bench by the Divide.

"You're pretty close to that priest?" Cain asked sharply.

"What business is that of yours?" Amy asked.

"Just asking," Cain said. "You seemed awfully concerned about him yesterday."

"Of course I'm concerned about him," Amy said, as she crossed her arms defensively. "He's the local pastor. A lot of people look to him for support and guidance. It'd be a big problem if he were hurt."

"Just asking," Cain repeated.

"Whatever," Amy complained, as she shook her head. "Good luck with everything, Cain. I expect my morgue and lab to be pristine in the morning. I'm sure security will keep an eye on things for now."

"It'll be clean as a whistle," Cain said. "I promise."

"It'd better be," Amy warned him.

Cain removed a white card from the inside pocket of his suit jacket. "Here, take one of my cards," he said, as he took out a pen and scrawled an additional phone number on the back.

"Why?" Amy asked.

"Because you should have it, but most importantly, we don't know exactly what we're dealing with here. If you get into any trouble or something doesn't seem right, you call me pronto. Got that?" Amy took the card and looked at it. "That's my direct cell number on there. You need me, you call. Even if you don't think you need me, you call."

After rolling her eyes, Amy placed the card in her pocket. Muttering a terse "goodnight", she walked to her office. Gathering her purse and keys, she headed out the door and entered the elevator. Once she was safely inside, Amy hit the button for the lobby. Letting out a loud sigh, she admitted to herself how tired she was. It had been a long day, both physically and emotionally. Her stomach was growling, which made her realize just how many meals she'd missed again. As she walked through the parking lot, and settled into her car, she was aware nightfall was merely an hour away. Definitely not enough time to relax on her bench and make it to her home in daylight. The roads leading to her log cabin were not well lit and she didn't want to take the chance of dropping off a cliff if she didn't have to. As she passed the covered wooden bridge that led to St. Francis Church, and her bench overlooking the Divide, Amy couldn't help feeling depressed. If she'd wanted to spend her days like this, she never would have left Boston.

Chapter Thirty Nine

Michael entered the bar and waited several moments for his eyes to adjust to the dim light. Late afternoon sunlight filtered in through the open doorway, but it didn't help. Looking around, he noticed two men in the back right corner of the room, playing a casual game of pool. A few of the smokers had sauntered back inside and nursed a beer while they tried to watch professional sports on an old television mounted near the ceiling. The sportscaster's monologue had competition from music playing on an old-fashioned juke box at the other end of the bar. Michael hadn't seen one like it since he'd left New Jersey. Intrigued, he walked over to check the song titles. There were vinyl records sitting upright in the clear top bubble, but he was disappointed when one wasn't picked up by the magic arm and placed on a turntable when the next song played. Song titles were listed on little white cards by each button. One was titled, 'Live Stream'. Michael tried to pick a song using the big plastic, chunky buttons, but he found they were simply decoration. Strains of 'I Can't Help

Falling in Love with You', sung by Elvis Presley, floated out from the jukebox. Smiling, Michael turned back to the bar.

Father Victor was seated on a stool, an icy glass of birch beer in his hand. Standing in front of Victor, with his feet planted and arms folded across his chest, was Tony Noce. A hulk of a man, he looked amused as he listened to the animated priest talk excitedly about going to the gym. Father Victor had been accustomed to working out in the boxing ring when he was back in Chicago. He'd bonded with Tony during his first week in Vermont when he realized they both shared a love of the ring and made a good pair of sparring buddies.

Father Michael walked over and perched on a stool next to Father Victor. "Father Michael, how are you? What's your pleasure?" Tony asked, as he used a dry towel to wipe the bar.

"I think I'll take one of those," Michael said, as he pointed to Victor's drink.

"You got it and on the house too," Tony said, with a laugh, as he slid a bowl containing a mixture of mini-pretzels and peanuts in front of Father Michael.

"Bless you, Tony," Michael said, as he watched him pull a thick, frosted, glass mug out from a refrigerator under the bar and fill it with soda.

"Least I can do, Father. Especially for all you've done for us," Tony said gently.

"How's Marty?" Michael asked, with concern in his voice. "I know Willow's been thinking about her a lot."

"She's doing well, thank you," Tony said, as he smiled at the sound of Marty's name. "She's going on three months sober and she's fighting hard."

"I'm happy to hear that," Father Michael said. "I'm sure Willow is pleased as well."

"I don't know about that," Tony said. "Marty says some days are still pretty hard, but she pulls out that little photo of Willow and she gets through it."

"Family can keep us strong, but temptation is one of our favorite Gospel topics," Father Michael said, as he hurriedly gulped some of his soda.

"Hey," Father Victor asked. "How is Father Doherty?"

Tony looked toward Victor and grinned. "Let me tell you, Father Patrick Doherty has become a new man. He's been sober three months and has really thrown himself into helping others. I'm sure he has a little more understanding because of his personal experience."

"God Bless the caregivers," Father Victor said, as he took a big gulp of his drink.

Tony turned to Michael. "I noticed you liked my new jukebox."

"I haven't seen an old-fashioned one like that in years," Michael said. "When I was a kid in New Jersey, I use to go a diner near my house to play with the jukebox. I'd get chased out after an hour or so. That brings back a lot of good memories," Father Michael said, with a smile. "This jukebox is a little different, though."

"That's because it's digital," Tony explained.

"Digital? Wow, it looks original from here."

"That's the beauty of it. It's actually a brand new model that my friend in the city told me about. It comes with preloaded songs you choose when you order. You know, specific for your establishment, but there's an area to request any song you want, because it's got a service to live stream music. You can request a specific song or enjoy the classic stuff from yesteryear."

"Fancy," Michael said, nodding his head. "I wanted to use the chunky buttons but they didn't work."

"No, they don't. When you want to request something you have to use the digital keyboard that pops up when you hit live stream, but that's not all," Tony said, mimicking the traditional pitchman.

As the priests began to laugh, Victor said, "Do tell."

Tony leaned toward them and whispered. "It's actually a security system."

"What?" They said in unison.

"It's got a camera mounted inside the clear plastic bubble," Tony said, in a hushed voice. "It's connected to a digital recorder in another room. The reason it's at the end of the bar is to video every transaction as well as any patron or employee that decided to help themselves to the cash register."

"Really?" Michael asked, surprise registering in his voice.

Tony straightened back up. "It's even got a wide angle lens for the rest of the joint," he said with a laugh, as he refilled their glasses. "Don't get me wrong, most of what happens in Hasco's, stays in Hasco's, if you know what I mean," Tony said with a nod and wink. "But it does come in handy if a fight breaks out or someone pulls a gun, which happens more frequently than we'd like."

"Who would've guessed?" Victor said.

Tony shrugged. "It's also used to catch people dealing."

"It's amazing what technology can do these days," Michael said, as he picked up his glass.

"Just think about it, an average city may have a million cameras yet we rarely notice them until we need the footage. There's a camera on every streetlight and ATM machine. The majority of public and private business establishments have security cameras on their buildings, lobbies, and main rooms. That's not even considering laptops and personal cell phones. Cameras are focused on us when we order at fast food places and then drive through windows when we pay, for cryin' out loud."

"That's really kind of disturbing," Father Michael said.

"Next time you're at a gas station, look up at the overhang. There's a camera positioned on every pump as well as the little booth in between."

"Big brother is watching," Michael said, referring to the George Orwell book. He shook his head as he lifted the icy birch beer to his lips.

"Yeah, and hopefully God is watching him. Well, enough of that," Tony said, as he leaned forward and rested his arms on the bar. "Can I interest you gentlemen in something to eat? We've got some great food. Our cheeseburgers are heavenly, but our chili fries are spicy as hell."

Father Victor smiled, "You know you don't have to ask me twice."

"Good, cause the more you eat, the slower you'll be," Tony said, with a laugh. Looking at Michael, "How 'bout you, Father?"

"As delicious as that sounds, I was already warned by Katie that she has dinner in the oven. I'll take a rain check, but I do expect to collect sometime soon."

"Anytime, anytime," Tony said, as he walked away to place the order with the kitchen.

Father Michael turned to Victor and said, "I'm gonna leave when I'm done with my soda, you'll be okay here?"

"I'm wonderful," Victor said happily. "I've been waiting to get back into the ring for a week. A good workout is just what I need."

"You'll get a ride home or shall I come for you?"

"I'm sure Tony can drive me over. If not, I'll call the rectory," Victor said, with a smile. "Why don't you go back to St. Francis and relax? Everything is fine, or we would've heard something. Small towns have very fast grapevines."

"That, my friend is very true," Michael said, lifting his glass to finish the soda. "And I'll bet they work faster than some of these cameras." Placing the heavy glass back on the bar, he wiped his mouth with a napkin and hopped off the stool. "I'll see you later," he said to Tony, as he tapped his arm. "Good luck tonight." As Michael walked out of the bar, he was already planning next week's homily on the watchful eye of God. The voice of Bobby Helms singing, My Special Angel, followed him out.

Chapter Forty

Driving up the hill that lead to her log cabin, Amy paused as she pulled around a bend in her driveway. Looking at her house, a pang of guilt washed over her as she realized what a snob she'd become living in Boston. The first thing she did, after signing the contract with Rocky Meadow General, was to call a real estate agent in the area and explain her immediate need for housing near the hospital. The agent told her there weren't a lot of places available, but she'd start a search immediately for a home to meet her needs. Several days later, the agent called back and was thrilled to inform Amy how lucky she was that a log cabin had just become available on a private wooded lot. Amy agreed to a rental with an option to buy and then quietly questioned her own sanity. She was a prestigious trauma surgeon from Boston, who was moving to a log cabin in the woods, to work in a small, but upcoming hospital in Vermont. She was glad the hospital in Boston only granted her a leave of absence instead of dropping her privileges. Amy knew she had to work through the emotional trauma of her family tragedy, but she didn't want to make her life situation worse. The plan was already in motion and she had no choice but to accept the log cabin.

When Amy came to Vermont for final arrangements, the real estate agent was thrilled to personally drive her to the rental. On the way, she talked endlessly about the area and its charms. Seeing the Divide for the first time provoked some strong childhood memories which Amy really needed at the moment. As they continued up the hill, the agent slowed the car and stopped when they rounded the same bend in the driveway. Seeing the log cabin for the first time, Amy paused and drew in a deep breath.

Before her was a gorgeous home made of white cedar logs that was raised off the ground and stood two stories high. The cabin rested on top of a stone foundation that was built on a concrete base, so the wood that reached the ground wouldn't decompose as quickly as it did in dirt. The house was completely surrounded by a large deck that held a gazebo on either side. In the middle of one gazebo, was an outdoor fire pit. The other gazebo housed a heavy wooden picnic table surrounded by benches. Littering the deck was beautiful, hand carved, wooden Adirondack chairs that looked restful and welcoming compared to the busy activity of the city. Near the house, there was a hand carved wooden swing.

One side of the house consisted of two story windows that faced a beautiful lake. The height of the hill, as well as the position of the deck and the house, allowed her to see the sunrise as well as the sunset from the same spot. She had a similar view through the magnificent wall of windows, while holding a steaming cup of coffee when it was cold outside. Amy was sure the view when it snowed in the winter would be gorgeous as well. As the agent drove to the house, she talked about the two-car garage that had a special plug to keep the car engine warm during cold weather.

When Amy heard the term log cabin, she expected a small broken down structure in the woods. Instead she was pleased to find a 2,000 sq ft home that was accented by wood, granite and local marble. The floors were wooden except for tile in the kitchen. The kitchen counters were made of granite and the indoor fireplace was accented by lovely stone and marble. Even the stairs climbing to the next floor were made of wood. Overhead, the polished wooden beams that supported the structure seemed more like accents than an essential part of the house.

"Don't you absolutely love it?" The real estate agent asked, as she gushed about the log home and the natural resistance of cedar to insects and decay.

"It looks like it should be a resort or something," Amy said in surprise.

"Well, it's just beautiful. It has a wonderful kitchen, three bedrooms, two and a half baths, and a loft. The Great room, with a cathedral ceiling, faces the lake as does the master bedroom upstairs. The guest room is on this level. There's even a little deck off the upstairs bedroom and the view is more breathtaking than down here."

"I'm absolutely speechless," Amy said, as she looked around the house. "I have to say, I'm rather shocked. When I got your call, I was expecting a small, cold little cabin, but this is completely opposite of what I imagined. It's really almost too grand for me."

"Well, there was a politician living here who recently retired and decided to move down to Florida with his family. The place came on the market and knowing that you were from Boston, I naturally thought you'd fall in love with it."

"You're right about that," Amy said. "Unfortunately, my salary is not going to be what it was in Boston."

"Well, I think you'll be surprised at the price too," the real estate agent said with glee. "And all the furnishings come with it as well." She was practically clapping her hands in excitement.

"Okay, let's sit down and you can give me the details," Amy said, as her stomach knotted up. After an hour of paperwork, Amy had signed a lease for a year, with an option to buy. Her monthly payments were still less than the rent she'd paid to live in Boston in a much smaller, less attractive place. When she finally moved in, she was almost afraid to be excited. It was too perfect.

Looking at the house, the memories flooded back to her as she took in the view. She wanted all the nature and beauty of Vermont and none of the violent ugliness that she'd left behind in the city. She'd been living in Vermont for six months now. So far, she only had a few regrets.

As she parked the car in the garage, her cell phone started chirping. Reaching into her bag, she grabbed the phone and checked the caller ID. Willow's name and number lit up the display.

"Hello? Willow?" Amy asked.

"Hi, is this a good time? Willow asked anxiously.

"Of course, honey. I told you to call me anytime and I meant it," Amy said, as she got out of her car and closed the garage door. "Are you okay?"

"Yea, I was worried, about you I mean," Willow said in a rush.

Recognizing her false bravado, Amy tried to console her. "I'm fine, don't worry about me, but I'm glad you called."

"You are?"

"Of course, I haven't had a chance to speak to anyone since yesterday. You looked so upset when I left the kitchen." Pangs of guilt washed over Amy as she realized she couldn't handle all her responsibilities and always be available for this poor teenager. That was one of the reasons she never married and had children. You can't serve two masters.

"I was kind of scared. There were so many policemen there."

"I know. Did you go home last night, by yourself?"

"No, Katie made a room for me at the Rectory. She called my guardian, but that woman wouldn't notice if I didn't come home for a week," Willow said, the hurt in her voice obvious.

"I'm so sorry, Willow. If I didn't have to be at the hospital or working with these FBI Agents, I would've been there to see you," Amy said soothingly.

"I know you would've," Willow said sadly. "Are you okay? I got so scared thinking something happened to you."

"I'm fine, honey," Amy said, as she reached the main floor of the house and put her purse and keys on the counter. "But I have to conduct 'official business' as they say."

"Oh, okay." Willow said, with a small voice that made Amy's heart clench. She sounded like a small, wounded child instead of the strong, confident sixteen year old she should've been.

"Where are you now?" Amy asked.

"I'm home, at my house," Willow said.

"Is your guardian there?" Amy wanted to know.

"Yea, she's in the living room watching TV," Willow said angrily. "I can't wait until I'm old enough for my trust fund, then I'm gonna throw her ass out of here."

Amy held back a chuckle. "That's a plan. But right now, she needs to be there with you."

"I wish she'd fall off a mountain," Willow said.

"Don't say that," Amy said, remembering the drama from several months ago. "Listen, once this is cleared up, let's go out for lunch. Did you get your driving permit?"

"No, next week and I can't wait," Willow said, with some excitement in her voice. "Will you drive with me?"

"I promised I'd take you," Amy laughed. "Did you finish the official driver's education yet?"

"I have two more hours and then I get my permit," Willow happily reported. "I want to make sure you'll take me driving, 'cuz I don't have anyone else to ask."

"Oh, honey, we'll go. I promise," Amy said into the phone. "Maybe Father Michael or Father Victor can take you, too."

"Yea, but I'd feel funny if I were with them. They'd make me more nervous," Willow said.

"Willow, I promise I'll take you. No hills at first. We'll just go on flat roads and then work our way up. How does that sound?"

"I already went up a hill and on a highway with my driving instructor," Willow said.

"Did they take you out at night?" Amy asked, thinking they had an extra brake in their car.

"No. No night driving," Willow reported.

"Well, things in Vermont can look a lot different at night," Amy said. "You have to go slower and be more careful in the dark. We'll take driving step by step if that's okay with you, but we'll go."

"Yay," Willow said, as she jumped up and down.

"Easy now, don't get too excited," Amy laughed. "What about a car?"

"The lawyer, Mr. Bradford, is getting a car for me with money from my trust fund," Willow said. "But he won't get me a new one because he's afraid I'll bang it up."

"That makes sense," Amy said. "It's not a bad idea to start driving an older car first."

"Yea, but it's my money," Willow said.

"I know Willow, but I do believe Mr. Bradford is watching out for you. As you get older, and wiser, you'll be more involved in handling your own money. But until the trust is all yours, he has to guide you."

"I can't wait," Willow said eagerly.

Amy laughed. "That's why he's in control, for the moment."

"I know," Willow said. "But I still can't wait."

"Me either," Amy said, as she heard a noise outside the window. Not wanting to alarm Willow, she said, "Let me go, I have to get my dinner ready, okay?"

"Okay, I'll talk to you tomorrow, right?"

"Of course honey, I'll see you at the hospital," Amy reassured her.

"That's right, I don't know what I was thinking," Willow said. "See you tomorrow."

"Bye, honey," Amy said, as she heard steps on the deck. Quickly hanging up the phone, she ran to the window to see who it was.

Chapter Forty One

Four FBI agents sat in the conference room located in the VIP wing of Rocky Meadow General Hospital. They weren't more than six feet away from the room where Jimmy Griffin was lying, lost in sleep from his narcotic.

"Did they finish processing Griffin's personal effects?" Cain asked.

"It's done, but there's nothing there to help us," one of the agents reported.

"Any sign of a flash drive?" Cain asked.

"No. They're still looking at the phone to see if they can get a lead."

"I'm not holding out too much hope for that," Cain said, as he looked at the team. "We don't know what we're dealing with here. Stay tight. I don't know if they'll try to broach the hospital or how important this guy really is to them. He may be holding back and has the flash drive hidden somewhere."

Sam Oakes, Cain's partner, was scheduled to stay at the hospital for the night shift. "The elevators and floors are monitored. We have an agent in the lobby tonight and I personally toured the place with the locals to make sure everything is locked tight. We break into two teams and pull alternating twelve hour shifts."

"Fine for now, but I want to get this guy out of here as soon as possible. I don't know where he's going yet, but we're working on it. I don't want anyone else at risk, especially innocent hospital patients," Cain said. The agents nodded their heads. "If anyone tries to get up here, they'll create a distraction so be wary of unusual activity on another floor. Let the locals handle it and keep this guy covered."

Sam half raised his hand. "Do you really think this computer nerd is holding back?"

"Not really, he looked too scared, but who knows?" Cain said, with a shrug as he got up from his seat. "From this point on, I don't want anyone using your regular case tracking software. I don't know what they're plugged into. Keep everything quiet for now. I have to get some updates to the head of the Cybercrimes Unit, so he can talk to the Director before the situation gets out of hand. Sam is running point for tonight. Any questions?"

The agents looked around and shook their heads. "Okay, stay sharp." As the men left the room, Cain turned to Sam. "You have any problems or even a quiver, you call me."

"You know it," Sam said, as he adjusted his vest and his gun.

"I don't think anything will happen, but if it does it could get ugly."

"We got it covered. Get the hell out of here and clean up, will ya? For Pete's sake, even your suit's wrinkled." Laughing, Cain adjusted his tie and jacket and said goodnight.

Chapter Forty Two

Amy looked at the deck through the bank of windows in the front of the house. The sun was setting. Normally, she didn't mind being isolated, but lately she was nervous. There was enough light to see a large raccoon scampering across her deck. She started laughing and chided herself for being so paranoid. Her stomach growling, she opened the refrigerator to find very little food inside. She'd have to go shopping soon. After pulling out a brick of locally aged cheddar cheese and some stale crackers, she made a small plate for herself. She found a bottle of White Merlot and opened it to breathe. Cutting the hardened edges off the cheese, she decided to slice an apple as well. Filling a wine glass with the Merlot, she picked up the plate and went out to the deck. Having been told to always have things ready, it took a moment to light the fire. Amy was glad she'd listened to that advice. Although the last couple of days were very warm, the night air cooled off considerably. The glow and warmth of the fire would help her relax, settle her nerves and allow her to think about this weekend. Pulling up an Adirondack chair with a thick cushion, she sat down with her plate and wineglass in hand. Watching the fire catch, Amy sat back against the cushion and closed her eyes. The cool night air felt refreshing as she listened to the crickets chirp noisily in the woods. Bullfrogs croaked near the lake which was aglow with the reflection of the moon. Hearing the logs start to crackle and pop, she let out a deep breath, picked up her glass and enjoyed her first sip of cold, delicious wine, as it slid down her throat. She started to hungrily eat the cheese and crackers, saving the apple for last. As Amy relaxed with her second glass of wine, mentally reviewing the events of the last two days, she saw headlights coming up her driveway. Not many people knew where she lived, but she doubted an attacker would announce themselves. Amy checked her cell phone for missed calls, but didn't find any. The car stopped at the base of the stairs and Father Michael eventually stepped out. Looking up toward the fire, he softly called out to her as Amy stood up and crossed to the wooden rail.

"Michael, I can't believe you're here," Amy called back. "Come on up."

Michael climbed the stairs and she met him at the top. The moment was awkward at first. She wanted to rush over and hug him when she saw his beautiful face and warm smile, but she wasn't sure what would be proper.

"I really can't believe you're here," Amy said again, her words tumbling over one another as she blushed. Was it nerves or wine? At the moment, she didn't care.

"Me either," Michael said quietly. "Willow called the rectory after you talked to her and told us you were finally home. We were worried and I wanted to check on you personally. Katie gave me your address."

"Well, I'm glad to see you. Here, come sit," Amy said, as she awkwardly guided him toward the gazebo. She pulled another Adirondack chair close to the fire.

"We've been pretty worried about you. A man gets murdered at the soup kitchen and then we haven't been able to contact you in more than twenty four hours," Michael explained.

"I'm so sorry. This whole situation has been horrible, hasn't it? How are you?" Amy asked, as she searched his face for answers.

"I'm fine," Michael said. "Especially, now that I see you're okay."

"I went to the emergency room when I was done in the OR last night, but you were all gone by then," Amy explained. "It was late, so I didn't call the rectory. Ernie told me your exam was okay."

"Let's just say it was an adventure," Michael sighed.

"Please thank Katie for leaving me food," Amy said. "I've barely had time to eat in the last two days. Oh, where are my manners, would you like something?"

"Katie just served dinner a little while ago," Michael said as he looked at the plate of hardened cheese and apple slices. "It looks like I should've brought some leftovers for you. There was plenty since Father Victor wasn't there."

Amy erupted into her first genuine laugh in days. "Better that you eat Katie's cooking than mine. How about a nice glass of wine? The wine is delicious."

Michael smiled at her. "Apparently, I may need to bring food more often than I thought. I'd love a glass of wine."

"Great, I'll be right back," Amy said, as she hurried inside. She came back to the fire pit with a tray containing a second wine glass, a full bottle of Merlot and a small bucket of ice. Jumping up, Michael placed a small table between the chairs. Amy put the tray on the table and sat down to pour for the two of them. As she settled back in her chair, she let out a heavy sigh.

"I hope I'm not interfering," Michael said, as he sipped his wine. "This wine is good."

"Not at all," Amy said. "When I first moved up here, I craved the isolation, but lately and especially after this weekend, I'm feeling lonely. Believe me, I welcome your company."

“Thank you,” he said, with a small smile looking down at his glass. “This place is beautiful. I think I’ve seen the back of it from one of my trail runs, but I didn’t realize you were staying here.”

“Apparently, I was lucky the real estate agent found it. I’m renting for now. It’s a little large for me, but it’s beautiful, especially when you sit and watch the lake.”

“Then why do you sit on the bench by The Divide so often?” Michael asked perplexed.

Amy took a sip of wine and smiled. “This may sound strange, but I’ve always found running water empowers me. I’d rather watch powerful, forceful water than a pond for instance. The lake is gorgeous, but watching The Divide is different, it’s cleansing.”

“Ah, yes, that’s one of my favorite quotes from the Bible,” Michael said, as he softly recited the words.

“For the Lamb at the center of the throne will be their shepherd; he will lead them to springs of living water. And God will wipe away every tear from their eyes. Revelation 7:17 NIV”

“Wow, that really says it all,” Amy said.

“Living water, as it’s described in the Bible, restores our spiritual health and keeps us strong,” Michael explained. “It’s also said the rivers of living water will spring from those that believe, so eventually, once your faith is restored, you won’t need the actual Divide, it will flow from within you.”

"I wish I was that strong Michael, but I'm not," Amy said softly, as she shook her head.

"You're much stronger than you think. You'll get through this, I promise."

"We'll see about that." After a few seconds of silence, Amy gently offered, "It's funny, but when I dream of water, I find it very frightening. I'm always trapped somewhere. What does that mean?" Amy asked, as she shrugged her shoulders.

"Well it may be exactly what it is, in other words you feel trapped by or anxious about something that can't be changed at the moment. The water may just be a symbol, not the actual problem," Michael said sipping his wine. "I don't know. I think we'd have to do a lot more work on that one."

"I've never told anyone that much about myself," Amy said, her eyes misting as she looked at him.

Michael was quiet for a few seconds. He wasn't sure if she was opening up to him or the wine was to blame, but he didn't want to press her on personal demons at the moment. "I'm here for you, whenever you want to share. I mean when you need me, I'll be there for you," Michael said, fumbling over his words. Blushing, he quickly said, "Not to switch subjects, but can you tell me anything about what's going on?"

"Well, I don't know how much I'm supposed to say, to be honest. There's confidentiality on a medical level as well as the FBI case." Amy curled her legs up in the chair as she watched the flames of the fire.

"Then don't say anything. I understand the importance of being bound by silence."

"I can safely tell you this," Amy looked at him. "Our murdered man was a homeless war veteran who happened to be in the wrong place at the wrong time. He was an innocent victim."

"I'm sorry for him and I'll pray for his soul," Michael said quietly.

"I read his history and I feel very bad for this man. It's possible he hasn't any family that will claim him, much less give him the honor he deserves."

"Amy, what are you trying to say?" Michael asked, as he looked over and saw her pained face in the firelight.

"I know I've been questioning my faith a lot, especially since my sister was killed, and I haven't been to church much," she said quietly. "I don't know this man's situation except he was listed as a Roman Catholic in his records."

"And?" Michael patiently waited for her to collect her thoughts.

"The social worker at the hospital will see if he qualifies for burial through the VA, but if no one claims him," she said and then hesitated. "I mean, would the church or I guess, would you be willing to give him a funeral?"

"I wouldn't have any problem offering a funeral mass for this man," Michael said to her.

"His name was Ray. Raymond Fuller and I'll pay whatever fee the church wants," Amy said hurriedly.

"That has nothing to do with it." Michael said as he looked at her and smiled. "I met Ray on one of my previous visits to the soup kitchen. But on Saturday, I participated in his last few hours and moments in life. I actually watched him die and I'd be honored to celebrate the repose of his soul."

"I don't know what I'm thinking. Maybe I'm just very sensitive to death right now or maybe I'm inebriated, but I don't want his life, his sacrifices, and his dignity as a person to end with being a case number and sent to a potter's field."

"Don't worry, we won't let that happen. I can see how upset you are," Michael said, as he reached over and touched her arm.

"Our lives should have more value than that. We need to realize the difference we really make in this world." Amy looked down and noticed her wineglass was empty again. She chuckled and said, "I think I'd better stop talking now."

"It's getting late and we're both exhausted," Michael agreed. "Do you have a busy day tomorrow?"

"I'm not sure, to be honest."

"Do you think you'll be able to get to the bench tomorrow afternoon? I'd like to talk more about this."

Amy looked over at Michael and searched his face. He was the friend she was looking for, the person she wanted to trust with her feelings and fears. Someone she could lean on and not have to constantly be a pillar of strength for. Why did he have to be a priest? "I'll try Michael; I swear I'll try to be there."

"Good, I'd like that," Michael said, with a large smile. "Well, I'd better go." Michael leaned forward and put his glass on the tray. He then lifted the entire tray as he stood. "Let me take this inside for you, you're tired." Placing her wine-glass on the tray, Amy reluctantly stood up and led the way inside the kitchen.

"Just leave it on the counter. I'll take care of it in the morning."

Michael nodded and gently placed the tray on the granite counter. "You've really got a beautiful home here," Michael said, looking around the room. Through the windows, the reflection of the moon on the lake was beautifully serene.

"Thanks," Amy said, as they slowly walked back out on the deck. She stopped at the top of the stairs and placed her hand on his arm. Looking up at him, she said, "Thank you, for checking on me."

He quietly gazed at her upturned face. "You're very welcome." After a few seconds, that seemed a lifetime, he reached out and hugged her to him. Feeling a heady rush of warmth at his touch and scent of cologne, she held him tightly for just a second or so and then he was gone. As she watched him hurry down the stairs, she smiled to herself and for the first time in days or even months, she sighed and felt happy.

Chapter Forty Three

The sun rose high the next morning and promised a beautiful day. A typical Monday would've found Amy running around, frantically getting dressed and hurrying to the hospital. She normally went to work earlier than required as the day was more productive when she worked ahead of schedule. Otherwise, more distractions presented themselves and her efficiency dropped sharply. Now that she was the acting medical examiner, the hospital provided replacements for her other duties and her schedule was more flexible. There were no set hours at the emergency room or clinic, in case she had to leave immediately. Amy rolled onto her side. The sun was shining through the large upstairs windows and the lake glistened below. It was a gorgeous, peaceful vision. Given the craziness of the weekend, she allowed herself an extra twenty minutes to lie in bed and think. Remembering the feel of Michael's arms around her, she smiled and hugged her pillow.

Originally, she'd planned to see patients in the clinic and relax on Saturday. Instead, it turned into the weekend from hell. From murder to FBI, unscheduled surgery and autopsies, it was insane. She closed her eyes to review, especially last night. She remembered everything she said and did, so thankfully she hadn't drank too much wine. Amy wished she could stay exactly where she was as the moment, lying in blissful peace, staring at the lake. But she knew she had to get up and go to work. She envisioned poor Mr. Fuller, still in the morgue. She knew she'd have to talk to Cain and he'd probably be a pain in the butt. Before getting up, she rolled over and thought of that precious hug from Michael.

Knowing Michael these past months made Amy realize how much she had withdrawn since her sister died. She'd wanted to deny the pain and grief, but couldn't and wasn't able to move on. She also recognized she'd been on the brink of burnout as a trauma surgeon and had no life outside of medicine. Being with Michael gave her a small stirring of hope and happiness, except for the fact that he was a priest.

For the first time, in a long while, she hugged her pillow and wept. She hadn't cried in six months and wouldn't allow herself to acknowledge the pain and loneliness. She was changing and this morning it washed over her like the cleansing water of the Divide. She didn't want to fight anymore. Either she'd survive or die trying. There had to be more out there and deep down she wanted to find it, with Michael. She knew she could find happiness and love, but she was looking in the wrong place. Regardless, it was time to start living again.

When the tears subsided, she threw the covers back and got out of bed. Pulling her t-shirt down to her cotton pajama pants, she padded to the bathroom. After cleaning up and washing her face, she went to the kitchen and made a strong pot of coffee. It was 8:30 in the morning, but it felt like noon. Toasting a bagel, she pulled jelly out of the refrigerator. When the coffee was done, she poured herself a large mug and added extra cream and sugar. Pulling on a sweater, she walked outside with her toasted bagel and coffee mug and sat down in last night's cushioned Adirondack chair. Positioned directly toward the sun, the warmth felt nice on her face as she let her head rest against the back of the chair. The deck was peaceful. Birds were flying overhead and Amy could smell the woods. Pine scent drifted toward her as well as the remains of the wood fire in the nearby gazebo. Small, white fluffy clouds lazily crossed through a sky of blue and she didn't want to move. She didn't want to go back to work and be reminded of pain, death and violence. She was too tired to fight today, but she had no choice.

Eventually, her coffee cup was empty and she couldn't put off the inevitable. Amy went back to her kitchen and washed all the dishes, including those from last night. She changed into a clean pair of scrubs, collected her things and got into her car. Driving down the hill, she slowed more than usual when she passed her bench in front of the Divide and the vision of St. Francis Church in the background. Amy vowed to get there today and hopefully, by late afternoon, she'd feel the power of the river and most of all see Michael.

Chapter Forty Four

The morning mass ended with a flourish as both priests recessed down the aisle with the deacon in tow. The deacon turned when he reached the last pew and walked back up the side of the church to return the Book of Gospels to the altar. Father Michael and Father Victor both continued out the back door and positioned themselves to greet the morning parishioners. Monday morning mass was more crowded than usual. Tourists helped to fill the church since it was the end of August.

"Father, you look so much better than yesterday," Florence said, as she approached him and held his hand. "You almost look like you're beaming."

"Thank you, Florence." Michael smiled down at her.

"I'm glad you took my advice and rested. After all, it was the seventh day."

"Yes, thank you. Bless you Florence, have a great day," Michael said, as he shook her hand. As she walked away, Father Victor leaned toward him and smiled.

"Yes, you do appear to be beaming today and much more relaxed than yesterday. I take it you found her?"

Michael said nothing and turned to greet the other parishioners. When all had departed the church, the two priests went back to the sacristy and hung up their vestments. The deacon was extinguishing altar candles and lights. Walking together, the two priests made their way from the church to the rectory where they joined Katie in the kitchen. The aroma of freshly brewed coffee was heavenly and both men waited while Katie filled their plates with bacon and eggs. She also put a plate of warm banana bread on the table, right next to the butter dish.

"Katie, this is delicious. I'm gonna have to run twice as far today," Michael said, with a laugh.

"Well, I'm happy you feel like running. When I think of what could have happened, I still feel weak in the knees," Katie said, as she moved around the kitchen. "It's nice to be back to routine."

"And, I'm happy that you're happy when you cook," Victor said, extending his plate for another serving.

"The Saints preserve us," Katie said, while serving Father Victor. She grabbed her coffee and casually sat at the table with them. Looking at Father Michael she raised her eyebrows and said, "So, I assume she was home last night."

Michael looked directly at Katie and said, "Yes, Willow was right. Amy was home and we talked for awhile."

In between sips of coffee, Katie said, "I knew it, because you look rather well this morning, if I may say so."

Michael made a face and said, "Actually, I'd rather you didn't." He took another sip of coffee and realized Katie and Victor were sitting at the table looking at him expectantly. "I don't know what you're waiting for. Katie, I followed your directions and got to the house. I didn't realize her place was so beautiful. The view from the deck, overlooking the lake is gorgeous." He turned to Victor, "I know, because that's where I stayed the whole time. By the way, she was eating an assortment of stale crackers and dried cheese, so I offered to bring her leftovers next time she worked late."

"I knew she wasn't eating well." Katie clucked and sipped her coffee. She continued looking at Father Michael, waiting for more details.

"She couldn't really tell me much about what was going on. I know the FBI is involved, but I don't know why. The man that was killed was named Raymond Fuller. He was a homeless war veteran who unfortunately stood between this Jimmy Griffin and a bullet."

"Poor man," Katie said, as she shook her head.

"Well, I can tell you he was well liked by the other people in the soup kitchen," Victor said. "They were very respectful of him and looked to him for direction."

"He was very popular among the homeless up there," Michael said. "Amy doesn't know that but I think it would make her feel better if she did. One thing that upset her was he'd be given a paupers burial if no one claimed him. I told her we'd offer a funeral mass when he was released from the morgue."

"You did?" Katie asked, with a smile. "That's very nice of you."

"It's the least I can do. He fought for his country and returned safely. Here, the poor man was simply trying to eat a good meal and was murdered as a result."

"I'll be glad to cook, if you care to have a small repast in the all purpose room," Katie said, as she stood and began to collect the empty plates.

"That would be very nice," Michael sighed. "I'm sure he'd be eligible to receive a free burial for his service to the country. Someone from the hospital is going to contact the Veterans Administration to check."

"No doubt," Father Victor said. "We had quite a few deaths like that in Chicago."

Looking up, Father Michael turned to Victor. "So how did the boxing match go?"

"Well, I showed him a thing or two," Victor said. A grin spread across his face as Father Michael continued to look at him. “Truth be told, we’re both out of shape. We started clinging to each other just to catch our breath.”

“You can always come on a trail run with me,” Michael said, with a mischievous grin.

“No thanks, I think I’ll start walking first,” Victor said.

“I’ll tell ya what you can start, a diet, that’s what.” Katie said, while wagging her finger at him. “I’ll cook for you, but it’s gonna be mostly protein and vegetables from now on. Less potatoes and bread, I think.”

“But Katie,” Victor protested, as she walked over to the sink.

“And only one dessert a day,” Katie threw back over her shoulder. “Now both of you move along, while I do the dishes.”

As they walked out the door, Katie heard Victor say, “Thanks, now you got us both in trouble.” Michael laughed all the way down the hall.

Chapter Forty Five

Amy parked her car in the doctors' lot and turned off the ignition. She was feeling better about the day and wanted to get started. The sooner she got her responsibilities done, the sooner she could leave. As she gathered her things, her cell phone began to ring. Thinking it was the answering service, she picked it up right away. "Dr. Daniels."

"We want the flash drive," the muted voice said.

"What?" Amy was surprised when she heard the caller's demand.

"The flash drive, doctor. We know you have it and want it delivered as soon as possible."

"Who is this? How did you get my number?" Amy said into the phone and realized the stupidity of her own questions. If Shepherd Force could hack international financial companies, they'd have no trouble tracking down her cell phone number.

"The flash drive, doctor." The emphasis on her title chilled her to her core.

"Look, you're not hearing me," Amy said. "First of all, the FBI took everything with them. They must have it."

"We don't think so. They would've tried to access it and they haven't yet. We would've known."

"What makes you think I have it?" Amy said into the phone as she shook her head.

"You'd better go back and talk to your patient. Deliver it immediately or there will be consequences. We'll start with that little teenager or maybe your priest friend. By the way, I hope you two enjoyed your campfire last night as it'll probably be your last."

Amy was shocked and her mouth fell open. Realizing the line had gone dead, she quickly looked at her phone. The caller ID didn't reveal a number she could use. It was one thing to go after her, but to threaten Willow and Michael was simply too much. Amy found her purse and rummaged through her wallet until she found the business card she'd been given by Cain. Hands shaking, she started to dial and then hung up immediately, thinking her calls were being monitored. Grabbing her belongings, she jumped out of the car and hurried into the hospital. She stopped at the first lobby phone she could find and had the operator page Willow. After a few quiet moments, Amy's headache started to return. When the phone began to ring, she grabbed the receiver in a hurry and said, "Willow, hello? Willow, is that you?"

"Amy?" Willow sounded confused.

Amy took a deep breath and closed her eyes. "Willow, where are you?"

"I'm on the second floor. They needed someone to bring ice to the patients' rooms."

"You need to meet me now. Stop what you're doing and find me at the clinic. I'll tell the head nurse I pulled you away. Please come right now."

"Okay, what's wrong?"

"Nothing, I can't talk at the moment. Just come to the clinic, immediately."

"Okay, I'll be right there," Willow said, as she hung up the phone. After pushing the ice cart back to the break room, she headed downstairs.

Amy almost ran through the lobby to get to the clinic. She took out the business card again and dialed Cain's number from the hospital's phone. After several rings, he picked up. "Cain."

"Cain, this is Dr. Daniels. I need to speak to you."

"I'm listening."

"No, I have to talk to you in person. It's important."

"What's this all about? Where are you?" Cain asked.

"I don't want to discuss it over the phone, but that bastard called me on my personal cell phone. Please come to the clinic and hurry." Amy hung up the phone and looked down the hall, hoping to spot Willow. When the teenager finally emerged from the elevator, Amy ran over and hugged her.

"Okay?" Willow sounded confused. "What's going on?"

"I wanted to make sure you're safe. You're staying with me for a little while. That FBI agent is coming to the clinic and I have to talk to him, but I'd rather be near you right now."

"Now you're scaring me," Willow said, as she looked around the hall.

"Don't mind me," Amy said. "I'm very nervous. Just do me a favor and hang here for now, okay?"

"Cool with me," Willow said, as she shrugged her shoulders.

Amy looked up and saw Cain getting off an elevator. He looked very sharp in a traditional dark blue suit with light blue shirt and sapphire silk tie. He quickly walked over to Amy when he saw her anxious face. "What's going on?"

"C'mon, let's go to the clinic," Amy said, as she guided Willow down the hall. When they reached the front desk, she asked Willow to wait with the receptionist while she spoke with Agent Cain. Firmly holding Willow by the shoulders and looking into her eyes, Amy said, "Promise me, that no matter what happens or who calls you, you will not leave here without me. Promise!"

"Okay, I promise. I will not move without you. Jeez," Willow said, as she slowly emphasized each word as she repeated them.

"Good!" Amy turned to Cain. "Come with me to an exam room."

Hidden inside the exam room, Amy turned to Cain and told him about the phone call. "He threatened my friends and used my personal cell, so there's no need to worry about the burn phone anymore."

"Let me see it," Cain said, as he held his hand out.

"See what?"

"Your cell phone. I want to look at the caller ID. Do I have your permission to track your phone? Otherwise I have to get another warrant and that could take forever."

"Of course, do whatever you have to." Amy dug in her purse and handed over the cell phone. Cain spent a few minutes looking at the recent call list and then asked for her number. When Amy gave it to him, he called a computer tech and recited the number over the phone. "Run it down, ping it and see if you can catch a tower or anything." Hanging up, he gave the cell phone back to Amy.

"Are you listening? He threatened me again. He kept telling me to find the flash drive or there would be consequences. He specifically mentioned Willow and my priest friend," Amy said, as she made quote marks with her fingers.

"Yeah, what about him?" Cain asked, as he watched her face.

"What do you mean?" Amy asked. "You mentioned him yesterday," Amy said. "What's the problem?"

"The problem is I need to speak to him. I want to go over his statement. We've been running around this hospital looking for a flash drive and the truth of the matter is, the person who's spent the most time with this Griffin guy is your priest friend."

"What are you implying?"

"Well, they were both in the soup kitchen together and the path."

"He told you he went to break up their fight."

"They both spent quite a bit of time in and around that lake. How do we know Griffin didn't give the flash drive to the priest for safekeeping?"

"He would've said something," Amy said quietly.

"Are you sure? Did the two of you discuss this case?"

"No, no we didn't," Amy said, as she remembered Michael wanted to talk about it. "I saw him, but I told him I couldn't discuss any details beyond the dead man's name."

"That's it?" Cain's facial expression indicated he didn't believe her.

"Yes, that's it," Amy said defensively. "We also talked about a funeral at St. Francis if no one comes to claim Ray Fuller's body. Michael said he'd offer the mass himself."

"Maybe he wanted to talk about it. Perhaps he has the flash drive, but didn't tell you once you shut him down." Amy remained quiet for a few seconds, annoyance and uncertainty crossing her face.

"He's a priest," Cain said. "If he's asked to keep something confidential, doesn't he have to?" Cain looked smug knowing she wasn't sure about anything. "If I was being stalked by a killer and I had some important information, I think I would give it to a priest for safekeeping."

"I think he would've told me," Amy said quietly.

"He could've given it to the priest as soon as he was shot. Maybe he thought death was near and didn't want to go down with the evidence. The police report said there was a time in the ambulance when the priest held his hand and prayed. I can understand that, but I've also been an agent long enough to know he could have easily palmed off a flash drive."

"You're ridiculous, you know that?" Amy made a face and shook her head at him. "What are you doing about all this? You have three people who've been threatened. Do we just wait for something to happen or what?"

"I need to talk to your priest friend. Call him and arrange a meeting place. In the interest of time, I won't make him go all the way up to Burlington. Once I believe his story, I'll read him in. Make sure it's a public place, preferably outdoors. I'm not doing this in his rectory." Amy looked at Cain without moving. "Go ahead and call him." Cain handed her a land line.

Amy shrugged her shoulders and dialed the rectory. After several rings, Katie picked up the phone. “St Francis Rectory, Katie speaking. May I help you?”

“Katie, it’s Amy,” she said, in a terse voice.

“Amy, how are you? We’ve been worried sick about you, dear.”

“I’m okay, but I need to speak to Father Michael. Is he there?”

“Are you sure you’re okay? Something sounds wrong,” Katie said with concern.

“I’ll be alright, but I need to speak to him right now. Can you get him for me?”

“I’d love to dear; let me see if he’s back from his trail run. One second, please,” Katie said, as she put the phone down with a clunk. After listening to some shuffling and muted voices in the distance, Katie came back on the phone. “He’s just come in, he’ll be right here.”

Amy let out a big sigh. “Thank you, Katie.”

“You’re welcome, here he is.”

After more fumbling with the receiver, Michael picked up the phone. “Amy, are you okay?” He sounded anxious and out of breath.

“Yes, I am. Are you? Has anything happened?”

“No, not that I’m aware of. Where are you?” Michael asked.

"I'm at the hospital. I'm with FBI Agent Cain and I have Willow with me. We need to talk to you right away."

"Sure, of course. Where and when?"

"Is fifteen minutes okay?"

"Absolutely, where do you want to meet?"

"I don't want to say exactly over the phone," Amy said, looking at Cain. They still couldn't be sure whether someone was listening to the call. "You know where we meet in the afternoon? My, ah, special place?"

"Yes," Michael said slowly, without elaborating.

"Meet us there in fifteen minutes. Don't bring your cell phone. I'll explain when we get there."

"Okay, I'll be there. Amy, I don't know what's going on but please be careful," Michael said into the phone.

Amy turned away from Cain. "I will, you too."

Chapter Forty Six

After arranging the impromptu meeting, Amy and Cain walked back to the reception desk to find Willow. Cain placed a call on his cell phone as Amy walked over to Kathy, the clinic manager. When she looked up, Kathy immediately knew something was wrong. "Is everything all right?"

"Yes," Amy told her. "I'm sorry but I've got to leave for a little while." Amy noticed Kathy looked at Cain out of the corner of her eye, trying to decide if her sudden leave was voluntary or forced. To ease the tension, Amy said, "This is Agent Marcus Cain of the FBI." On cue, Cain flashed his badge.

"Oh," Kathy said, as she looked over the badge. "I'd heard that someone was murdered and there was some unusual activity in the hospital."

"Yes, all true and as you know; I can't go into the details," Amy said. "But I, ah, have to help Agent Cain do something." Amy looked at Kathy without blinking.

"Okay," Kathy said nicely. In an unspoken attempt to see if Amy needed help, Kathy asked, "Do you want me to call anyone for you?"

"No, I'm fine, really. Willow is coming with us, too."

"Are you coming back?" Kathy asked.

"At some point," Amy said vaguely. "I know I have patients scheduled."

"Speaking of which, Helen has her follow up appointment today," Kathy reminded her.

"Oh, I completely forgot. Can you call her and reschedule? Make sure she's feeling okay, please?"

"No problem," Kathy said, as she made a note.

"If she has any headaches, dizziness, nose bleeds, anything unusual, call an ambulance for her to come in and be seen at the ER," Amy said, remembering the follow up was for a head injury.

"Okay, no problem," Kathy replied. "Your other burning message is from Dr. Applebaum."

"Did he say if it was an emergency?"

"Actually, he said it was personal and I wouldn't be able to help him," Kathy said, with a smile that would make a Cheshire cat proud. "He left a specific number for you to call when you're available."

"Thank you, I'll get back to him later," Amy said stiffly as she shoved the message in her purse.

"C'mon, let's go," Cain said, as he looked at his watch.

Amy waved her hand to Willow to come join them. As they neared the lobby, they were met by Sam.

"Sam's coming with us, to stay with Willow," Cain said, as he guided them out the glass revolving doors in the front of the hospital. Amy had her arm around Willow's shoulders.

"Good, I'm glad you're finally taking this seriously," Amy said. "Can Willow and I go in my car? You guys can follow us?"

"You can bet on that," Cain said.

Amy ushered Willow into her car. She backed out of her parking space and left the hospital. Agent Cain and Agent Oakes closely followed in a dark sedan. "What's going on?" Willow asked. As they sped over the covered wooden bridge and onto the grounds of St. Francis Church, Amy tried to explain as much as she could to Willow without scaring her. Amy needed her to be aware, but not to the point of panic.

"We're going to meet Katie. You and Agent Oakes can spend some time with her while I meet with Father Michael and Agent Cain."

"Can't I go with you?" Willow whined.

"I wish you could sweetie, really I do, but it's not a great idea right now," Amy said, trying to console her as she guided the car into the parking lot.

"I hate this," Willow yelled, as she crossed her arms and crunched up in the passenger seat.

"I know you do and so do I as a matter of fact. You probably don't understand this, but I want to make sure you're safe," Amy said patiently.

"Why does this keep happening?" Willow asked, as she angrily shook her head.

"I don't know. My job, I guess. Sometimes I have to deal with bad people, or their victims," Amy said thoughtfully. "This time, I'm keeping you near me until this whole thing is done with."

"Even overnight?" Willow asked hopefully.

"I don't know. Let me talk to Agent Cain and see what he thinks. After that, we'll have to call your guardian. I didn't get a chance to call Mrs. Russo yet, either."

"You mean Nurse Ratched?" Willow asked, while she glowered. "I can't stand her."

"Well, I will say she has a strong presence about her," Amy said, as she tried to smother a grin.

"I guess a battleaxe is pretty strong."

"Willow," Amy said in surprise.

"That's what they call her behind her back," Willow said, with a look only a teenager could conjure.

Amy turned off the engine and pulled out the key. "C'mon. Let's go see Katie." Amy shoved her purse and cell phone under the front seat. She kept the keys in her hand while she got out of the car. Willow kept grumbling as she unbuckled her seat belt and followed.

"One more thing," Amy said.

"What's that?" Willow asked.

"Please don't use your cell phone. If you need to call someone, use the land line in the rectory, but try not to talk on that too much either."

"Why?" Willow asked as she shrugged.

"I can't explain it all, but it has to do with a hacker," Amy said. "So, no cell phone or internet or that other stuff you do with your phone."

"A white hat or a black hat?" Willow asked, as she cocked her head to the side.

"What? I don't follow you," Amy said.

"A white hat is a good guy, hello?" Willow said with a face.

"As opposed to a black hat or bad guy?" Amy asked with a smile, as she rang the bell to the rectory.

"Bingo."

"Well, in this case I guess it would be a black hat," Amy said, trying to ignore Willow's surly mood. The two agents came up behind them as Katie opened the front door.

Katie smiled when she saw them. "Dr. Amy, Willow, how nice." When she saw the two FBI agents standing behind them, she quickly said, "What's wrong?"

"Nothing, Katie," Amy said, trying to calm her. "Everything is okay. This is Agent Cain and Agent Sam Oakes of the FBI. They were at the Burlington soup kitchen on Saturday. I hope you don't mind if Willow and Agent Oakes stay with you, while Agent Cain and I talk to Father Michael?"

"No, not at all," Katie said, as she stepped back and opened the door wider. Willow went inside and when Sam reached the doorway, he displayed his gold badge to Katie and followed. Looking at Amy and Cain, Katie asked, "Are you two coming inside?"

"No ma'am," Cain said, with a charming smile. "We'll be out here."

"Amy?" Katie looked at her for agreement, remembering the situation from a few months ago.

"It's okay, Katie. Really, you can relax. We're just gonna talk out here," Amy tried to reassure her.

Katie shot Amy a warning look that asked, 'are you safe?' When Amy nodded and smiled back at her, Katie stepped inside the foyer and closed the door. As Amy and Cain walked away, Amy saw the curtain on the side window flutter.

Chapter Forty Seven

"Where are we going?" Cain asked, as he followed Amy away from the rectory.

"To one of my favorite spots," Amy said, as she continued to walk. "It's a great spot, so I hope this adventure doesn't ruin it for me. There's no electricity, cameras or computers there."

Cain was silent as they walked, but Amy didn't speak. Deep in thought, she realized she didn't know much about Father Michael. Last night, she was ready to become emotionally dependent on him and today he could admit he had the flash drive all along. Maybe he knew more about the whole situation and didn't want to tell her. As she and Cain walked towards the bench, her stomach knotted inside. She didn't know what to expect. Every time she let herself trust someone, she got hurt and didn't want to go through it again.

"So, is this it?" Cain asked, as they neared her bench.

"What did you expect, a safe house?"

"Just asking," Cain said defensively.

"Normally, this bench is a very quiet and peaceful place," Amy explained. "The mountain view, the river, and the solitude make your problems all seem rather insignificant when you sit here."

"It is a beautiful spot," Cain said, as he nodded and looked around. Amy took a seat on the bench and Cain stood to one side, waiting for Father Michael. Within minutes, they spied the priest walking toward them from the church. Amy jumped up to greet him.

"Michael," Amy said, as he took her hand. "This is Agent Marcus Cain from the FBI."

Father Michael nodded at Cain and extended his hand. "Hi, nice to meet you."

Cain returned the priest's handshake. "Father, please have a seat." Cain then turned to Amy and said, "I'll need to speak to Father Michael alone. Would you go back to the rectory and wait?"

"Seriously?" Amy asked. "I arranged this whole meeting and assumed I'd be part of it."

"Not initially. You can wait by your car if you prefer, but I need to speak with him in private," Cain said, his facial expression warned no questions asked.

"Okay then, I guess I'll be in the parking lot," Amy said with obvious irritation in her voice as she turned and walked away.

Father Michael sat on the bench while Cain perched himself on the black handrail to his left, so he could face Michael.

After a few seconds of silence, Michael said, “I don’t know what this is all about, but how can I help you?”

“I asked Dr. Daniels to set this meeting up. I could’ve come to the rectory or made you come to Burlington, but I thought it might be better to keep this as simple as possible,” Cain explained.

“Thanks for that consideration. Katie would’ve been upset with a lot of commotion.”

“You’re welcome,” Cain said with a nod. “I wanted to go over your statement from Saturday night. I need to hear, from you, exactly what happened. You were there during the shooting; just tell me everything you remember. Any detail may be important, so take your time.”

“Of course,” Michael said. “We’d been asked, by the Archdiocese, to help at the soup kitchen in Burlington. Things seemed to be going well. As a matter of fact, most of our guests had finished their dinners.”

“Go on,” Cain encouraged him.

“I was collecting the garbage. The gentleman who was killed, Ray Fuller, went outside for a smoke,” Michael said, trying to remember.

“Then what?” Cain asked.

“The other fellow, Jimmy, must have followed him out.”

"How long have you known these gentlemen?" Cain asked.

"I've met Ray a few times at previous dinners. Saturday was the first time I ever saw Jimmy," Michael answered. "He was eating at one of the tables and I asked if he wanted anything else."

"Okay," Cain pressed him to go on.

"Anyway, I was near the back door with the garbage and I heard yelling outside so I looked down the path and saw the two men arguing. Naturally, I went down there to try and calm them."

"Do you know what they were arguing about?"

"I heard Jimmy say he wanted his things. He was upset. He accused Ray Fuller of stealing his belongings and said he wanted them back. Ray denied it. They were arguing about the jacket Ray had on. Apparently, it was Jimmy's jacket. He recognized it because the sleeve had a large tear up the side."

"What was so important about the jacket?" Cain demanded.

"Jimmy said he had something important in it. He said the jacket and the rest of his things were stolen on Church Street and he thought Ray had been the one who took them."

"Okay, so what happened next?"

"Well, Ray said he found the jacket next to a dumpster and put it on because he was cold. Jimmy didn't believe him since the weather's been so warm lately."

"So maybe Ray finds the jacket at a dumpster or maybe he steals it, but he's wearing Jimmy's jacket. Then what?" Cain asked, looking straight at Michael.

"Jimmy kept repeating there was something important in the jacket and he wanted it back. Finally, Ray took it off and threw it at him. Jimmy picked it up and went through the pockets and he didn't find whatever he was looking for," Michael explained. "So he put the jacket on to check again."

"Go on," Cain urged him further.

"Ray started yelling that he didn't take anything but stopped mid-sentence and fell over," Michael said clearly, his voice showing signs of strain.

"Uh-huh," Cain waited.

"It took us a few seconds to realize he'd been shot. I think another bullet hit a tree or something. Jimmy started screaming. I grabbed his arm and we ran down the path. Someone was chasing us, I know that. When we got to the cliff, the only choice was to jump or be shot," Michael said nervously.

Cain sat on the bench looking at the priest. After a few seconds, he quietly asked, "What aren't you telling me?"

After fidgeting for a few seconds, Michael started to speak. "Well, to be honest, he didn't jump. I pushed him off the cliff."

"Why?" Cain asked.

"Well, he just stood there, saying 'we're gonna die.' The guy was coming behind us and we didn't have time to wait, so I just grabbed him and prayed as we went over."

"How do you know it was a guy?" Cain asked.

"I'm not sure. I guess I must've gotten a glance at some point."

"Then what happened?" Cain asked sternly.

"We hit the water. The guy chasing us was still shooting, so I grabbed Jimmy and swam under the dock by the boat house."

"Did you get a good look at the shooter?" Cain asked.

"No, like I said, I'm pretty sure it was a man," Michael said as he slowly shook his head. "Everything happened so fast, yet it seemed like years in slow motion. Then, Jimmy said he was hit and he was bleeding, so I held on to him. I don't know exactly when he got shot. We stayed like that until I heard Father Victor's voice. I yelled for help and he started scrambling down the cliff. He pulled us out of the water and then a boat arrived with officers on it."

"Did Jimmy say anything to you? Did he give you anything?"

"No, he was quiet. Actually, I was scared I had killed him with that little stunt," Michael said nervously.

"You're probably the only reason he's alive right now," Cain said. "But, I'm gonna ask you one more time. During the whole time you were in the kitchen or the water or boat or in the ambulance when you, ah, prayed together, did he say or give you anything?"

"No, nothing. Nothing at all. Why do you keep asking me that?"

He turned towards Father Michael to gauge his reaction to the information he was about to tell him. "Jimmy Griffin apparently had a flash drive that contained sensitive information stolen from his company. He either lost the flash drive or it was taken from him."

"Wow," Michael said, with genuine surprise.

"Yes, the flash drive is still missing and we're trying to make sure he didn't give it to anyone," Cain said, staring straight at Michael.

"He didn't give it to me, that's for sure," Michael said in a hurry.

"I hope not, for your sake. If we found you were holding it for him, you would be prosecuted." After another few seconds of stony silence, Cain waved to Amy to come back to the bench. When she arrived, Michael slid to the side to make room for her to sit.

"There's more to the story," Cain said. "This is where Dr. Daniels becomes involved. This information is classified and it is not to be shared, with anyone. Do you understand?"

"Yes, of course," Michael said nervously.

"We believe Jimmy was forced into committing a cybercrime, internet theft, by a hactivist group." Cain watched Michael closely for his reaction. "We believe it had something to do with Shepherd Force."

Michael looked at Cain and asked, "What's Shepherd Force?"

"It's the name of a very elusive activist group that's wanted for cybercrimes. Mr. Griffin told us the flash drive had their insignia on it. When they didn't get their property back from Mr. Griffin, we think they came looking for him," Cain explained. "We're still looking for the flash drive, but he swears he doesn't have it."

"I don't know anything about that," Michael said. "The only Shepherd I know is the one we preach about; God, that is. Why do they call themselves Shepherd Force?"

"They're an activist group who are 'shepherding their flock'. They see their flock as being made up of average citizens who are being fleeced or taken advantage by private corporations or sometimes political committees or organizations."

"That's interesting," Michael said.

"Why?" Cain asked.

Michael was thoughtful for a moment. "Shepherding has been around for six-thousand years. A shepherd's job was to keep their flock intact and protect it from wolves and other predators, even if they had to lose their life to accomplish that. God is known as our Shepherd. In Christianity, we refer to Jesus as The Good Shepherd. Shepherds are important to many religions. They sold wool to survive. The prophet Moses, and King David, were both considered shepherds."

"What's the significance of the crook?" Cain asked. "I wonder if this group has religious leaders involved."

"Well, a crook is a shepherd's staff with a hook at the end. Shepherds used them to control their flock. If a sheep was out on the edge of a cliff, the shepherd would use the crook to pull the sheep back in. In a religious sense, a crook or a crosier is a ceremonial staff carried by high ranking prelates. For instance, bishops and archbishops all have a shepherd's crook as one of their insignias. The whole concept of the crook is quite detailed and symbolic. The designs, the materials used, even the direction it's held are all significant. That would actually make a very interesting homily," Michael rushed on. "Why is this so important to the activist group?"

"That's their symbol or mark," Cain said. "We've dealt with them before and they can be a nasty international group. I don't know why they chose a crook, but like I said, I was wondering if religion plays any part in this." Cain was thoughtful for a few moments. “We managed to catch another hacker in a different state who was given a similar flash drive. We haven’t been able to get any info from that drive, but we know what it looks like. At the very least, it identifies the group. They didn’t go after that flash drive like they are now.”

“Why not?” Michael asked.

“Who knows?” Cain said as he shrugged. “The information may not have been as valuable.”

“Well, whatever it is, they want it back and they’re willing to kill for it,” Amy said.

“And that brings us to the second reason for this meeting,” Cain said as he turned toward Father Michael. “There’ve been continued threats. They have Dr. Daniel’s cell number and it’s probably cloned so they know every call she makes. That’s why it’s important for us to know your involvement.”

“There’s no involvement, Cain,” Father Michael said defensively, as he looked directly at him.

“Like it or not, you’re involved. Unless they get that flash drive, they’ve threatened to kill Dr. Amy, your friend Willow, and yourself.”

Michael turned to Amy. “Is that true?”

Amy nodded her head and swallowed hard. “I’m afraid it is. They called me this morning. Willow can’t go through this again and I'd just about die if anything happened to either of you."

"So what are we doing about it?" Michael asked Cain.

"I'm getting to that," Cain said.

Without waiting for an answer, Michael turned to Amy. "Why don't you and Willow move into the Retreat House? There's safety in numbers, plus we have very little here in the way of computers or internet. You and Willow are too isolated in your homes."

"He's got a point," Cain said to Amy. Looking back at Michael, Cain asked, "Do you have cameras on your grounds?"

"No, actually we don't," Michael answered. "But after this year, I'm thinking of putting them in."

"Really, this is ridiculous. I can't stay here," Amy said. "I need to be in the hospital every day. What am I suppose to do when I go to work or there's a body I need to see as the medical examiner? We can't all go together and I can't stay here until this blows over because it could take months."

"True," Michael said. "But you'd be welcome as long as you'd like."

Amy's face turned red and it didn't go unnoticed by Cain. She looked down at her hands for a moment. When she looked up again, she said, "I'd like Willow to stay here. I'd rather she be here with you and Katie instead of that clueless guardian. At least, I'd know she's with someone who cares about her."

"Done," Michael said. "What about you? Is there any way I can convince you to stay?"

"We can assign a protective agent to Amy," Cain said. "She'd be able to work but have a shadow for awhile. We need her to be in her normal routine for now."

"Oh really? Why is that?" Amy asked.

"Because you're the only point of contact with Shepherd Force," Cain said. "If you go into hiding, they'll come after you even more."

"What if I don't want to be the point of contact?" Amy asked.

"I think that choice was made for you, by them," Cain pointed out. "They're not likely to walk away if they think you have something worth a lot of money to them. If you run, I guarantee they're going to chase you."

"That's great," Amy said sarcastically. "I couldn't hide if I wanted to. That's fine because I have to go back to the hospital and finish the autopsy report for Mr. Fuller anyway. I want to see if anyone claimed him."

"And if they didn't?" Michael asked.

"If not, we give him a proper funeral when the body is released and hopefully he'll get that free burial," Amy said. "Cain, how much longer until you're done with him?"

"You're the medical examiner," Cain said. "When you're done, we're done. We took all his personal effects."

"His manner of death was obvious and I'm signing him out as a homicide, so basically I'm done. I have to check with Alex and see if there's been any claim on the body. If not, and if social services finished talking with the VA, then we're ready to go."

"I could do the funeral on Wednesday," Michael said. "That would give us two days to have a director prepare the body." Michael turned to Amy. "What funeral home does the hospital use for unclaimed persons?"

"I have no clue. I'll have to go back and ask."

"Well, let me know so Katie can get the details," Michael said. "We'll arrange the service when the body is released, whether it's this week or a month from now."

"I think we should wait to see what develops with Mr. Griffin," Cain said. "We don't want to offer Shepherd Force an opportunity to come after you."

"I thought you said they protect average citizens," Michael said.

"Yes, but on a national level. I'm sure they'll have no qualms about losing a few to protect the many," Cain replied. "Especially if you got in their way."

Amy turned to Cain. "You'll make sure arrangements are made for Willow and Father Michael and everyone else at the church? They'll be protected until this is over?"

"Yes and you too. You'll be assigned an agent for now."

Amy turned to Michael. “Can you have Katie get Willow’s things and talk to her lawyer?”

“Consider it done,” Michael said.

“Tell them she’s going on retreat. I don’t want any information leaked out. You understand? ” Cain asked.

They both nodded their heads in unison. “We’ll have a local patrol watching the church property for now.”

“Okay,” Father Michael said. “I have to tell Katie something.”

“Tell her it’s just a precaution, but no details. Understand?” Cain said. “As I recall, she was at the soup kitchen on Saturday. She knows we’re looking for a killer.”

“Got it, but I don’t like to lie,” Michael said.

“Technically, you’re not.” Turning to Amy, Cain said, “It’s time for us to go.”

A small shadow of fear passed over Amy’s face as she turned to Michael. “Please tell Willow I said good-bye,” Amy pleaded with Michael. “I’ll be in touch as soon as I can.”

“Of course,” Michael said. He then watched with a forlorn look on his face as Cain and Amy walked back toward the parking lot.

Chapter Forty Eight

Amy drove back to the hospital, followed closely by Agent Cain. Together, they walked toward the elevator. Amy needed to make rounds for the day and check on Jimmy Griffin's progress. The sooner he healed, the sooner he'd be out of her hospital. In the elevator, Amy pressed the button for the fourth floor. Once the doors closed, she turned to Cain and said, "What about my phone? What should I do about that?"

"Keep it. It actually helps us if they use it as a direct contact. You gave the FBI permission to monitor your phone, so I'd keep your conversations strictly about business and assume nothing you say is confidential."

"That's just great," Amy said, with a stony look.

"You should also know certain phones can be turned into a recording device by tech savvy people." Cain said.

"What do you mean?" Amy asked.

"Some of the newer cell phones can be used as a receiver. Your conversations can be heard, as long as you're near the phone," Cain said, as he tried to explain. "Even if the phone is turned off. Do you understand?"

"So you're telling me if I have my cell phone turned off, but it's in my pocket and I'm speaking to someone, my conversation can be overheard."

"That's correct," Cain said. "So keep your cell away from you during sensitive conversations, but we still need it as their point of contact."

"Great, what about Willow? Will she be in danger if she calls me?"

"Listen, if they wanted her number, they'd have no problem finding it. Anything personal should be done face to face, and don't indicate meeting times or places over the phone with verbal or text messages."

"What if I want to call you?" Amy asked nervously. "Will they hear everything I'm telling you?"

"Probably," Cain shrugged. When he saw the look on Amy's face, he tried to calm her. "That's the reason we don't talk about things over the phone. I'll give you a burn phone for safety. It'll have GPS tracking on it, so at least I'll always know where the phone is. Don't use it unless your life is in danger. Don't call and leave me thoughts or theories about anything. We'll discuss important things in person, if we have to."

"You got it, Cain," Amy said, looking overwhelmed. The elevator reached the VIP floor and they disembarked.

Together, they walked down the hall. Cain stopped at the door of the conference room. He called his team for an impromptu strategy meeting and wanted to get started.

Amy continued on to Jimmy Griffin's room. On her way, she called the Director of Nursing to inform her that Willow had to leave and wouldn't be back. After hanging up, she reviewed Jimmy Griffin's chart. She found Jimmy lying in bed with his head turned toward the wall. Checking his vitals for temperature and oxygen saturation abnormalities, she put on a pair of vinyl gloves and proceeded to check his wounds. Placing a new sterile bandage on his arm, she went to work on his chest and asked how he was feeling.

"As good as you can feel when you've been shot, had surgery and a bunch of FBI agents up your butt," Jimmy said sarcastically.

"Yeah, but you put yourself in that position to begin with, didn't you?" Amy asked with a shrug. "I mean you openly admit to doing what they're accusing you of."

"Yeah, so what?" Jimmy said. "Do you know how many people are out there getting screwed over by information on their computer?"

"Not really, but it almost makes me glad I don't use one very much," Amy said as she worked.

"It was supposed to be easy. Get the flash drive, deliver and disappear." Jimmy said angrily. "It would've been simple if some friggin' jerk hadn't stolen my stuff."

"Well, I can see you're really broken up over your choice to commit a federal offense to begin with," Amy said sarcastically. She pulled the tape a little too harshly.

"Ow," Jimmy yelled. "Watch it, will ya?"

"So sorry," Amy said. "This wound dressing should've been easy. Just pull, rip and run."

Jimmy quickly looked up. Amy knew he'd gotten the point. She stared directly at him. "Listen, I'm taking a lot of heat over this stupid flash drive and your decision to commit cyber theft," Amy said. "I don't want to be involved with any part of this situation, but it's too late for that. You caused all this. Right now, there's not an agent up our butts. If you really have it hidden somewhere, tell me and I won't let them know how I found out. You're never gonna be free of these agents and I want to get Shepherd Force off both our backs."

"Whad'dya mean?" Jimmy asked.

"Your so called friends still want their flash drive," Amy said angrily. Now they think you gave it to me or someone else for safe-keeping. All I know is, if one of my friends gets killed because you're being a dirt bag, the FBI will be the least of your problems. You'd better hope you never come back to this hospital or any other one I work at." Jimmy's face blanched when he heard her threat. "Now, for the last time. Do you know where the flash drive is or not?"

"I swear I don't know where it is or I would've never followed that guy to begin with."

Amy realized what he said made sense. Obviously, the activist group didn't have it or they'd stop harassing her. Jimmy Griffin didn't have it and neither the FBI nor the hospital had it. The question was whether or not Shepherd Force would accept that as an answer.

"When am I getting out of here?" Jimmy's whiny question broke through her thoughts.

"As far as I'm concerned, you're outta here as soon as they pick a place to take you to," Amy said. "I'll let Agent Cain know."

"Thanks for nothing, doc."

"You're an ungrateful bastard. You should be thanking Father Michael for saving your pathetic life," Amy said, through clenched teeth. "The rest of it will be decided by the FBI."

Chapter Forty Nine

After making notations on Jimmy's chart, Amy informed Cain that Jimmy was well enough to be discharged, as long as medical care was arranged at his next destination. Leaving the floor, she went down to the morgue to check on the status of Ray Fuller. Her office in the autopsy suite was usually quiet, but not today. Amy had to admit the allure of working with the dead was the silence. Sitting at her desk, she rested her head in her hands and closed her eyes. After a few minutes, she began to read the written copy of Mr. Fuller's autopsy findings and found nothing amiss. The wounds were as described and the toxicology report was completely normal. The case status showed his body hadn't been claimed and the social service worker was still trying to get information on the free burial. If no one claimed him, he'd probably be a guest of the county coroner for thirty days. Then, he'd either get a free burial as a morose parting gift from the government for his service to his country, or he'd be cremated.

Amy picked up the phone and called Alex. "Is everything okay with the morgue?"

"All's well," Alex said casually.

"How about Mr. Fuller?" Amy asked. "By the way, who does the hospital use for unclaimed bodies?

"He's back together and ready for pickup," Alex said nonchalantly. "And the hospital contracts with Murphy's Funeral Home for unclaimed patients."

"Great, thanks Alex. Are you sure there haven't been any problems?" Amy asked again. "Nothing missing, no break-ins, etc?"

"Not a thing," Alex reported. "Calm down."

"Okay, I wanted to be sure," Amy said. "Thanks, you do a great job.

Amy called St. Francis Rectory next. She took a few minutes to explain to Katie that the body of Ray Fuller was going to be released to Murphy's Funeral home, but it would probably stay there until someone from the hospital finished looking into the burial. Once that was worked out, Murphy's would call St. Francis to get details for the funeral.

"You're a caring doctor," Katie said, as she scribbled the information on a pad, located on the hall desk.

"Katie, speaking of caring, I want to thank you for watching Willow until this blows over," Amy said, with passion in her voice. "I'm worried sick about that girl."

"Yes and we're all worried about you. I know you have to work, but I'll be putting an extra plate on the dinner table tonight. Willow needs to see you and I want to be sure you have a good meal, so please stop by," Katie said.

Amy laughed as Katie eased her tension. It was more of an order than an invite, but with Katie's cooking, you didn't need to be asked twice.

"I'd love to come. I'll be there as soon as I can get out of the hospital. Thank you, Katie."

"We'll be seeing you later then, dear. Goodbye," Katie said, as she hung up the phone.

Amy leaned back in her desk chair and let out a big sigh. It'd only been forty-eight hours since the incident at the soup kitchen but it felt like a month. Next, she needed to go check the clinic and tell Cain that Ray's body would be released. As she was reaching for her bag, her cell phone rang.

"Dr. Daniels," Amy answered with a tired voice.

"Hey, Amy, it's me," Lou Applebaum's bouncy voice boomed through the phone.

"Hey Lou," Amy groaned to herself. "What's happening?"

"I wanted to touch base about Thursday night. We'll go to the medical society meeting, and then I made reservations for dinner in Diamond Point, NY. I thought we could take a look at the riverboats on Lake George too."

"That's nice, Lou, but …." Amy began.

"You know you have to present at the meeting, right? The medical examiner is supposed to give a report," Lou reminded her.

Amy paused for a minute. "I don't know what to present. I've only been doing this a short time."

"Just introduce yourself and they'll let you know what they're looking for."

"Do I need stats?" Amy asked.

"Since it's only been a week or so, just tell them your experience so far."

"I don't know, Lou," Amy said slowly.

"C'mon, Amy. With all that's going on around here, you need to get away for awhile anyway. A drive by the lake and a nice dinner will make you feel like a new woman," Lou cajoled.

"I guess," Amy said. "Okay, we'll try it. But, Lou, you don't even know the half of it and I can't really tell you right now. If anything happens, I may have to cancel."

"Think positive, Amy. I know I am," Lou said cheerily, as he hung up the phone.

Amy grumbled to herself. Think cheerily. The whole situation had gone from bad to worse and Amy didn't know how to fix it. She grabbed her purse, slammed her desk drawer closed and headed upstairs to dump it in Marcus Cain's lap.

Chapter Fifty

Amy had trouble finding Agent Cain. She went up to the VIP floor, looked in all the rooms and asked the other agents. No one had information or cared to share if they did. Realizing her fatigue and anger had something to do with lack of a meal as much as Cain's attitude; she went to the hospital café for a bite. She grabbed a diet cola for some caffeine and a sandwich that had been left behind by the lunch crowd. Sitting in a corner, Amy relaxed as she ate lunch and thought about the situation. She didn't give a hoot about the flash drive or Jimmy Griffin, except for the fact that Willow and Michael had been threatened and she was getting tired of being held hostage for everyone else's agenda. Hopefully, it was an empty threat for her friends, but Amy couldn't be sure. Obviously, the flash drive held something important, but she didn't have it and as the old proverb says, "you can't get blood out of a stone." The flash drive simply wasn't available and if it was, someone wasn't talking.

Now, a little more energized after eating, Amy was collecting her things when her cell phone rang. Thinking it was

Cain returning her call, she quickly opened her phone. Not a second went by before she realized her mistake.

"Have you found it?" The muted voice asked.

"Listen, whoever this is, no we haven't found it. As far as I'm concerned, it doesn't even exist. I can't help you," Amy said into the phone feeling frustrated. "Just leave me and my friends alone!"

"I believe you," the voice said.

"Look," Amy started to say and then stopped, perplexed. "What did you say?"

"I believe you don't have the flash drive," the voice said. "When someone tries to use it, we'll know."

"Then why are you hounding me? I'm just trying to do my job," Amy raised her voice and several people in the café turned to look at her.

"Because you have Jimmy Griffin and he had the flash drive. He may be hiding it and you're helping him. This could all be a set up by the FBI."

"Well if he is, he's not telling me where," Amy said. "Lord knows, I've tried."

"Tell him this, he has twelve hours to give us that flash drive when he's released or you'll all die. We'll be watching and waiting." The line went dead.

Amy's heart pounded in her chest. Exhausted again, she sat down and tears streamed down her face. Using the palms of her hands, she wiped the tears away from her cheeks.

She was tired of being threatened, being afraid and having to measure every conversation and action in her life. And, she realized, that her epiphany was not just about this patient or the flash drive. It started with her sister's murder and continued from there. She finally realized she'd have to face her fears from within, no matter where she was, or she'd be held hostage for the rest of her life. She always was a fighter and she wasn't going to stop now. Maybe going out with Lou was a good idea. Let them follow her and leave Rocky Meadow alone, but she had to warn him that being with her may not be safe! First she had to find Cain. Amy couldn't release Griffin until they had a better game plan in place, but how long could she hold off? She got up and took the elevator back to the VIP floor.

As the doors opened on the fourth floor, she spied Cain going into the conference room. She called out to him before another agent tried to close the door in her face.

"Cain! Wait, you have to talk to me," Amy yelled.

Cain turned round to face her and noticed her red, swollen eyes. Walking toward her, he said, "Are you alright? Did something happen?"

"He called again," she said quietly.

"What did he say?" Cain asked, while taking her arm and guiding her into the conference room. "Come sit down and relax." He poured her a cold glass of water. Looking up, he addressed the few men standing around. "Gentlemen, give us a few minutes, please." As the briefing for the local police was delayed, Cain used his cell phone to text someone as they sauntered out. He looked at her again and said, "Okay, take your time and tell me everything."

"He said he believed I didn't have the flash drive, because he'd know when someone used it, but he thinks Jimmy is lying and has it hidden."

"That doesn't really make sense," Cain said. "If he knew where it was, Jimmy wouldn't have been in that soup kitchen."

"You know that and I know that, but apparently they don't. He also said if we don't produce the flash drive within twelve hours of Jimmy's release, everyone is going to die." Amy's voice trailed off as she started to get upset.

"That changes things. Obviously, Griffin's not going anywhere until we figure this out," Cain said, as he patted her arm for reassurance and handed her a tissue.

Amy blew her nose and wiped her tears. "Just so you know, Ray's body is getting released today. Murphy's Funeral Home will hold him until he can go to St. Francis. Do we have any risk there? Are we endangering more people?"

"I don't think so. I doubt they'd think a flash drive would be hidden on a dead man's body? Especially, one that's been examined thoroughly inside and out by now."

"I haven't a clue. I'm asking before this becomes more ridiculous."

"Well, let me worry about that," Cain said in a quiet voice. "For now, we need to buy time. How long can we keep Griffin in the hospital?"

"I don't know. Different hospitals have different policies." Amy reached into her bag. "Here, you can have my cell phone. I'm don't want it anymore. Maybe you can do something with it."

"Actually, we've been tracking your cell phone since the first time he called. You gave us permission to clone your phone. We've been recording your conversations with him."

"What?" Amy asked, now clearly confused.

"You're doing fine," Cain said. "You're our main contact. Put your cell phone back in your bag. If he calls again, just keep holding him off. Tell him Jimmy's got medical complications or an infection and he needs to stay for antibiotics or something. You'll figure it out."

"I don't believe it," Amy said disgustedly.

"Every time he calls, we get another opportunity to track him or a tower close to him. During the call we ping his phone and then backtrack to all the places it's been redirected through, but we can only do that during an active conversation. We'll get him soon. You're doing great."

"You could've clued me in! So, I walk around as bait for you guys?"

"We've got you covered," Cain said. "I promised."

"Listen, I'm supposed to go to a medical society meeting on Thursday and Dr. Applebaum and I discussed it over this phone, so I guess everyone knows about it by now. As the medical examiner, I have to give a report."

"Okay," Cain said. "Just relax and go about your business. The more normal things appear, the better it is. I told you yesterday there was no confidentiality for any of your conversations."

Amy couldn't believe he was being so matter of fact, so calm and controlled. This had to be a technique they learned at Quantico, but then again his life wasn't being threatened.

"Okay, I'm going," Amy said, as she shrugged her shoulders and got up from her chair. She felt exhausted as she left the room and waited for the elevator. She couldn't wait to leave the hospital and run to St. Francis and her bench.

***

"You look spent," Michael said, as he held her hand while Amy told him exactly what had happened. Confidentiality with Michael wasn't as important now that he was involved.

"I'm exhausted," Amy admitted. "This is a nightmare. I thought I'd have a quieter life living in Vermont, but so far it's worse than Boston. At least this time I have an FBI agent as a shadow. She followed me here and she'll follow me home too."

"That's the agreement we made with Cain," Michael pointed out. "This too shall pass." Trying to lighten the mood, he said, "Believe it or not, that's not actually a Bible verse."

"Most of the phrases that help me come from medical textbooks. As long as this goes away, I don't care where it's from."

"Try to relax for now," Michael said, as they sat on the bench. "Worrying isn't going to help anything. For the most part, it's out of your control. You need to step back and let faith kick in. If Cain said he'll handle it, I believe he will."

"I spend my whole life trying to control things," Amy said as she laughed. "My anxiety is much worse when I can't."

"That my friend is what anxiety is all about," Michael agreed. "It's time to rest your brain, start trusting again and let someone else take charge."

Amy stared up at him for a minute. "If you say so," she agreed as she sat back and watched the turbulent water flow by.

Chapter Fifty One

The next few days passed uneventfully, but Amy was wary. During the day, she worked in the hospital and spent her evenings at St. Francis with her friends. She was jumpy, especially when her cell phone rang. Jimmy Griffin still hadn't been released. The hospital administration was told he wasn't ready, but Amy knew better.

Amy had an agent trailing her regularly. She was thankful she got to use the bathroom by herself. At night, the agent would follow her to dinner at St. Francis, so Katie set a place for her too. Amy thanked Katie for caring for Willow and keeping her protected. Although it was a horrible situation, Willow seemed to be blossoming from the special attention she was getting. Amy acted as the protective Aunt while Katie took the role as Willow's grandmother. They'd spend afternoons in the kitchen, baking cookies and making dinner. Katie was glad she had an extra pair of hands to help her at the rectory and Willow seemed to enjoy learning to cook. Amy and Michael would sit in the library after dinner and talk before she went back to her house for the evening.

Amy spent Wednesday afternoon in a hospital conference discussing upcoming department budgets. There were proposed changes for areas that had overspent and sanctions if it continued. Strangely, when the discussion rolled around to increasing profits, Amy's cell phone started ringing. She tried to mute her phone, but then all the cell phones in the room started ringing simultaneously. The result was a total cacophony of beeps, musical songs, buzzing noises and odd tones that had everyone jumping for their mobile devices. Realizing the hospital wasn't responsible for a system-wide message, Amy could only deduce this was more intimidation from the hacktivists. Eventually, the noise stopped and the meeting put on hold. Amy didn't verbalize her theory, but it didn't matter since the administration was getting upset anyway. She felt like she was under a microscope and couldn't figure out how Shepherd Force was monitoring her. She was only slightly comforted by the fact that Cain and the FBI were monitoring them, but Amy had no idea if they were making any progress. Cain didn't provide any information, he simply collected. Amy overheard Sam say the FBI finally got the video tapes from Vandersen Group and they talked to Jimmy's supervisor. She assumed they finished going through Jimmy's apartment, personal accounts and car. Beyond that, everything was strictly 'need to know', which meant she was told nothing.

***

Thursday afternoon arrived and Amy got ready to meet Dr. Lou Applebaum. He'd called her last evening, as promised, for her address and to confirm the time of the medical society meeting. Not wanting to give any information over the phone, she'd suggested they leave from the hospital. Amy brought her evening clothes in a small tote bag and changed in the locker room.

Sitting in the ER, Amy was charting on her patients when Lou walked in. He wore an expensive business suit and a smile that could power a small city. She smelled expensive cologne when he approached her.

"Hi, Amy. Are you ready to go?" Lou had never been so excited to go to a medical society meeting. He tried to skip out on half of them, but if that was the only avenue he could use to spend time with Amy, he was ready and willing to serve.

Amy looked up with a smile and said, "Sure am. You look very handsome in that suit."

"Thanks, I appreciate it," Lou replied, as his grin got wider.

Amy wasn't sure, but thought he was preening for a moment. He was an attractive cardiologist and had more than his share of nurses trying to catch his eye, especially in his current attire. Yet, Amy would rather go sit on a bench with Father Michael than face meetings and fancy dinners with

Lou. She wondered for a minute if she should go back to counseling.

"You're looking lovely yourself," Lou said, with appreciation for her black dress and pumps.

"Thank you," Amy blushed as she accepted the compliment. She'd chosen a black dress that hugged her body when she moved. A single strand of pearls lay softly around her neck. Amy wanted to be dressed nicely enough for dinner but not overdressed at the meeting. When she'd been living in Boston, she'd primp as much as possible since the majority of her life was spent in scrubs covered by a white lab coat. Since moving to Vermont, she didn't find the need to spruce up. Amy realized how much she missed some of the brightest attractions of Boston. The concerts, plays and fancy dinners were important in retrospect. Maybe Lou was right. Leaving the immediate area, having a nice dinner and relaxing just might restore her mood. "I need to get my purse," Amy said, as she stood up. "I'll just be a minute."

Lou nodded and smiled appreciatively as she moved away from the nurse's station. When she returned, they walked to the parking lot and got into his car. He held her door until she was fully positioned in the front seat and had her safety belt on. Closing the door, he quickly scooted around the car and climbed in the driver's side. After securing his seat belt, he guided the car out of the parking lot and headed for

Route 4 West. The day was lovely, not as suffocating as the last weekend had been. Amy stared at the scenery as it passed and realized she was relaxing. There were lovely patches of forests, with views of mountains and refreshing lakes in the distance.

"You're so quiet," Lou said. "Everything okay?"

"Yeah, it's been a really bad week," Amy said. "I wasn't expecting this to happen."

"So if you don't mind my asking, what's with all the FBI activity in the hospital?" Lou asked, as he closed his window. Amy would've preferred driving with the windows wide open. She liked the fresh scents that accompanied a warm summer and the wind blowing through her hair, but knowing a crazed wind-blown effect wouldn't look good at the medical society meeting, she acquiesced to closed windows and air conditioning.

"Gee Lou, I don't know how much I can share with you," Amy said with a shrug. "Believe me, I'd love to tell you everything, but you know how the saying goes, 'then I'd have to kill you.'"

Lou laughed as he drove on. "Not to upset you, but you know people are whispering about you in the hospital," Lou said gently, as he quickly glanced at Amy to see how she'd react.

Amy groaned and shook her head. Things couldn't get worse. "What are they saying?"

"Well, the staff doesn't know you," Lou explained lightheartedly. "When you first came to Rocky Meadow, there were hints you were involved in a murder or crime in Boston. To be honest, no one knew if you were the victim or a murderess. Some people thought you were here in a witness protection program."

Amy laughed out loud at the absurdity of the suggestion. "I see. You know I use to be a famous chef and when they choose my cover they thought trauma surgeon would be low key, right?"

"I guess that doesn't make sense when you think about it," Lou agreed with a grin.

"Next rumor?" Amy asked.

Lou went on. "Well, the witness protection thing really picked up a couple of months ago when you were almost killed."

"I see, but wouldn't I have moved if my cover was blown?"

"That's what we thought, so then there was a suggestion you were a highly trained CIA operative, who also happened to be a trauma surgeon."

"This is all quite entertaining. Please go on."

"Well things died down for awhile, but then our regular medical examiner takes a sudden leave of absence and you become the medical examiner."

"So?"

"Within a few days, the hospital is crawling with FBI combined with the fact you really haven't connected with a lot of friends. Some people are getting nervous."

"You can't be serious?" Amy asked astounded.

"Yes, I can," Lou assured her. "There hasn't been this much activity around here, ever. Use to be, we were excited if we saw a dead raccoon in the road."

Amy couldn't help laughing.

"Before I hang around with you too much, I want to know one thing," Lou asked.

"What's that?" Amy said as she started to grin.

"Are you one of the good guys or the bad guys?"

Amy's next laugh was well enjoyed and infectious. She felt the tension leaving her body as she relished the tenacity of gossip. Had she known there were this many vile rumors circulating about her, she would've guessed it'd be about her and a certain priest, not an undercover position in the Federal Government.

"Lou, I can't tell you anything more than the fact I'm definitely with the good guys," Amy said laughing. "But it may not be a great idea to be out with me tonight. You could be in danger. I'd understand if you want to cancel dinner and go back right after the meeting."

"Are you kidding me? I knew there was something about you. You're definitely not like the rest of the doctors."

Amy was still chuckling as they pulled into the parking lot of the municipal building where the meeting was being held.

Chapter Fifty Two

Cain sat at the conference table to answer his cell. The report was quick and brief. Amy was in the company of another physician and they were headed West on Route 4. A second car had followed them away from the hospital and it wasn't FBI. Cain made sure his agents remained far enough behind to watch both cars. He'd asked for license plates and descriptions. He wanted as much information as possible before he had his agents take out the second car. So far, they determined it was a rental. Officers were on their way to the agency. They'd collect information on the driver that rented the car, along with the driver's license photo and insurance card. It'd be even better if they'd used a credit card, but Cain didn't expect miracles. He expected results. The last two phone calls to Amy's cell had been traced to towers in the United States. The origin of the calls was on the Eastern Seaboard. They needed another day to pin it down. There must be something really important on this flash drive. They may never know, but once they caught even the smallest hacktivist, the dominoes would fall. They had Jimmy Griffin in custody. One more break would make a big difference in the case. Sam was busy watching Willow and Father Michael. Cain was in charge of protecting Amy. She wasn't happy about being the point of contact, but he hadn't suggested that anyway. Amy was strong; she'd be okay, especially if he had anything to do with it. Shepherd Force targeted her for some reason, so they'd use that fact to track them. Things would happen soon, he was sure of it.

Chapter Fifty Three

Amy looked at her watch for the sixth time in the last fifteen minutes. The medical society meeting was boring and she was having trouble concentrating. Various physicians, representing their assigned or chosen specialties, droned on about statistics in monotone. Amy was sleepy, especially since she hadn't slept well for the past week and she didn't want to risk being rude by falling asleep in front of the speaker. Sitting in her chair, she started to deeply pinch her right thigh hoping she could inflict enough pain to stay awake. Her eyelids felt as if they weighed thirty pounds. She reached for the bowl of ice to try something cold. Perhaps caffeinated soda would help. Amy had written many prescriptions for sleeping aids, but none could compare to this tedious monologue. If the pharmaceutical companies could bottle this presentation, insomnia wouldn't stand a chance!

Amy looked up when she heard her name. The current presenter had finished and was happily introducing her as the most recent addition to their team. He was quoting her prestigious credentials although she had no idea where he had obtained them and Lou was smiling like she was his star pupil. On cue, she stood up and advanced to the makeshift podium. She had no papers to read from or reports to present. When the smattering of applause quieted down, Amy cleared her throat and introduced herself. She explained her position would be temporary, but she was assigned to be the Rocky Meadow medical examiner until her predecessor could return. There had only been two deaths since she started. One was a local Rocky Meadow gentleman who died of a sudden heart attack from coronary artery disease and the other was the result of a gunshot wound. There were no questions since hunting accidents occasionally happened in Vermont. She didn't point out that the gunshot victim was murdered. Save that detail for the next meeting if things were cleared up by then. After a few moments, Amy sat down and the next physician started his report about boating accidents that resulted in emergency room visits.

Amy's bag was resting next to her when she felt the tiny vibration from her cell phone. She was eternally grateful to the person who was texting her, until she saw the message.

Stop Stalling – release the patient.

Amy didn't know what to do. Looking for the source of the text, her phone indicated Blocked. Trying to be discreet, she forwarded the text to Cain's cell number. Her phone immediately vibrated.

Stop forwarding texts, release the patient.

Amy almost dropped her phone. She looked up, apologized and excused herself from the meeting. Stepping outside the front door, she texted the hacktivists back.

Not ready yet. Leave me alone.

The reply came within seconds.

You R stalling. DON'T.

She typed using the small fingerboard.

Will discharge as soon as I can.

She pressed send and waited.

Watch your back – getting angry. Did he tell you hiding spot?

Her stomach started to clench.

No- don't know location!

Pressing send, she listened to the small sound that indicated her message was delivered. Within seconds, another reply.

Watching – always! Don't screw with us.

Not knowing what else to do, she called Cain. When he didn't answer, she left a message on his phone telling him what had happened. She realized Shepherd Force may be listening, but she felt it was important that he knew.

"Everything okay?" Lou asked, as he came outside looking for her. Not expecting to hear his voice, she jumped at the sound.

"You scared me," Amy said, as she held her hand over her heart.

"You looked upset when you left the meeting. I wanted to make sure you were okay," Lou said.

"I'm fine, I had to make a call," Amy said hesitantly.

"Oh, your government buddies. I get it," Lou winked. "Your secret is safe with me."

Amy laughed. "Lou, there is no secret."

"Then I can tell everyone?"

"Absolutely not! I mean, I'm a trauma surgeon who happens to be working and living in Vermont. There is nothing beyond that."

"I understand," Lou said with a smile.

Amy looked at him for a few minutes. "Let's go back to the meeting."

Reseated, Amy tried to concentrate on the current presentation. Thankfully, her cell phone was quiet. With luck, Cain was able to get the message and track them. Her phone might as well have been a public address system at this point. The last presenter finished his statistics and the meeting was adjourned. Amy was immediately surrounded by many physicians who wanted to know more about her and invite her to their monthly dinner at the steak house next door. Lou looked at her over someone's head and shook his head 'no' several times. Amy begged off saying she had another meeting to attend and gradually separated herself from the crowd.

"Well, that was uncomfortable," Amy said, as they walked out to the car.

"I'm telling you, you're the hottest thing that's hit the Vermont medical system in years," Lou laughed.

"I came here to live in obscurity," Amy explained, while shaking her head.

"Then next time wear a shift instead of that dress," Lou said, while making an appreciative face with his eyes.

"Stop it," Amy said with a smile. She blushed as Lou opened the car door for her. After she belted herself in, she pulled out her cell phone again. Looking at Lou, "I'm sorry; I just need to check on Willow."

"How's she doing?"

"She's staying at St. Francis Rectory for now. Katie is so good to her. That guardian of hers does nothing."

"How about her mom?"

"As far as I know, Marty has been sober for three months but she's still in long term rehab. She goes up to the detox floor with Father Doherty and talks at the group meeting. Tony helps her quite a bit, too."

"I'm glad to hear it. Hopefully, Willow will get her mom back for good one day," Lou said softly.

"That's very sweet of you," Amy smiled. She remembered Lou had to go see his parents several months ago when one of them was hospitalized. Amy made a mental note to ask him about them over dinner, but at the moment she needed to call the rectory. She dialed as he started the car and left the parking lot. Neither one of them noticed the cars that followed them.

After several rings, the phone was picked up. "St. Francis Rectory." It was Michael's voice.

"Hi, it's Amy." She suddenly felt very awkward being in the car with Lou while having this conversation.

"Are you alright?" The concern in his voice was evident.

"Yes, I'm fine," Amy said. "I wanted to make sure you and Willow were okay."

"We're fine. I missed you at dinner," Michael said. "Katie told me you had a meeting."

"Yes, a medical society meeting," Amy told him. Why was she feeling guilty? What a crazy thought. "I probably shouldn't talk on this cell phone very long," Amy said, knowing that he'd understand.

"Can I call you tonight? Make sure you're back safe?" Michael asked.

"Sure or if I can, I'll stop by quickly," Amy said in a rush. "Okay, gotta run." Amy disconnected the call. Blushing again, she put the phone in her purse.

"Everything okay?" Lou asked.

"Yes, I think so," Amy answered, while looking out her window at the passing scenery.

Lou drove along Route 4 West and then eventually connected with Route 149 until he reached NY State. He continued until he was on Route 9 North and then drove to Beach Road. Once they reached Lake George, he slowed and parked. They got out of the car and walked along the street. The view of the lake was gorgeous and Amy was amazed at the riverboats.

"I'd suggest a boat ride, but we already have dinner reservations," Lou said, while staring out at the lake. "Maybe next time?"

"It looks like it'd be a lot of fun," Amy said, hesitating as she picked up the reference to another date.

"We'd better go if we want to make that dinner," Lou said nicely. They walked back to the car together and got in. Lou restarted the car and headed north towards Lake Shore Drive. They drove towards Diamond Point and Bolton Landing and stopped at a lovely restaurant, situated on the lake. The car was whisked away by a valet as they went inside. After waiting several minutes, they were shown to a table on a veranda overlooking Lake George. The night air was warm and calm and the shoreline looked beautiful under the glow of evening lights. Amy wished she could forget everything and drink in the beauty of her surroundings. It was all so relaxing, but she knew she had to go back to Rocky Meadow sometime.

She was handed a menu and their waitress began to recite the specials for the evening. The selections looked delicious and reminded her of the fancy restaurants in Boston. Amy and Lou conferred and decided to share a bottle of Pinot Grigio. They started with a delicious appetizer of asparagus risotto mixed with aged parmesan cheese. Next, they were served a classic, chilled Caesar salad with freshly made garlic croutons. Amy could have stopped there. She'd become accustomed to eating smaller meals since moving to Vermont, but the next course was Maine Lobster dripping with seasoned butter. Small tenderloin was served on the side with freshly roasted vegetables. Amy enjoyed every morsel and ate slowly so she could savor the flavors. Their conversation drifted from the hospital to medical school as well as their childhood. She didn't discuss Boston or the reason she'd moved to Vermont. Lou sensed the topic was not approachable and didn't pursue it. They even skirted the awkward questions about why they were both single. Amy took the opportunity to ask about Lou's parents and discovered they were now in an assisted living facility.

The table was cleared once they finished eating and brushed for crumbs. After ten minutes, they were served a small platter of strawberry tiramisu, almond cheesecake and chocolate torte. Amy had never tasted strawberry tiramisu, but it was delicious. All this was washed down with a caramel cappuccino.

"Lou, I can't believe we just ate all that food," Amy said, as she finished her coffee.

"I told you it was a great restaurant," Lou said with a smile. "I'm really glad you liked it."

"I won't be able to move for three days," Amy said. "I'm stuffed, but it was worth it."

"I thought you'd enjoy it. You've looked so stressed lately; I thought this would be a nice way to relax."

"How did you find this place?"

"Well, to be honest, a few of my patients mentioned it."

"I'm sure eating like this all the time would stir up some heart disease."

"Once in awhile, it's okay as a treat. You'll just have to exercise more."

"That's an understatement, but it was heavenly. Thank you so much," Amy said again as she smiled. "The company, the food, the lake and even the weather is perfect." Lou's smile was broad which left Amy wondering if she shouldn't have been so effusive.

"The last time I ate like this was probably several years ago, to be honest," Lou said. "But I thought this occasion, our first date, was worthy of none other."

Amy was smiling on the outside, but panicking on the inside. To Lou, she said, "Well, thank you again for a lovely dinner."

"You're most welcome. I have another treat planned for you. I hope it works out."

"Really? What else could top this?" Amy started to get nervous.

"There's a beautiful waterfall a little way up the road," Lou said. "I wanted to show it to you."

"But it's dark," Amy pointed out with a grin.

"I know, but during the summer it's lit up with colored lights at night. Obviously, it's not as big or fancy as Niagara Falls, but it's breathtaking all the same, especially the view from the top."

"Sounds lovely," Amy said, not wanting to be rude.

Lou paid the enormous bill with cash and they left the restaurant. The valet brought the car around and helped Amy into her seat. She had to admit she hadn't had a night like this in a very long time. Talk about being wined and dined.

Traveling up the road, they listened to soft music. They were both quiet and relaxed as a result of the wine and heavy food. Lou was driving more slowly than usual and explaining a bit about the area as he drove. He tried to pull to the right when he noticed a car tailgating them in the rearview mirror. Night had fallen and the two lane road was climbing to a higher elevation. There wasn't much room to pull off to the side and Lou didn't want to speed, for a variety of reasons. He was hoping that the lit waterfall would provide an opportunity for him to put his arms around Amy. He'd been imagining how it would feel to hold her in his arms for a couple of months and so far the night had gone perfectly.

The lights in his rearview mirror continued to creep closer and Lou had no choice but to speed up. He looked over and made sure Amy had her seat belt on. The road was becoming narrow and there was always the danger of an animal appearing out of nowhere. A sudden stop under these conditions could prove treacherous. The car drew closer but there was nowhere to stop. Amy looked at Lou and realized something was wrong. "What's going on?"

"I don't know. Some idiot is right behind me. I think I saw him leave the restaurant after us. He's probably drunk and could get us all killed if he doesn't slow down," Lou complained.

Amy's stomach began to clench. The beautiful afterglow of a delicious meal disappeared in an instant. "You know these roads, right?"

"Yes, but everything looks different at night," Lou stated. "I normally like to drive a little slower on these roads."

"How often have you been to this waterfall?" Amy said, trying to lighten the mood, although she was feeling anything but calm.

"A few times, but never with a beautiful woman like you," Lou said quickly. He was talking to her, but Amy noticed he was watching the rearview mirror more than he should've been. She was also acutely aware he'd had at least a half bottle of wine which wouldn't help his reflexes any if he needed them quickly.

"Maybe I should slow down and stop. I can tell him to go around because he doesn't seem to understand I can't drive much faster on this road," Lou said.

"No," Amy shouted out.

"What? What's wrong?" Lou asked, as he glanced at her.

"I don't know, maybe nothing," Amy said in a hesitant voice but she knew stopping would make them sitting ducks if the person behind them was part of Shepherd Force. "Don't stop." The road was becoming smaller and there were steep drops off the side.

"Amy, I don't know what to do," Lou said. "I can't drive much faster. We could miss a turn and ..." Lou didn't want to voice the thought.

"Keep going as safely as you can," Amy said.

"We're almost at the top now," Lou said. "I'll be able to pull into the road that leads to the waterfall. Then that idiot can go as fast as he wants."

"Okay," Amy said, as she gripped the arm rest. She didn't know if it was the wine and heavy food or anxiety but she was starting to get nauseous. Amy was thankful Lou couldn't see her face in the dark. Their turn came up fast and Lou quickly jerked the wheel to the right. The car skidded as the back wheels fishtailed on gravel in the road. Lou was able to straighten the car and began to slow down until he realized the car behind them made the turn as well. Looking in the rearview mirror, he saw the headlights coming toward them. "What the hell?" Lou said, as he navigated the small parking lot. He didn't want to drive straight off the top of the cliff and still had his foot lightly on the brake. He wasn't more than twenty feet from the end of the cliff when their car was rammed from behind. Amy screamed and grabbed the arm rest near the window to steady herself.

Lou jammed on the brakes and his body tensed. The car skidded and stopped. The driver's side was now facing the drop. Lou noticed the car behind them start charging again and he quickly shoved his foot on the accelerator. His car took off, spraying gravel as it peeled out of the turn. Not having a choice, Lou had to go back out the same driveway he'd just entered. As his speed picked up, he was praying no one turned into the driveway to avoid a head on collision. His prayers were answered as he reached the end of the driveway and made a left onto Lake Shore Drive. He'd driven a mere five feet when he almost collided with a dark colored Ford just reaching the top of the hill. "I don't know what the hell is going on,"

Lou yelled out. "Does this have anything to do with your government friends?"

"I don't know," Amy said, as tears flowed down her face. Her hands were shaking and she felt dizzy. "Just keep going, until we reach a public place."

"I'll try," Lou said, driving as quickly as he could down the hill. Within a few minutes, the headlights were blazing in his rearview mirror again. "Damn!" Lou yelled out, as he realized the other car was rapidly gaining speed behind them. He continued to drive as fast as he could, taking the twists and turns at a dangerous speed. Several times, the car lost traction and skidded on leaves and brush located along the side of the road. At last, the lanes were beginning to get wider and the elevation wasn't nearly as high as it had been, but still high enough for an accident to be fatal.

Amy sat frozen in the seat next to him. She kept saying, "I'm sorry. I'm so sorry." She thought about using her emergency phone to call Cain, but it was in her bag which was now resting somewhere around her feet. She prayed it wasn't under Lou's feet or in the way of the brake pedal. Tears streamed down her face. She held on to whatever she could to steady herself.

Lou continued to drive at breakneck speeds for the road they were on. At least, this area was familiar to him. His pupils were dilated from the adrenaline rush, so the night didn't seem quite as dark as before. The car that followed kept trying to get close enough to ram them again. Lou knew that a small cliff was coming up in the next turn. There was also a small road that led to a campground next to the cliff. He didn't warn Amy of his plan but as they reached the turn he yelled, "Hold on." Jerking the wheel, he angled the car to the right and headed into the small hidden campground road as he heard Amy scream. The car behind them was not as quick and the scene was surreal as the car drove straight off the road and dropped about thirty feet. As Lou slowed down on the campground road, a sudden bang rang out from below. The continued noise of breaking glass and a car horn blaring could be heard through their closed windows. He couldn't remember what was at the bottom of the cliff but was hoping it was nothing more than rocks and trees. He didn't remember campsites or a moonlit beach being there. Lou didn't feel any sympathy for the jerk in the car, but hoped there were no innocent people caught in the way.

Amy trembled in her seat and sobbed.

Lou quickly ripped off his seat belt and leaned over to hold her. "Amy it's okay, we're okay," he said close to her ear as he soothed her hair. "Are you hurt?" Amy shook her head from side to side as well as she could against his face. "I'm okay, just upset."

"I'm so sorry," Lou said. "I don't know what the hell happened, but we're okay."

Amy pulled away from him. Her face was wet with tears and her mascara was smeared down her cheeks. Her nose was running and she wiped her face with the back of her hand. "No, I'm the one who's sorry. I never should've gone out with you."

"We had a great time," Lou began.

"NO!" Amy said, as her breathing became ragged. "I could've gotten you killed. I never should've gone out with you."

"Amy, we're okay. I'm fine."

"I couldn't stand it if someone got killed because of me," Amy said, as she shook her head. "Please, I need my purse."

Lou felt around by their feet and located her bag under her seat. He picked it up and handed it to her. Amy quickly rummaged around and located the throw away cell phone Cain had given her. She dialed his number and waited for him to pick up. Meanwhile, Lou noticed another pair of headlights in his rearview mirror. The car slowed and stopped, but something wasn't right. No one got out of the car or called to them. Lou immediately drove into the campground where they reached a small building. He circled to the back and turned off his headlights. Amy was talking to Cain, trying to explain what happened, but stopped when she noticed they were behind the office. Without hanging up, she turned to Lou for an explanation.

"I don't know what's going on, but there was a second car," Lou said, watching the road. "Something's not right and I wasn't gonna sit there."

Amy relayed that information to Cain. She purposely didn't say where they were in case someone was listening. There was silence for a minute as Amy listened to the response. Lou continued to watch the road that led into the campground, but the second car didn't appear. No one was working in the little office so they remained hidden.

"Now what?" Lou asked, as he turned toward her when she hung up the phone.

"The police should be on their way," Amy said. "We're not moving until we see flashing lights."

"That was your, ah, friends?" Lou asked gingerly.

"It was someone from the FBI," Amy told him. "There's a car in this area. As a matter of fact, we've been followed all night by a couple of cars," Amy said angrily. "I can't tell you anything more than that and we're forbidden from telling the police anything more than we were chased down the hill."

"What the hell?" Lou asked shaking his head.

"Lou, I'm so sorry," Amy said starting to tear up again. "They're checking to make sure the agents who followed us are okay. I have no idea who's at the bottom of that cliff, but I'm not looking to find out unless I have to."

"Amy, it's okay. I'm quite sure you didn't have this planned."

"How can you believe I'm a secret agent now?" Amy asked with a laugh. "Not too many operatives start screaming and sobbing when their life is in danger."

"Yeah, but not too many women get to have a car chase after dinner. It certainly was different," Lou said with a laugh. "I still think you're very different from a typical doctor and I'll bet this has something to do with that whole FBI thing going on in the hospital."

"Well, I aim to please, Lou," Amy said with a laugh. "Just wait until the second date."

"I can't wait," Lou said with a grin.

Chapter Fifty Four

"You what?" Michael choked into the phone.

"I'm okay," Amy reassured him. "I was almost in a car accident, so I'm not coming over tonight and I didn't want you to worry."

"Now, I'm more worried," Michael said peevishly.

"Listen, it's late and I'm kind of tired so I'll talk to you tomorrow," Amy said quietly. "Just take care of Willow for me, please."

"She's fine, Amy. You're the one I'm afraid for."

"Is Agent Oakes still there?" Amy asked.

"Yes, but why do you want to know if everything is okay? What aren't you telling me?"

"I wanted to be sure," Amy replied. "Listen, I have to go. I'll call you tomorrow, I promise. Good night." She hit disconnect on her phone. Amy felt bad not telling Michael more, but at the moment she didn't know if the car at the bottom of the cliff belonged to Shepherd Force or a drunkard.

Amy and Lou sat in his car behind the small campground office until they saw a patrol car pull up with flashing red lights. Within minutes of speaking to the officer, the entire area was packed with emergency vehicles. Additional police cars, an ambulance, tow truck, fire truck and the FBI car crowded down the little road that led to the campground. Even Cain made a personal appearance and was now making his way toward them. He stopped when he saw Amy's face.

"Are you okay?"

"Not really," Amy said. "What's going on?"

"They pulled a body out of the wreckage," Cain said.

"Any idea who it is?" Amy asked, as her stomach knotted.

"Not yet, but we'll know soon," Cain said, as he looked at them.

Turning to Lou, he said, "The local police will want a statement from you. You might want to speak to them now while the details are fresh."

"Of course," Lou said. "I'll find the officer and get started."

Cain looked at Amy, his facial expression difficult to read. "They're sending the body to Rocky Meadow General, so it might be a good idea for you to go home and get some rest. You'll have a busy day tomorrow."

"Do you think it was them?" Amy asked quietly.

"I have no idea," Cain said. "Perhaps you'll find some answers in the morgue. Even if it was, we don't know if they meant to scare or kill you. I imagine we'll be hearing something soon."

"That's not very encouraging," Amy said.

"We're doing the best we can, but until this is settled, you shouldn't be far from home."

"I'm sorry I went to that meeting."

"Things are heating up, go home," Cain said, as Lou walked back toward them.

"Fine, we'll go. You know how to reach me."

"Sure do. I'll see you in autopsy tomorrow," Cain said, with a nod, as he turned and walked away. Lou and Amy climbed back into his car. After putting on their seat belts, Lou guided the car around the remaining emergency vehicles and headed toward Lake Shore Drive. He slowly drove back to Vermont. Both were quiet after their dinner and brush with disaster. Lou was edgy and looked into the rearview mirror more often than necessary. There was a car behind them, but Cain told them they would have an escort home.

Lou drove straight to Amy's house and pulled up to the garage when they got there. He got out of the car and walked around to open Amy's door. At the same time, a car quietly pulled into the drive and parked behind them. Two agents got out of the car.

"Ma'am, I'm Agent McNeil," the first one said while flashing his badge. "Agent Cain wants us to walk you to your door and check the house."

"Okay," Amy said. "We'll all go together." The four of them climbed the stairs to the deck and approached the glass doors. Amy and Lou were told to wait outside while the two agents went through the house, searching rooms and checking closets.

"Are you sure you want to stay here?" Lou asked, while watching the agents move through the Great Room.

"Yes Lou, it's fine," Amy said with resignation.

"Seriously, you could come back with me."

"No, I don't want anyone or any other place involved," Amy said. "Go home, please."

"I don't know what's going on, but...," Lou's voice trailed off as the agents moved to the second floor.

"Unfortunately, it has to stay that way for the moment," Amy said, looking up at him. "Thanks for a wonderful dinner."

"My, ah, pleasure," Lou said. "What about that second date you mentioned?"

Amy smiled. "I think I need to get some things settled in my life right now. Please, let's give it some time."

"We can go slowly. I know things are hectic and I'm not trying to pressure you, but when you're ready, I'm ready."

"Lou, I really appreciate that and I had a nice time, but I'm not able to date right now," Amy said, indicating the agents coming down the stairs. "Maybe soon, we'll see."

Lou leaned down and gave Amy a kiss on the cheek. "Whatever's going on, be safe. I'll see you in the hospital tomorrow."

"Thanks Lou. I'm really sorry this happened."

"It wasn't your fault," Lou said. "Talk to you real soon." Lou smiled as he touched her cheek. As the agents came back, he turned and left the deck. Amy continued to watch until he reached his car and drove off.

"Looks like a real nice guy," Agent McNeil said, with a lopsided smile.

Shaking her head, Amy turned around. "He is a nice guy. Are you sure he's not in danger?"

"Cain doesn't think so," McNeil said.

"Let's hope Agent Cain is right," Amy said with disgust.

"Yes, ma'am," McNeil said. "He told us both to stay here tonight. We'll be keeping an eye on you. One of us outside, one inside, if it's okay with you."

"Whatever," Amy said. "I'm exhausted and I'm going to bed. There's stuff in the fridge and coffee on the counter."

"Thank you, good night ma'am," McNeil said, as he looked around the deck.

Chapter Fifty Five

Friday morning started out gray and drizzling. Amy rolled over in bed and looked at the somber landscape. The house was quiet and a few seconds passed before she remembered two agents had stayed overnight. Getting out of bed, she put on a robe and padded to the kitchen. Agent McNeil was walking on the deck and the other appeared to be dozing in the living room. She reached for the coffee pot and accidentally banged a nearby saucepan. The agent on the couch jumped up with his hand on his gun and frightened Amy. Agent McNeil came running over to the windows to see what was happening.

"Whoa, easy there," Amy said holding her hands up defensively. "I just wanted to make coffee."

The agent stared at her for a few moments and looked around. Agent McNeil walked into the room and loudly said, 'stand down.'" Slowly, the sleepy agent lowered his gun and relaxed.

Taking a deep breath, Amy turned back to the coffee. She filled the pot with water, placed the filter, spooned in the dark roast coffee grounds and plugged in the pot. "I'm making ten cups because it looks like you could use some too." As she started toward the bedroom, she yelled over her shoulder, "The cream is in the fridge, sugar in the cabinet."

Closing the bedroom door, she gathered a clean set of clothes for the day and locked herself in the bathroom. Undressing, she quickly jumped into the shower when the water turned hot. Having watched too many movies depicting crazed killers attacking in the bathroom, she cut her wash time to a total of seven minutes while peeking around the shower curtain. Drying off, she quickly donned her clean clothes. Although her hair was wet, she tied it in a knot on top of her head. This was not the day to worry about fashion. Amy wanted to get to the hospital as soon as possible. She had another difficult autopsy scheduled and wanted to get the agents out of her house. Although they were assigned to protect her, Amy found them intrusive.

When she was dressed, she returned to the kitchen. Both men were sipping the strong brew and looked more alert. Amy sympathized with them, having personally spent many long hours in the hospital, operating through the night, while families and detectives slept in awkward positions in the waiting room. There was a very distinct feeling to being on duty while the rest of the world slept. At times it was exhilarating, but exhausting as well and she didn't miss it a bit.

Amy poured coffee into her travel mug and added cream and sugar. Offering a refill to the agents, she unplugged the pot and threw out the grounds. As they drank their coffee, she asked them about the evening and learned the night had been quiet. There were no attempts to invade her home and their night glasses hadn't picked up any activity in the woods.

Grabbing her coffee and purse, Amy and the two agents left the house. She had driven to the hospital the day before and was planning on retrieving her car after dinner, but Lou had driven her straight home. Amy got into the back seat while the two agents piled in front. After securing themselves, Amy was chauffeured to the hospital by the FBI.

As the car pulled up to the emergency room entrance, Amy noticed several nurses, smoking outside. Their heads popped up as soon as the vehicle came to a stop. Amy felt the staff staring, as one of the agents jumped out of the car and opened the back door. She lowered her head, grabbed her purse and got out. There couldn't be more than several people outside, but Amy had the impression a hundred eyes were watching her. The rumor mill would be buzzing today. She couldn't wait for Lou to bring back the latest theory about her clandestine activities in the hospital.

She held her head high and walked briskly into the emergency room. Behind her, one of the agents was on his cell phone. When the call finished, they got back in the car and drove off. Approaching the front desk, Amy looked over the board to see how many cases were in the trauma rooms. The night had been quiet and most of the rooms were empty. Waving to the nurse at the desk, Amy walked to the elevator and pushed the call button. When the doors opened, she entered and pushed the button for the basement. She couldn't help but notice one of the nurses, who had been outside smoking, was now whispering to the nurse at the desk. Looking up, they saw Amy's stony face and stopped talking while the elevator doors slid closed. Oh yes, the rumors would be good.

Amy arrived in the basement and made her way to the morgue. Alex was arranging a man's body on the steel table, in the center of the room, and Amy assumed it was the body of the man who drove off the cliff. Smiling, Alex looked up and waved in her direction. She smiled back and made her way to the locker room. Storing her things, including her cell phone in the locker, she retied the hair on her head, made sure her scrubs were clean and returned to autopsy.

"Morning Alex," Amy said. She appreciated his hard work, dedication and attention to detail. There'd been a physician's assistant in Boston who worked cases with her in the operating room. She'd been excellent as well. The impact of a good assistant was incalculable and Amy made a mental note to let Alex know. She also decided to call her previous assistant when she found time. Prior to now, she'd distanced herself from contact with anyone from Boston in order to minimize the emotional impact of what had happened there. Perhaps, she was starting to heal, as she missed them.

"Ready to go when you are," Alex said softly. "Are you okay to do this? I heard there was more drama last night."

Amy looked toward Alex. "It's ridiculous at this point. Did you get a file or any paperwork on this guy?"

"Not really. He's listed as John Doe in the computer, Case file 12641. The FBI was here a little while ago and took his fingerprints. Maybe they'll come back with something interesting."

"Well, in the meantime, let's get started." Amy put on her gloves and gown and carefully looked over the body with a magnifying glass. Photos had been taken and she reviewed them while shaking her head. Alex washed the body while Amy reached up and turned on the overhead microphone. "This is Dr. Amy Daniels dictating the external exam of John Doe, Case file 12641, Caucasian male, approximately 5'10", 175 lbs. Turning to Alex she asked, "Have you ever seen anything like this before?"

"No, can't say I have."

"I used to see plenty of strange things in the trauma suite. Ugly way to die, isn't it?"

"Looks like it hurt, that's for sure."

As Amy reached up to turn the microphone on again, Cain walked into the autopsy suite. Amy lowered her hand as she didn't want anything they said to be recorded.

"Good morning," Cain said with a nod.

"Morning," Amy said, a little too curtly.

"Did you sleep well?" Cain asked.

"As well as one can expect with two strange agents in her house and a potential killer on the loose," Amy said testily.

"For your protection," Cain said.

"I suppose it was," Amy said, as the corner of her mouth curled a little. "Do you have any information on this guy?"

"Well, the best I can do," Cain said and stopped when he took a closer look at the body. "What is that?"

"It's a tree branch, Cain."

"That's a nasty way to go," Cain said while shaking his head.

"When the car went off the cliff, it crashed into a small grove of trees. Either the windshield broke right away or the tree branch broke through and drove itself straight into his chest. Apparently, he was speared right into the car seat, but I have to read the field report to get more details."

"That's brutal," Cain said.

"I'm sure it was. Death came quickly, he hemorrhaged internally and from his throat."

Cain paused for a minute. Amy distracted his attention and asked her question again. "Do you have any information on our John Doe?"

"Not much detail," Cain began. Looking at Alex, he said, "Why don't you take a break for a few minutes?"

Alex took off his gloves and untied his gown. Walking away, he said, "I'll be back in ten."

"Thank you Alex, I'm sorry," Amy said, as he left the room. Once the door closed she turned back to Cain. "Okay, go on."

"I am limited to what I can tell you, but since you were almost killed, I will tell you this. The fingerprints came back to a mercenary by the name of Gustov. We've heard of him, but we're going back in the database to get more information. We ran his passport and we know he arrived in the US about ten days ago. I've got agents showing his photo to the local hotels to see if we can find where he's been sleeping."

"What about a phone?" Amy asked quickly.

"We found one in the car and they're running it now for numbers, prints and data."

"So, you think this is the guy that killed Ray?"

"He's been linked to Shepherd Force. Beyond that, I have no idea. There was a .22 caliber gun in the car as well.

Ballistics is running it to see if it matches the bullet that killed Raymond Fuller."

Amy winced at his bluntness.

"I'm sorry," Cain said. "If we don't learn to distance ourselves from the emotional impact, we die."

"I get it, really I do," Amy said, knowing she'd had to do the same, over the years.

"The thing is, we don't know if he was trying to kill you. He may have only wanted to scare you. We know he followed you from the hospital parking lot, because we had him under surveillance the whole time."

"Apparently not close enough when we went up that hill," Amy said sarcastically.

"Look, if he wanted to take you out, he could've killed you anytime. He could've attacked while you were walking into your meeting or out of the restaurant. He's a trained assassin and didn't need to wait for the cliff."

"Cain, I'm fairly worn out with being bait and I don't want to do this anymore," Amy said tiredly. "Jimmy Griffin has been ready to go for five days. Please call your base or office or whatever it is, find a place to send him and get out of the hospital."

Cain held back his reply when he noticed Alex return to the autopsy suite. Turning to Amy, he smiled and said, "I'm going upstairs. I'll touch base with you in a couple of hours. Try to relax."

“Relax?” Amy said incredulously. Why did women always get accused of being histrionic when they were emotional or passionate about an issue? Amy felt like slugging him.

“We’ll discuss this later,” Cain said, when he saw the fire in her eyes. He turned and left the autopsy suite. Alex smiled as he watched him go.

Chapter Fifty Six

Willow pushed the grocery cart through the aisles as Katie filled it with the food she'd need to cook for the weekend. Father Michael had come along but spent most of his time conversing with parishioners in the store. Rolling her eyes at Willow, Katie shook her head and they went on to the next aisle. Trailing behind, an FBI agent dressed in casual clothes followed from a distance.

"I'll need potatoes and I have to get the ingredients for stuffing," Katie said. "I need to buy more food with extra people around."

"Everybody loves your cooking," Willow said. "It's really good."

"Well, thank goodness you're staying with us. You've helped me a lot. It was bad enough making sure Father Victor was full. Now I have other guests coming for meals on their breaks."

Father Michael snuck up behind them and let out a hearty laugh when he heard Katie complain. Turning she said, "You weren't suppose to hear that Father."

"But I did, Katie. That's what happens when you're a great cook."

"We might as well open a soup kitchen. What's the difference?" Katie said, with a small smile.

Father Michael continued to chuckle. He knew Katie loved cooking and liked to feed people even more. There'd been at least one agent in the rectory since the threat was made against Willow and himself. In addition, other officers seemed to visit and catch up on details during meal time. They were fairly well protected and no one was getting by Father Victor at the food table.

"Willow, can you get one of those five pound sacks of flour for me please?" Katie asked, as she pointed to the shelf on Willow's side.

"Got it. What else?" Willow asked, as the food laden cart got heavier with each aisle.

"We'll need several gallons of milk and enough butter to make the food. Oh, and don't let me forget rolls. They can have bread and butter while they're waiting," Katie said, as she looked over her list. Turning to Father Michael she said, "If this keeps up, I'm gonna give a bill to that FBI agent. What's his name, Cain?"

"Yes, Katie. Marcus Cain. He seems to be a good man. I know he's doing as much as he can to protect Amy while trying to catch these guys."

"He'd better 'cause if something happens to Dr. Amy, I'm gonna be very upset," Katie said softly.

"It'll be fine Katie. Where is your faith?" Michael squeezed her hand and smiled at her. Remember Proverbs 3:5 NIV "Trust in the Lord with all your heart."

"I hope so," Katie shot a worried look up towards Father Michael. "Let's check out and get home so I can start dinner. Willow try that line, I think it's pretty short."

Willow guided the cart into the third checkout line of the small food store located on the edge of Rocky Meadow. None of the major food chains had made their way to town yet. As they put the food on the belt, Katie looked at the register clerk. "Why little Charlie Miller, is that you?"

Charlie blushed as she singled him out. "Yes Katie, it's me."

"My, how you've grown. Father Michael, you remember Charlie Miller, don't you?"

"I sure do," Father Michael said with a smile, as he reached over and shook Charlie's hand. "One of our best CCD students to date."

Charlie's face turned crimson from the attention. He started to check out their food as he murmured a soft, "Thank you."

"Charlie, how old are you now?" Katie asked, with a smile.

"Seventeen, ma'am," he replied, as he kept working to ring up the food.

"Why, Willow is sixteen," Katie said with a smile. "You two should get to know each other."

It was now Willow's turn to color as she realized Katie's attempt at matchmaking. Willow wanted to scream out, "Awkward," instead she gave a nervous smile and stared down at her sneakers for the next several minutes.

"Do you go to Rocky Meadow High?" Charlie asked, as he picked up the potatoes and put them in the cart.

"No," Willow said, as she shook her head back and forth.

"Willow is staying with us at the rectory for now. You'll have to stop by and visit sometime, Charlie. After Sunday mass, perhaps?"

"Yes ma'am," Charlie said with a little smile, as he finished ringing up the order. "Your total is $196.88."

Father Michael leaned over Katie and handed him the parish credit card. They'd established an account at a local bank years ago which made the bill paying much easier month to month. The Sunday collection was counted by several parishioners on Monday, and then deposited in the church bank account. The deposit slip was shown to Father Michael for confirmation and logged into the bank ledger.

After swiping the card several times, Charlie's face turned red again. He looked up and stammered as he shrugged his shoulders. "I'm sorry, but it says declined."

"What?" Father Michael asked in a surprised tone.

"It's not going through," said Charlie. "Do you have another card?"

"No, that's the only card for the Parish. I don't have a personal credit card," Father Michael said.

"I got rid of mine when my husband passed away," Katie said.

"I'll get one when I'm eighteen," Willow said. "Then I could pay for you."

"I know you would dear," Katie said with a smile, as she squeezed her hand.

"I don't understand why this happened," Father Michael said. "I know we put a nice deposit in the bank on Monday." Clearly, the whole group was embarrassed. Charlie put on his light and the store manager, Ed Baker, came over to help. The FBI agent trailing them sidled closer to the checkout counter as he noticed things were not going as planned.

"Father Michael, how are you?" Ed greeted them warmly.

"Ed, nice to see you." Father Michael shook his hand and was relieved to see a friendly face.

"How can I help?" Ed asked, as Charlie shuffled his feet and looked anywhere but at the register.

"Um, the card for the church wouldn't go through," Charlie said and shrugged.

"Here, let me try it," Ed offered, as he took up Charlie's position. "Maybe it's been demagnetized." Ed swiped the card with the same result. The transaction was declined with the message to call the bank for further details.

"Should we put the stuff back?" Willow asked Katie quietly. Katie shook her head and squeezed Willow's arm.

"Well, I'll call the bank now," Father Michael said. "What should we do with the food in the meantime?"

"Tell you what, Father," Ed said. "We're gonna pack the food in your car. Take it home and then worry about the bank. You can always come back and pay me later, I still trust you."

"Why bless your beautiful heart, Ed," Katie beamed. "That is so nice of you."

"Katie, do I get a free sausage sandwich at the next picnic?" Ed asked, with a laugh.

"You can have two for being so kind," Katie said with a large smile.

Ed looked up at Father Michael and said, "Between you and me, a lot of credit cards haven't gone through today, so don't take it personally. Apparently, there's some fraud going around, so the bank put a stop on everyone's money."

"That makes me feel better. What if someone has an emergency?" Father Michael asked.

"I guess you have to go to the bank and get the cash. A real pain in the bummer if you know what I mean," Ed said with a grin.

"Bless you again, Ed," Father Michael smiled as he shook his hand. "And you too, Charlie. I'll be back with cash as soon as possible."

"I know you will, Father. Have a pleasant day," Ed said as he waved.

Katie was shaking her head and talking as they made their way to the car. Charlie watched Willow walk away and almost couldn't wait to go to church this weekend.

Chapter Fifty Seven

Amy sat at her desk in the morgue and signed paperwork. She had spent the earlier part of her morning completing the autopsy on the mercenary. Together, she and Alex removed the branch that served as a stake to Gustov's heart. His fingerprints were retaken as well as general x-rays of his chest and abdomen. After completing the external exam, documenting tattoos and scars from previous gunshot wounds, Amy efficiently opened his chest to attempt an internal exam. The organs that weren't macerated were weighed, measured and removed. Her conclusion was obvious. Gustov had died from blunt force trauma to the chest secondary to a motor vehicle accident.

The rest of the morning was spent documenting her exam and dictating her findings. Her report was to be typed and placed in her file within two hours. As she studied her notes, the phone on her desk rang. Taking a deep breath, she answered with a coolness reserved for an unwanted caller. "Dr. Daniels."

"Amy? Is Amy there?"

"Oh, Michael, hi. It's Amy," she said with a sigh of relief.

"I wasn't sure for a minute," he chided. "You sounded quite official."

"To be honest, I thought it would be another message from our so-called friends," Amy confided.

"No, it's just me. How are you?"

"I'm okay, tired, but okay," Amy said softly.

"I know you mentioned something about a car accident," Michael began.

Amy realized she hadn't told Michael about the events that had taken place last night. He only knew about the medical society meeting. She felt awkward telling him that she'd gone out to dinner with a colleague and chided herself for thinking that way. She wasn't cheating on him. What a strange thought. She didn't want to go into detail about the car chase or the agents hovering over her all night long either. Maybe another time, but not now.

As she spoke, a secretary came into her office and placed a pink message on her desk. Amy glanced at it briefly. A meeting with administration had been requested as soon as possible. Uh oh, that didn't sound good either.

"Michael, can you hold on for a second?"

"Of course, sure."

Amy put the call on hold and looked up at the secretary. "What's this all about?"

"I don't know. Someone just called down and wants to see you, now if possible."

"Do you know what it's in reference to?"

"No ma'am, I sure don't."

"Okay, that'll be all for now," Amy said, as she excused the secretary. She turned her attention back to the phone. "I'm sorry; I've just been requested to give a command appearance to the administration."

"Uh oh, that's not good, right?"

"Probably not," Amy said. "I'm sure they're not happy with something. I'll have to go talk to them but I should be done soon."

"Otherwise, you're okay?" Michael asked again, his voice concerned.

"Well, I'm holding together for now," Amy said. "But it hasn't been fun."

"Sorry to hear that. Do you think you'll be able to meet me at our bench in a couple of hours?"

"I'm gonna try to get out of here as soon as possible," Amy said.

"Stay for dinner. Katie has been cooking her little heart out and I think Willow really needs to see you again. She's been upset she couldn't have her driving lessons this week."

A pang of guilt washed over Amy. Her intentions were always in the right place, but time and situations got away from her. "I'll be there. I promise. Meet me at the bench two hours from now, okay?"

"Wild horses couldn't drag me away," Michael said, sounding very happy.

"Great, gotta go, see you later." Amy said and gently hung up the phone. Seriously, she'd almost died last night. No matter the consequences, she was going to take time and visit her friends and loved ones.

"Excuse me, Dr. Daniels," a loud voice filled the room. Cain walked in and sat on the only chair available. He was lucky it wasn't filled with case files and paperwork.

"Agent Cain," Amy said as she acknowledged him. "How can I be of help and where do we stand with our macabre situation?" Amy asked tiredly.

"You'll be happy to know that Mr. Griffin will be transferred to a federal prison tonight."

"Thank the Lord," Amy said happily.

"We're trying to keep it quiet for now. Only one other person knows about the transfer beside you and me. We don't want anyone blowing up our little convoy or anything."

"There's a happy thought," Amy said sarcastically.

"Speaking of blowing things up, we had our team check your car since it was in the lot all night. I'm happy to say, no car bombs were found."

"Thank you for checking but you don't have the keys. Should I even inquire how you opened it? Amy asked, staring at him with an annoyed look on her face.

"That's privileged information," Cain said with a grin.

"Forget it, I apparently have no private life or material objects anymore," Amy complained. "Listen, while you're here, take a walk with me upstairs?"

"Why?" Cain asked suspiciously.

"Because I've been summoned to the administration office," Amy explained, not breaking eye contact.

"Is that a bad thing?"

"Yes, and I'm sure it has to do with all the activities you're involved in. He can bite your head off at the same time he bites mine."

"Would he really do that?" Cain asked surprised.

"He would if he's getting a lot of complaints," Amy said, as she straightened her desk and pulled her computer close to her. "Before we go, I want to see if my dictation is done. I can show you some interesting details from the autopsy." Amy waited a few seconds for the computer to boot up. After her screen saver displayed, she went into reports and pulled up the case labeled, Gustov, Case file 12641. She motioned Cain closer and clicked on the photos of his tattoos.

"I recognize that," Cain said, as he studied the photo. "It's the mark of a Ukrainian gang that does not do nice things in the world."

"I thought so," Amy mused, as she moved around the report. "I want to show you another photo of his old gunshot wounds as well." She kept moving her cursor but the report wouldn't respond to her commands. Getting frustrated, she said, "I don't know what's going on with this thing." She closed the program, hoping it would work if she reopened it. Her tactic was successful and Gustov's report once again filled the screen, but as they looked at it, the words slowly disappeared. One by one, the pages were replaced by strange symbols that were incomprehensible to Amy and Cain.

"Oh damn," Cain said, as he took over the keyboard. His fingers flew as he began typing in various commands.

"What's going on?" Amy asked, watching him type. It was obvious he knew his way around a computer.

"It's Shepherd Force," Cain said, as he softly cursed again. "They're inside your program and they're erasing the entire file labeled Gustov."

"You're kidding me?" Amy asked, as she stared at the screen.

"Unfortunately, I'm not," Cain said, as he punched in more commands.

"Are they erasing everyone's file?" Amy asked with alarm.

"No, it looks like the only file they're deleting is Gustov."

"I don't believe this," Amy said, looking at the computer.

"Well, believe it or not, it's happening," Cain said again as the screen went blank. After a few seconds, large words appeared to be floating in the middle of the screen, Flash Drive, Flash Drive.

"There goes my dictation," Amy said, throwing her hands up. "There's no protection against Shepherd Force, is there?" As she turned to look at Cain, she asked, "I'll still have the dictation, right?"

"Is it on tape or digital?" Cain asked, as he closed down the computer.

"Oh," Amy paused. "I'm pretty sure it's digital."

"Then I wouldn't count on it being found," Cain said, slowly shaking his head back and forth.

"I can't stand this," Amy said, as she shifted in her chair. "Well, it's a good thing I have several copies of my handwritten notes and I made photocopies of all my diagrams. I'll give them to you now, in case someone decides to come in and torch the place looking for them."

"Let me help you," Cain said, as they put the entire paper folder in a manila envelope. "I'll hang on to this."

"I'm glad Griffin's leaving tonight. I want to get this whole thing over with," Amy said anxiously.

"Easy now, we're working on a plan," Cain said, trying to calm her.

"Well, I'd love to hear it when you're ready," Amy said sarcastically.

"C'mon," Cain said. I have another conference on the fourth floor. Let's go see your boss and take care of the paperwork for Griffin."

"It'd better be quick because I'm leaving to talk to Father Michael and Willow shortly," Amy said, while grabbing her purse and phone out of her desk. Looking at her phone, she noticed Lou had called several times.

"That's good, in fact that's better than what I had in mind," Cain said. "Let's do the paperwork and then we'll all meet back at the same place the three of us visited last time." When Amy looked a little confused, Cain continued to prompt her. "You know, where there are no phones or cameras." Obviously, he didn't want to announce it not knowing if anyone could hear them.

Amy understood what he meant and shook her head in agreement. Of course, she realized he meant the bench at St. Francis. "Okay, if we need to," she agreed.

"I have to make some calls, but I'll be there in an hour," Cain said. They were quiet as they rode up the elevator. Together, they went to administration and quelled some of the rumors that were circulating the hospital without giving any direct information.

Next, they went to the VIP floor. Amy examined Jimmy Griffin one last time. She wrote his prescriptions and discharge order. They couldn't hide the fact he was leaving, but gave no information on where he was going. When Amy was done, she stood up and slung her purse over her shoulder. Glancing at Cain, she left the nursing station and entered the elevator with an agent who would follow her to St. Francis.

Chapter Fifty Eight

Father Michael hung up the phone and was looking forward to seeing Amy. He'd left the food mart, and gone to the bank where they confirmed what Ed, the store manager, had told him. There'd been a breach of security and all accounts were temporarily on hold until passwords were checked and information verified. Father Michael went through the account and reset the church information. He also called a member of the parish finance council to explain what had happened. When all was done, he withdrew the cash he needed for the groceries and went back to the food mart. He personally met with Ed and gave him the money, with a copy of the receipt, as well as a personal blessing for being so kind. As he left the store, he thought of one of his favorite passages relating to food in the Bible.

"Taking the five loaves and the two fish, and looking up to heaven, he gave thanks and broke the loaves. Then he gave them to the disciples, and the disciples gave them to the people. They all ate and were satisfied." Matthew 14:19,20 NIV

Had Ed not trusted them, they would've taken something from the food pantry. That food was just as good, but he didn't want to deprive another family who needed it. Father Michael would've fasted before he'd let that happen. Fortunately, Katie was talented enough to feed a lot of people on a small budget.

As he drove back to St. Francis, he was sure the breach had something to do with Amy's situation. He wanted to discuss it and decided to call her as soon as he reached his desk. Michal always trusted in the Lord, but he'd been worried about Amy and hearing about the near car accident almost threw him into a panic. Thankfully, he'd see her soon.

Chapter Fifty Nine

Amy left the elevator at a brisk pace. Jimmy Griffin was being discharged in a few hours and she was relieved. Eagerly, she crossed the lobby to get to her car and St. Francis. She was hoping to spend some time alone with Michael before Cain showed up and unveiled his final plan. Amy also wanted to visit with Willow after dinner.

"Amy, wait. Dr. Daniels." Amy turned from the lobby glass door and saw Lou. She waited until he reached her, puffing from his short sprint across the room. "Hey, I've been trying to get hold of you all day."

"I'm sorry, Lou," Amy said, with a smile. The agent assigned to follow her stopped across the lobby. "It's been a crazy day."

"Are you okay?" Lou asked. "I mean after last night, I was worried."

"You're so sweet," Amy said, which brought a smile to Lou's face. "I had a hard time falling asleep." She leaned closer to Lou for a conspiratorial whisper. "Those two agents stayed all night."

"They did?"

"Yes, and I was worried about you but they said you weren't in danger and apparently they were right."

"But you were worried?" Lou asked, with a smile.

It took all of Amy's self control not to roll her eyes and make a face. "Of course I was concerned. We could've died last night."

"But we didn't."

In an even lower tone Amy said, "No and to make it worse, I had to do the autopsy on the car victim today."

"Really? Do you know who he was?"

"Sort of. I could tell you, but as the saying goes, 'then I'd have to kill you," Amy said with a grin.

Lou hesitated for a moment until he got Amy's joke. He laughed and leaned toward her again. "Hey, everyone is talking about you today. The rumors are going wild about you and the FBI. Now they think you're a trauma surgeon who's also a high profile agent. I think some of them went to administration to ask if they were in danger."

"I'm sure," Amy said. "I was already called to a mandatory meeting up there, with Cain."

"Really? What did you tell them?"

"Not much, we did a little sidestepping for now. But then again, there's nothing to tell them. I'm just a trauma surgeon from Boston, end of story!"

"Will you tell me the truth someday?" Lou asked, while his eyes surveyed the lobby.

Amy laughed. "You already know the truth, my friend," Amy said, as she looked at her watch. "Listen, I've really gotta go, but I'll talk to you soon."

"Promise?"

"Yes, I promise," Amy said, as she crossed her heart and quickly left the hospital. Lou was a nice guy. Good looking, lonely, and probably ready for a relationship, but unfortunately, she was a far cry from commitment and her only concern at the moment, was seeing Michael.

Chapter Sixty

Amy sped through town as fast as she could. She drove through the wooden covered bridge and made a left onto the short road leading to St. Francis Church. She parked at the back of the parking lot, locked her car and headed for the bench. The day was beautiful, warm and breezy, a perfect summer day. Amy could smell a campfire nearby, as someone got ready to unwind for the weekend. Had this been any other Friday, she'd be getting ready to relax and enjoying the fact that work was done for the week.

Nearing the bench, she spotted Michael, waiting for her. Dressed in his clericals, he was facing The Divide, watching the sparkling river flow by. He must've heard her coming because he turned and smiled when she was still ten feet away. Jumping up, Michael came toward her and enveloped her in his arms for a tight hug before he let her go.

"Hi, how are you?" Michael asked, as he searched her face.

"Better now," she said with a smile. "There's so much going on that I haven't been able to tell you. All the phones are monitored and everything is being watched."

"But you're okay?"

"Yes, I'm fine," Amy said to reassure him. "How are you?"

"I'm well, thank you." Michael said, with a smile. "Katie and Willow can't wait to see you."

"As soon as we're done with Cain, we can go spend time with them."

"Cain's coming? What's going on now?" Michael asked, perplexed.

"I don't know exactly, but we're meeting to discuss some plan. You have the best spot since there are no cameras, or surveillance here. Jimmy Griffin is being discharged tonight," Amy said, but stopped abruptly and looked up at Michael. "You can't tell anyone that."

"I hold many secrets more sacred than that," Michael said.

Amy paused for a second. "Shepherd Force is going to expect a flash drive within twelve hours so we need a plan."

"They'll go away after that?"

"I can only hope so," Amy said. "They're holding us hostage for something we don't have."

"Yes, but they don't know that, do they?"

"No, and we're going to keep it that way," Amy said with a frown. "You know, use it to our advantage."

"Lord, please bless us. I hope it's a good plan," Michael said, while crossing himself.

"That makes two of us," Amy said. They both turned when they heard a branch cracking beneath someone's weight and saw Cain approaching the bench. He had a purposeful stride and a grim look on his face.

"Whatever's on your mind doesn't look good," Amy observed from his body language.

Cain paused for a moment before speaking. "Everything's okay, we've come up with a plan for Shepherd Force." Turning to his left, Cain nodded and said, "Father Michael."

"Agent Cain," Father Michael said, as he nodded.

"And that plan would be?" Amy asked, looking directly at Cain.

"As you know, once Griffin is released, Shepherd Force will be expecting a flash drive to materialize within twelve hours," Cain started.

"Yes, I already know that, did you happen to find it?" Amy asked.

"I have no idea where it is and Jimmy Griffin continues to deny he knows the location." Looking Father Michael straight in the eye, Cain said, "You're certain, Father Michael, you have no knowledge of this flash drive or its whereabouts?"

"Absolutely not," Father Michael said, as he held Cain's stony stare. "I wouldn't play games with this."

"Alright, moving on then," Cain said, as he looked straight ahead and took a deep breath. "As I mentioned before, the FBI has a damaged flash drive from a previous encounter with Shepherd Force. We weren't able to extract any data, but I think we can use it to get rid of them."

"And?" Amy asked.

"And what?" Cain replied.

"There has to be more to your plan. You wouldn't just offer it up to be a nice guy," Amy said with exasperation.

"We try to do it in a way that we're able to get some information when they come to collect it," Cain said, as he shrugged.

"You think they'll fall for it?"

"The drive we have is damaged. They won't be able to access anything. It's that or nothing."

"Okay," Amy said slowly, trying to understand.

"This is where you come in," Cain said, turning to face Amy.

"Me? Why do I have to be involved?"

"Because you're our point of contact," Cain explained quickly. He was met with total silence. "What I need you to do is contact them from your phone and set up the meet."

"Gee, no problem," Amy said a little too sharply.

"Calm down," Cain said, as Michael put a hand on her arm. "The last couple of times you were contacted, it was with a burn phone. There's a number in your recent calls list you can use. We know the phone is being monitored, believe me they'll see it." When Amy hesitated he said, "If not, they'll be looking for you when he leaves the hospital."

"I'd have to get my phone, it's locked in my car," Amy said.

"Then go get it, let's get this done," Cain said.

After a few seconds of silence, Amy left the bench to go to the parking lot. Fear was evident in her face. Michael turned to Cain. "Are you sure she'll be safe?"

"We'll do the best we can to keep everyone safe, Father. It's better to contact them now then to wait till he's discharged and they're chasing us. At least we may have an advantage."

"Let's hope for the best," Michael said, as he watched Amy return to the bench with cell phone in hand.

"Okay, Cain," Amy said, as she heavily sat down on the bench. "What should I do next?"

"You're going to place a call to the burn phone number. I'm sure it won't be answered, but they'll recognize your phone number and try to contact you. When they do, you'll tell them you have the flash drive and we set up the meet. Don't agree to come alone or to any private place. We need to be able to set up surveillance."

"I'm sure I'm going to screw this up," Amy said nervously, as she held the phone.

"You'll be fine. That's why we're doing this together," Cain explained. "I'm sure they'll want to do it as soon as possible and we want it to be a safe drop."

"You mean no more innocent victims, don't you?" Amy said.

"We don't want any victims," Cain said. "We just want to deliver the flash drive. Before we start, I have to make a call to make sure we're all set up. I'll be back in a few minutes. Don't do anything till I get back. You got that?"

"Loud and clear," Amy said, making a sarcastic expression as she watched Cain walk off.

Chapter Sixty One

Katie looked out the kitchen window and watched Cain walk around the church property. “Does anyone know what Agent Cain is doing?”

Following Katie’s gaze, Father Victor said, “He’s the FBI agent that’s been in the hospital all week. I don’t know exactly what’s going on, but he’s a big part of it.”

“Do you think Father Michael knows he’s here?” Katie asked, while she continued to watch Cain.

“I’m sure he does. I know Dr. Amy and Father Michael have both spoken with him several times. He’s been in the hospital every day I’ve gone in to offer communion to the patients. Seems like a fair man.”

Katie made a face as Cain walked out of their view. “I hope everything’s okay. I don’t want any more trouble around here. It’s been hard enough to keep Willow from getting anxious.”

"I know," Father Victor said, shaking his head. "Agent Oakes is in the other room. I'll go mention it to him, just in case."

"Thanks, I appreciate it. I need to get back to dinner. I hope Amy will be joining us tonight," Katie said happily.

***

Amy and Michael waited on the bench until Cain finished his phone call and returned. Nodding to Amy, Cain said, "Let's do it, then. Go to your contacts and dial the number they used the last time they called you."

"Okay," Amy said, as she started to fumble with the phone. She found the number and hit "text" by mistake. "Crap, I hit text message."

"It's okay, actually that's better," Cain said.

"So what do you want me to say?" Amy asked anxiously.

"Here, give me the phone," Cain said, with his hand held out. After a few seconds, he typed the following words,

Griffin being discharged tonight. Finally told me where flash drive is. I'll turn it over if you go away, permanently.

"That should do it," Cain said. "The text was delivered. Now, we wait." Five minutes went by until Amy's phone emitted a tone indicating a text message was coming in.

ACCEPTED. Meet at St. Francis Church, base of St. Francis Assisi statue at prayer walk by woods. 45 minutes.

"Well, that wasn't long at all, was it? Why does it have to be at St. Francis?" Amy asked.

Cain was busy typing a message on the phone and hit send. He waited until the message was delivered.

Amy nervously asked, "What did you say?"

"I told them we don't have the flash drive yet. We have to wait until Griffin is discharged."

Not two minutes later a response was received.

Midnight at statue. You'd better be alone. Tell FBI to back off or there will be severe consequences.

Cain read the response out loud. "What do you think?"

"I'm not going out there alone and get shot," Amy said with a face, as she grabbed the phone from Cain and started typing.

"Whoa, what're you typing? Don't make promises I can't keep," Cain said quickly.

"Here, look for yourself," Amy said as she hit send and handed him the phone back.

Not coming alone. We'll put the drive by the statue and then leave. Take it and go away. We're not waiting around. Leave us alone.

"Okay, that's okay," Cain said, as he watched the phone. The response came quickly.

Just you and the priest. No FBI! Leave the flash drive and go.

"Oh no, I didn't want that," Amy said, as she read the message aloud. "I don't want Michael involved and I don't want anything to happen to St. Francis"

"It's fine," Michael said. "I'll go with you. We'll be safe with the Lord's help."

"No, wait a minute. What about Katie, Willow or Victor?" Amy asked in disbelief.

"We'd have surveillance from now until midnight," Cain said. "There'll be an agent inside with them as well. The roads will be closed so no one can get over the bridge and I'll try to put spotters in the woods and near the prayer walk. After that, we hope for the best."

"Quite frankly, after what happened today, Katie would come out and beat them with a broom, if she could," Michael said.

Amy and Cain both stopped and looked at Father Michael. Cain asked, "What happened?"

Father Michael recounted the whole tale of the food mart and the bank. "I really think it's all related. Plus, we got a letter from the bank today, informing us that a breach occurred. All credit cards and accounts are frozen until the account holder sees a bank manager."

"That inconvenience, in today's economy, is just the tip of the iceberg," Cain said, while nodding his head. "The hacktivists usually steal millions to fund their bigger operations. Even if we catch this guy, it's a small link in a large chain."

"Do you really think St. Francis will be safe?" Amy asked.

"I believe so." Cain turned to Father Michael. "Tell me about your property, Father."

"St. Francis is cut off from the front by The Divide and the side by the mountains. You can see anyone coming in from the road during the day. The back is flanked by the woods so you can easily sneak in there, especially in the dark."

"I can't surround the place and I can't guarantee there won't be gunfire," Cain said. "The statue could get damaged, but all they want is the flash drive. You leave it and get out."

"As long as no one gets hurt and we can put an end to being held hostage, let's do it," Michael said.

"We could try to find agents that look like you," Cain said. "But, I don't know if we have enough time."

Michael turned to Amy. "You're very quiet. What do you think?"

"Let's get it over with," Amy said, turning to Cain.

A few seconds went by as Amy handed the phone over to Cain in total silence. He typed in a message to agree to their terms and hit send. "That's it then, it's all set up. I'll keep the phone for now. I want my tech guys to go over it and I want it monitored in case they change their mind."

"Do whatever makes you happy," Amy said to Cain, as she turned to Michael.

"You don't have to do this. You're not involved and I don't want you to get hurt."

Michael looked at Amy's eyes for a few seconds. He slowly smiled and said, "Alea iacta est."

"What does that mean?" Cain asked, watching the two of them look at each other.

"It's Latin for 'The die has been cast'," Amy explained. "We've passed a point of no return. The decision has been made. We'll go together."

Cain looked at them in silence and said, "Fine. I've got calls to make and I have to talk to Sam. I'm going back to the rectory and I think you should come with me."

Michael and Amy got up from the bench and slowly followed him like baby ducklings on their way to a tsunami.

Chapter Sixty Two

"How are you holding up?" Katie asked, when she finally let go of Amy. They were standing in the rectory foyer. "I've been worried sick about you dear."

"Fine," Amy answered with a smile.

"You're not fine. I can tell by your eyes," Katie said, as she stood back to study Amy's face.

"Let's just say I'm doing the best I can right now," Amy said, as the two men crowded in behind her.

"If you say so, dear," Katie said looking at her. She then looked at Father Michael and Cain standing behind Amy. "We have company for dinner this evening?"

"Katie, my love," Father Michael said with a smile. "You don't mind, do you?"

"Nice to meet you again, Katie," Cain said, with his most charming smile.

"Welcome, Mr. Cain," Katie said. "Come in, come in everyone. Relax, dinner will be ready soon."

"Katie, I'll come to the kitchen with you," Amy said, her eyes pleading for escape.

"Of course dear, I need someone to help me toss the salad," Katie said, as she turned toward the men. "Why don't you go into the library and wait while we put dinner on."

Nodding and murmuring, Cain and Father Michael went into the library. They were surprised to see Agent Oakes and Father Victor already seated on a couch. A small afternoon spread of cheese and crackers, cookies as well as coffee and tea, was set up on a sideboard. Cain opened his cell phone and started making calls as he picked out something to eat.

Continuing down the hall, Katie told Amy how worried she'd been about her and Willow.

"Where is she?" Amy asked, looking around the kitchen.

"Why she's up in her room at the moment," Katie said, as she surveyed the stove. "But I've been keeping a close eye on her."

"Katie, I can't thank you enough for all you've done," Amy said, as she gave her shoulders a squeeze. "She told me the legal guardian assigned to take care of her barely acknowledges her. I know she's come a long way since you've been teaching her to cook."

"Well, thank you dear, but she's been splitting a gut to talk to you," Katie said, as she put a head of lettuce on the table. “She wants to get back to her driving lessons and now she knows boys are looking at her as well.”

“She’s a beautiful girl, why wouldn’t they?”

“We know that, but she’s just figuring it out. That poor thing, her mother abandoning her and her grandmother dying like that,” Katie clucked and shook her head. “Thank goodness you took her under your wing this summer.”

“She reminds me of my niece,” Amy said quietly, as she started fiddling with the salad. “I don’t know if you know Katie, but my niece is in a coma. My sister was killed and my niece was shot, but she didn’t die.”

Katie looked horrified as she rushed over to Amy and hugged her hard. “That’s awful. How old is the poor girl?”

“Same age as Willow,” Amy said, as she turned back to the lettuce. “I never had time to get married or have kids so I spent as much time as I could with my niece. Now I wish I spent more.”

“Where is she now?”

“A neurological institute. They take good care of her. I check on her regularly and they call me with any changes.”

Katie couldn’t find a way to look more dismayed then she did at the moment. “I’m so sorry to hear that, dear, and I’m so sorry to hear about your sister dying.” A single tear slid from her eye as she got choked up. Turning away from Amy, she quickly moved to the stove and began to stir the contents of the pots.

"I didn't mean to upset you, Katie. I guess I wanted you to know why I'm so upset at Willow's situation. I want her to be happy and if I can help her in anyway, I will." Katie continued to stir and was silent, so Amy went on. "That's why I can't keep going through drama all the time. I just want some peace and quiet. Nice calm days to move through."

Katie finally turned from the stove. "Don't worry about Willow. Together we'll take good care of her." After a few seconds, she continued. "The Lord certainly has his own plans sometimes, doesn't he? The thought is that overcoming our difficulties is simply another step toward becoming stronger, faithful women." Katie shook her head. "Yes, the Lord has his plan, although I may not agree with it at times."

Realizing that Katie was referring to difficulties in her own life, Amy stayed quiet. She promised herself, one day, she'd take the time to get to know Katie better.

One of the pots boiled over and Katie rushed to turn off the stove. The tension broke as she asked Amy to help her set the table for dinner.

Chapter Sixty Three

Once dinner was ready, Katie called the men to the kitchen. Normally she would've used the dining room for guests, but there'd been police and FBI agents in and out all week. The table in the kitchen was wooden and could fit up to ten people. Over the years, scars had been left by various guests and workers that ate there. Although not the fanciest piece of furniture in the rectory, it was one of the most beloved and contained years of memories filled with warmth, companionship, love and support. The church was beautiful and the dining room was impressive, but the kitchen table was where the color of life's moments was played out on a daily basis. Willow came downstairs and was thrilled to see Amy. Running to her, Willow threw her arms around Amy's neck and squeezed tight. She rushed to tell Amy everything that had happened in the last few days and made her promise to take her driving soon.

"The lawyer says I have to get a used car, but it'll be a good one," Willow said with glee. Amy knew Willow was destined to be a wealthy woman, once the trust funds left to her by her grandmother were turned over. Then she'd be able to buy whatever car she wanted. For now, Amy wanted to help Willow realize that she deserved unconditional love in her life. Willow would mature into a beautiful woman one day, but Amy hoped she'd get a chance to be a normal teenager for awhile.

The men walked in and sat at the table. Katie had platters of food, set out family style, which they passed around several times until everyone's plate was full. Cain ran in after finishing another phone call. When he was seated, Father Michael said a prayer of thanks for the abundant food on the table, as well as the safety of loved ones.

"This is delicious," Cain said, as he heartily finished his plate.

"I'm surprised you can taste it dear, the way you're wolfing it down," Katie admonished him. "You're supposed to take time to relax and enjoy your meal."

Cain looked up. "Sorry, ma'am. I haven't had cooking like this in a long time."

Oakes looked at him over the table. When the meal was about finished, Cain looked up and said "I'd like to take a minute to discuss a few important things about tonight."

"Tonight? What's going on tonight?" Father Victor asked, looking from Cain to Father Michael.

Finally Cain spoke. "This evening, we're going to have an FBI exercise going on outside. Agent Oakes will be with you all in the rectory, but you must stay indoors and away from the windows."

Willow's face paled, as she began to get alarmed. "It's okay," Amy said, as she put her hand on her arm. "You'll be fine, I promise."

Cain broke in. "Everyone has to stay here at this point. We're closing off the road to St. Francis. We can't let anyone in or out from now on. That's the only way to ensure everyone's safety."

"What about me? I have to go home and get ready," Amy said. "Plus, I'm on call."

"Not tonight and I'm sure Katie has an extra room you can rest in," Cain said, looking toward the housekeeper.

"Of course we do, dear, and we'd love to have you stay," Katie said, as she looked at Amy with a smile. "I don't know what's going on, but if Agent Cain says it's safer for you to be here, then you must stay."

The small group sat around the table looking awkward and alarmed. Amy opened her mouth to speak and after a moment said, "Okay then, I'll stay."

She'd asked herself why bother to spend a restless evening at her log cabin when she could be at St. Francis with Katie, Willow and Michael.

“Agent Oakes will take care of everyone. You’ll be fine,” Cain said with a reassuring nod of his head. “Katie, thank you for a delicious meal.”

“Would you like some coffee, dear?” Katie asked with concern.

“I can’t stay, but I’d love some for the road,” Cain said, as his cell phone continued to ring. As Cain answered the phone once again, Katie handed him a traveling cup filled with dark roast, cream and sugar. Still talking, he turned and left the kitchen.

Chapter Sixty Four

After dinner, Willow and Katie cleared the table and washed dishes. Amy called the hospital to arrange coverage for the operating room and ER. All medical examiner duties would be held for now. Cain asked Amy and Father Michael to take another walk with him to the Divide. The night was cooler than last week, but the sky was clear. Stars twinkled above as they walked toward the water.

"I wanted to let you know what's happening," Cain said quietly, as they continued to walk forward. "Throughout the night, my agents will be divided working surveillance and transporting Jimmy Griffin. Access to the wooden covered bridge is now cut off with a Bridge Closed construction sign. By the time the town comes to check, we'll be long gone." Cain was silent for a few seconds. "We all need to meet in two hours. I'll have the flash drive by then."

"What about Shepherd Force?" Amy asked.

"I'm sure they're on their way, if not here already. We can't close the woods. They wouldn't have chosen this place if they hadn't already scoped it out. They're watching us, watching them, you know how it goes," Cain said, with a forced smile. "It'll look like the FBI will all be leaving soon. The men that stay behind will be hidden. Don't forget, they'll want to follow us when we transport Jimmy tonight. I'm sure they don't have enough boots on the ground to watch both operations, although they'll try."

"As long as everyone's safe," Father Michael said.

"We hope so Father, but we can't be sure," Cain said with a shrug. "The adrenaline rush is the part of the job some of us live for."

"That's what some of us need to get away from, Cain," Amy said flatly.

"You have a beautiful church and some gorgeous peaceful grounds here, Father," Cain said. "I'm trying to get this done as quickly as I can, with the least amount of collateral damage."

"I appreciate your concern," Father Michael replied with a nod. "I don't want anyone to associate St. Francis with violence. The property has served as a place of retreat for three hundred years. There's a lot of history here, but always with the greater goal in mind."

"Sounds like I should check in on my next vacation," Cain said, with a grin.

"You never know who's walking here alongside you," Father Michael said quietly as he looked at Cain. "I would have you turn your attention to Exodus 25:8NIV

Then have them make a sanctuary for me, and I will dwell among them.

"That would be a pretty big gun for our side," Cain admitted, as he looked up at the stars. "Let's go with our plan and let the Lord handle the rest."

"Amen to that," Father Michael said. "I believe that'll work."

"I hope so," Amy said softly.

"I need to walk you two back to the rectory to be safe," Cain said with concern. "Once we get there, please don't leave the building until I come get you."

"That doesn't inspire a lot of confidence," Amy said, looking up at him.

"Just trying to keep it all covered, that's all," Cain reassured her.

The trio walked back to the rectory with ample light provided by the stars. "Good luck with transferring Jimmy Griffin," Amy said to Cain. "I can't say I'm sorry to see him go. The hospital's been in an uproar all week."

"The Federal Government thanks you for your hospitality," Cain said, with a small grin as they stopped at the front door of the building. "I'll see you two later." When Amy and Michael had gone inside and locked the door, Cain turned and walked off into the darkness.

Amy and Michael watched him leave through the side window. For just a moment, Amy felt anxious for him.

"Judging from the look on your two faces, I'd say we should prepare for the Armageddon," Katie said, from behind them.

"Oh," Amy jumped as she covered her heart with her hand. "Katie, you scared me."

"Didn't mean to do that, dear," Katie said, as she touched her arm. "It's just that it's late and I thought you might be getting tired. I waited here so I could show you to your room for the evening."

Amy turned and looked at Michael. An awkward moment of silence passed between them before Amy said, "I'll see you later."

"I'll be here," Father Michael said, as he smiled at her and squeezed her hand. "I'm glad you're safe."

"Am I?" Amy said. "Let's hope so."

"Go rest," Father Michael said, as he turned and walked down the hall.

Katie walked Amy upstairs to show her the room she'd been given. As she opened the door and turned on the light, she said, "This is a lovely room and one of our nicest."

"Please don't go out of your way, Katie."

"I'm not dear and I'm very glad that you agreed to stay. Otherwise, I'd be worrying about you." Katie walked in and turned around. "This room is named for St. Bernadette. Perfect for you," Katie beamed, as she turned on the light at the bedside.

"Katie, I remember her name. Why do you think this is perfect for me?" Amy asked, as she toured the room.

"Why, she was born in Lourdes, France. The family was poor and she had a lot of medical problems, Cholera, asthma and then eventually tuberculosis. That's why it's perfect for you, being a doctor and all. Anyway, she's famous for seeing a very beautiful Lady above a rose bush in a grotto in Massabielle. That was Jesus's mother, the Blessed Virgin Mary. In one of the visions, Our Lady told Bernadette where to dig and a spring appeared." Katie turned to Amy and asked. "Have you ever been to Lourdes, France, dear?"

"No, Katie, but it sounds beautiful."

"You definitely need to go," Katie said, as she smoothed the bed cover. "Anyway, the spring water from the grotto is believed to have a special ability to heal. Every year, Lourdes has millions of visitors looking to drink or bathe in the water from the grotto for healing."

"Yes, I loved hearing that story when I was young," Amy said, as she recalled her Sunday school lessons.

"It's a beautiful one, to be sure," Katie said.

"I don't remember what happened to her," Amy said.

Katie smiled, "Well, because of her visions, she received a lot of unwanted attention and moved to the hospice school, run by the Sisters of Charity Nevers. Sadly, she died at the age of thirty-five from her tuberculosis, but she was blessed with the Marian apparition. There's a book about her on the bedside table. She's also the patron saint of shepherds. You really should go to Lourdes, dear. It's quite inspiring."

"I'll plan to do that, someday, Katie," Amy said, as she gave the woman a hug. "Thank you for this great room." Inwardly, Amy thought it was fitting she'd spend the next hour in the presence of the patron saint of true shepherds.

"Relax and be well, dear."

"Thank you," Amy said, as Katie left and closed the door.

Chapter Sixty Five

An hour went by and Amy was ready to go downstairs. She'd felt restless and couldn't relax. She'd washed up in the bathroom and rested on the comfortable bed, waiting for the hour to pass.

Walking down the stairs, the aroma of strong coffee drew her toward the kitchen and when she went inside, she found Katie, Michael and Agent Oakes. There was warm apple pie, complete with whipped cream, in the center of the table. Amy made her way into the room and joined the group. Katie quickly placed a steaming mug of coffee in front of her as well as a plate and silverware.

"Hello dear, how are you?"

"I'm a little nervous," Amy reluctantly admitted. "But I feel rested."

"This is a great place to relax," Michael said, with a smile over the top of his coffee mug.

"Would you like something to eat? I can make a sandwich."

"No thank you, Katie. My stomach is in a knot. Please sit and relax. I don't feel like eating."

Katie refilled everyone's coffee cup before she sat down. Together, they sipped coffee and purposely avoided talking about the evening's activities. Amy sipped the delicious brew, but felt like she was a child again, waiting the agonizing few hours until a dreaded dental appointment. Cain hadn't said the land line was off limits, so she called the hospital to check for messages and informed them she'd need to have continued coverage. Willow bounced into the kitchen, her youth demonstrating resiliency and courage. Perhaps it was the magic of the retreat house or the Lord's presence or Katie's cooking, but it was wondrous all the same and brought a smile to Amy's face.

At eleven o'clock, Cain knocked on the front door and Katie went to let him in. Together, they walked into the kitchen. There was a distinct sensation of nervous excitement or energy in the air, not the dreaded feeling of doom that Amy had expected. Cain sat down and pulled out a small clear bag that held a black flash drive. On it was stamped a shepherd's crook in gold, surrounded by the letters, 'S' and 'F'. Amy and Michael stared at it for several seconds.

"Wow, to think all this drama has been about a tiny little thing like that," Amy said, as she shook her head.

"It may be tiny, but it can hold a vast amount of information," Cain said, as he carefully placed the flash drive back in the bag.

"Let's just hope they buy it," Amy said, as Father Michael made the sign of the cross.

Chapter Sixty Six

At quarter to twelve, Father Michael opened the front door to the rectory and he and Amy stepped out. To the entire world, it appeared they were alone, but Amy knew there were several sharpshooters nestled in the trees, keeping watch over them. Years ago, it was shepherds keeping watch over sheep. Amy couldn't help but notice the analogy. Cain had made them wear heavy bullet-proofed vests and Amy's hands trembled as she held the plastic bag with the flash drive. Michael held her other hand tightly and together they walked, in the dark, toward the statue of St. Francis of Assisi. The moon cast enough light to see their surroundings with ease. Their job was to simply place the bag at the base of the statue, then turn around and walk back to the rectory. It was easy enough, no problems. She was with Michael. She trusted him with her life, yet her heart was racing and she was having trouble filling her lungs with air. Perhaps she was having a flashback to almost being murdered in the same area, in the same moonlight, several months ago. Amy couldn't stop thinking about the trauma patients she'd seen with bullet holes in their heads.

Bullet-proofed vests work fine if your enemy aims for your heart. Why hadn't they come up with a suitable helmet for the average law enforcement officer?

Small beads of sweat broke out on Amy's forehead and she felt dizzy for a few seconds. Stopping to regain her balance, she looked up and saw Michael smiling down at her. His smile was radiant and perhaps she was hallucinating, but he seemed to be surrounded by a glow. The moon was behind her, so it couldn't be moonlight. Amy was very frightened. Her eyes moistened as she looked up at him with fear in her heart. Michael looked down and placed his right hand on her cheek. He leaned over and kissed her on the forehead while he whispered, "He walks right beside you, depend on your faith." Amy closed her eyes for a moment, took several deep breaths and felt stronger. It was all up to the Lord now. "Okay," she said, smiling at Michael. "I believe."

Hand in hand they slowly walked toward the statue. When they got there, Michael crossed himself as Amy knelt forward to put the little plastic bag at the base of the marble figure. One would think they were a normal couple placing flowers to honor the Saint, who was the patron of animals and the environment. Slowly, Amy stood up and together they walked back, arm in arm, to the rectory. Amy had to resist the urge to tear across the lawn as time seemed to speed back up to normal. When they reached the front door, it was opened instantly by Cain.

Amy let out a little yell as Michael laughed and they hugged each other tightly in the hall. Father Victor and Katie stood behind Willow in the doorway that led to the kitchen. Agent Oakes, wearing a bullet proof vest, stamped FBI in big while letters, stood guard near them with gun drawn and faced the windows. Cain, in his vest, had his gun ready and talked into a cufflink microphone linked to his ear piece.

Outside, the hidden agents waited and watched. They were instructed to observe, wound if necessary, but not kill. The FBI wanted information, not to kill the messenger. All remained still, but it was too quiet. Everyone was on high alert; even the birds and animals felt the unnatural eerie silence that filled the air. Seconds ticked by.

All at once, the area burst into action. Flash grenades filled the air; small explosions were followed by big clouds of gray smoke. FBI agents began to yell and run across the grass. Cain shouted orders into the microphone attached to his shirt. As in slow motion, he turned to Oakes and yelled, “They’re using tear gas, damned tear gas.” He turned back to his microphone and said, “Everyone, masks on now!”

As the smoke began to fog the windows of the rectory and seep under the doors, the small group started tearing up, noses running. Katie moved to gather them together and herd them toward the kitchen. “Everyone, let’s get to the basement." She turned to find the large priest. "Father Victor, please help me open this door." Katie pointed to a partially hidden, heavy, thick wooden door behind a white hutch. Victor pushed the cabinet to the side with ease and pulled the heavy wooden door open. Five of them rushed down the wooden stairs to the basement below. Cain and Agent Oakes stayed upstairs in the kitchen and closed the heavy door to protect them.

Amy ran to Willow and hugged her as hard as she could. "Willow, everything's fine, we'll be okay."

"I'm alright," Willow said, looking up at her with a smile. "It's kind of like a neat adventure."

"You're not scared?" Amy asked her.

"The minute you came inside the rectory, I knew everything was cool," Willow said, as she grinned.

"I love you so much, you're such a brave kid," Amy said, as she continued to hold her tight. At the base of the stairs, Father Michael, Katie and Father Victor lit some candles to get their bearings. The small group continued to stand in the basement, listening to the muffled sounds of agents running, yelling and reacting to the effects of tear gas.

Amy noticed a tapestry hanging on a concrete wall to their left. The tapestry appeared to be moving and Amy slowly walked over to get a closer look. The cloth was a deep purple and had what looked like a religious symbol on it. Amy moved the tapestry to the side and found a crack in the wall, through which she felt cool, fresh air. The candlelight cast an eerie shadow, but in the center of the wall, was the same symbol as the one on the tapestry. Amy tried to push the stone, but it felt hard and solid. She looked around and noticed several solid wooden doors in the walls of the basement. Behind her, Father Michael whispered to Katie, while Victor and Willow stood to the side.

Outside, white smoke filled the night air. The agents had put their gas masks on, but not before some of them started coughing. For a few, the gas worked on their corneal nerves, causing pain and tears to flood their eyes, effectively blinding them to the activities around them. No one saw the two men dressed in dark clothing and gas masks run over to the statue, take the flash drive and run back to the woods.

Chapter Sixty Seven

"Requiem Aeternam dona eis, Domine, et lux perpetuae luceat eis. Requiescant in pace. Amen," said Father Michael. After pausing for a breath, he continued on in English. "Eternal rest, grant unto him, O Lord."

"And let perpetual light shine upon him," repeated the small congregation sitting in the church.

Amy sat in the wooden pew of St. Francis Church and half listened as Father Michael said the surreal funeral mass. It'd been two weeks since the showdown outside the rectory. The last funeral Amy attended was her sister's, just about a year ago. It had been hard to concentrate then as well. As she listened to Father Michael's voice continue to recite the Eternal Rest Prayer, her mind drifted back two weeks.

They stayed in the basement until all was quiet and one of the agents came to find them. The basement had been cool and more importantly, the air was surprisingly fresh. Amy was familiar with the effects of tear gas from her chemical warfare disaster training in medical school. As a student, she'd been required to slice a particularly potent onion without using a shield or any protection. Syn-propamethial-S-oxide, found in onions, was only one minor component of tear gas and it was awful. It worked by irritating the eyes, nose, mouth and lungs and caused victims to have sneezing, tearing, coughing, difficulty breathing, as well as pain and temporary blindness. She was thankful it was non-lethal chemical warfare and no one was hurt. The original flash drive must have contained some very important information. Maybe it was better the real flash drive had never been found.

Unfortunately, poor Raymond Fuller died for it. The government, helped along by Cain and the FBI, finally came through with a final resting place for him. Raymond was getting the full funeral he deserved for fighting and dying for his country. Today's congregation was small. Father Michael and Father Victor concelebrated the mass and Father Doherty and Deacon Eddie were on the altar as well. Amy and Katie sat together in the first pew. Behind them, some of the regular parishioners came to pray for Mr. Fuller though they'd never met him. Florence and Ted were there and surprisingly, so was Helen and Harold. Helen had done well after her accident and had been more than happy to have Ernie recheck her several times to make sure there was no permanent damage. Agent Oakes attended the funeral, as well as Katie's friend, Sue. Patrons from the Burlington soup kitchen were told about the services and eager to celebrate Ray's life. They were his only family when he died. A gracious bus owner had offered to provide transportation, free of charge. Willow was sitting in the back pew with her mother, Marty Davis, and her mother's boyfriend, Tony Noce. Marty was trying to spend as much time as she could with her daughter, while being in rehab; their progress was slow as Willow was still trying to understand how a mother could possibly walk out on her infant daughter.

Amy kept going back to the thought that Mr. Fuller's death didn't make sense and the man who murdered him was dead as well. They still didn't know if Gustov had orders to kill or scare them. Perhaps Gustov had taken matters into his own hands. They'd never know. Amy thought back to Katie's comment about how the Lord had his plan, although we don't always agree with it.

When the mass was over, the coffin was turned toward the back of the church. As the funeral director made the preparations to wheel it down the aisle, Amy recited the 23rd Psalm she'd learned as a little girl.

The Lord is my Shepherd; there is nothing I shall want. He makes me lie down in green pastures, he leads me beside quiet waters, and refreshes my soul. He guides me along the right paths for his name's sake. Even though I walk through the darkest valley, I will fear no evil, for you are with me; your rod and your staff, they comfort me. You prepare a table before me in the presence of my enemies. You anoint my head with oil; my cup overflows. Surely your goodness and love will follow me all the days of my life, and I will dwell in the house of the LORD forever. NIV

Amy watched the coffin go down the aisle and started to cry as she remembered the same scene for her sister. She felt Katie's hand reassuring her she wasn't alone. When Amy turned around, Katie handed her a tissue and together they left the pew and followed the coffin out the door.

The tiny congregation left the church and gathered on the sidewalk under a bright sunny sky. They watched as Mr. Fuller's beautiful wood coffin was placed inside a silver hearse. Walking toward Amy, the funeral director handed her a United States flag, folded into a small triangle. "Mr. Fuller had no family and Father Michael felt you should receive his flag for your concern and respect for his life contributions and value to society." Amy accepted the flag with tears running down her face. Turning around, the funeral director, in a voice loud enough for everyone to hear, announced there would be no graveside service. Instead, everyone was welcomed to a repast kindly being donated by Tony Noce at Hasco's Bar and Grill.

Father Michael walked over to stand next to Amy, as Katie went to check on Willow. He leaned over and said, "You're going to Hasco's, right?"

Amy turned to face him. "Yes, I was planning to go."

He helped her dry her tears and said, “Can you wait a few minutes? I’d like to go with you, but I have to hang up my vestments first.”

“Of course, Michael,” Amy said, with a wide smile. “I’ll be waiting right here.”

Michael beamed down at her and finally said, “Great, I’ll be right back.”

Chapter Sixty Eight

Music filled the air as the guests laughed and talked at Hasco's. Amy waited for Michael and then drove the two of them to the repast. The rest of the funeral congregation had drifted in as well. Alcohol was not being served, but the grill was smoking and platters of cheeseburgers, fries, hot dogs and sandwiches were being passed around, as well as plenty of cold soda. The guests of the Burlington soup kitchen were thrilled and helped themselves to heaping portions of food. Katie stood next to Father Victor and Father Michael and beamed as she watched Ray's friends eat. When Father Victor tried to grab the tray, she gave him a frown until he let go. "You'll have your turn, wait a little while."

Michael put his arm around her. "Katie, my love, why do I get the feeling that you and your friend Sue were the ones responsible for calling Ray's friends and arranging transportation, as well as a lot of good food?"

Katie looked at him with a sly smile. "Why, whatever do you mean, dear?"

Father Michael laughed. "I know you would've cooked for all these people but you deserve a break. You've worked very hard these last several weeks."

"Oh, go on, Father Michael," Katie said with a laugh. When he didn't say anything, she said, "I mean really, go on." Father Michael laughed harder and turned to find Amy. She sat at a small table speaking quietly with Willow.

"I don't want to," Willow was saying, as she shook her head.

"It's okay," Amy reached over and took her hand. "Your mom just wants a chance to talk to you. She's working so hard at the rehab with Father Doherty."

"I wouldn't know what to say," Willow said, as she screwed up her face.

"Just ask her how she's feeling. She knows she's not in charge of you or anything, but she's hoping you'll forgive her one day."

"Maybe I won't want to," Willow said, as she sulked.

"Just go talk with her," Amy cajoled.

"Oh, alright already," Willow said, as she jumped up from the chair and started to stomp over to her mother. Halfway there, she turned toward Amy and stuck her tongue out. Amy had a hard time suppressing a laugh.

"This chair taken?" Michael said, as he pulled it out and sat down.

"Yes, apparently, by you," Amy grinned.

"Then you won't mind if I take the one on this side," an unexpected voice said.

Amy turned and saw an attractive man in an expensive suit. "Cain! You made it," Amy said, as she and Michael smiled at him. He seemed like an old friend after everything they'd been through.

"Wouldn't miss it for the world and I'm starving," Cain said, as he grabbed a platter of cheeseburgers and sat down. "How are you guys doing?"

"Pretty well," Father Michael said. Amy and Father Michael each accepted a plate with a cheeseburger and fries from Cain. "How 'bout you?"

Cain took one of the cold glasses of soda that Amy poured from a pitcher in the center of the table. "Been busy, I can say that. Otherwise, everything's okay."

Amy looked at Cain, as she took a drink, and put her soda glass back on the table. "How's Jimmy Griffin?"

"As well as can be expected. He's currently in a Federal holding facility." Looking at Amy, he smiled and teasingly said, "Doctor, his wounds have healed nicely and medically he's stable."

"I guess I'm happy to hear that," Amy answered, nodding her head while she surveyed her cheeseburger.

"Have you had any more trouble?" Cain asked them with his mouth full. He looked at Amy and said, "I was hoping you would've called me." He was wearing another nice suit and his tie was tucked to the side to protect it from falling food.

"Not since the showdown," Amy said, looking at Michael for reassurance. "I haven't heard of anything from the hospital and I don't think there's been any trouble at St. Francis."

"Everything's been peaceful," Michael agreed.

"Good, I'm really glad to hear that," Cain said, as he poured ketchup over his fries.

"Easy with those fries, Cain," Amy said with a laugh. "I don't want to see you in the hospital ever again."

"Thanks a lot," Cain said, feigning hurt feelings.

"It's a shame," Amy said, as she looked at Cain with a serious face.

"What's a shame?" Cain asked, with a frown.

"It's a shame, we went through all that and you didn't catch anyone," Amy said slowly. "I'm very glad no one was hurt and Shepherd Force went away, but I'd be even happier if you caught someone."

Cain popped a fry in his mouth and looked at Amy. "You may not want to hear this, but we didn't actually want to catch anyone."

"What?" Amy asked incredulously, as her voice started rising. "Are you kidding me?"

"Now, just hold on there little lady," Cain said in his best cowboy voice.

"I'm sure Cain will explain it to us," Michael said, as he put his hand on Amy's arm to calm her.

"Go ahead, I'm all ears," Amy said to Cain. "And by the way, you owe me a new cell phone."

Cain washed down his fries with another gulp of soda and turned to Amy. "You know the flash drive we gave them was damaged, right?"

"Yes, I clearly remember you saying that."

"Well, they weren't able to use it."

"Okay, so why is that important?"

"Before I gave you the flash drive, the FBI installed a tiny RFID device on it."

"English translation, please?" Father Michael asked, as he looked at Cain.

"It stands for Radio Frequency Identification Device. The plan was they hopefully took the damaged flash drive back to their evil lair, so to speak. Once we planted the RFID on the flash drive, the FBI could track its physical location."

Amy stopped eating and looked up at Cain. "Did it work?"

"Actually, it did. We collected a lot of good information," Cain said happily. "It led us to a fairly big player that will probably "rat out" more of the organization. But you do realize there are thousands of cybercrimes committed daily? We'll never catch all the hactivists, but if we can shut them down, we can prevent some serious cybertheft and save a lot of headaches. Shepherd Force is a big group right now and believe it or not, their ultimate goal is to help the common man. They just commit crimes to do it. Usually, when we catch one of these guys, they're more than happy to work for us instead of going to jail."

Michael smiled and nodded his head while Cain talked.

"We don't want to kill anyone," Cain said with a shrug. "But we've got a whole Cyber Division designated to fight internet crimes."

"That's really interesting," Michael said, with a grin.

"Why do you say that, Father?" Cain asked, with a calculating look on his face.

"Well, actually a Biblical reference," Michael answered. "You remember hearing about Cain and Abel in Sunday School?"

Amy and Cain both nodded their heads at the same time. "Yes, but please, go on," Amy encouraged him.

"Adam and Eve were in love. Eve became pregnant and gave birth to Cain. Later, Eve gave birth to her second son, Abel. If you remember, Abel kept flocks and Cain worked the soil. Abel was a very important shepherd, protecting his flock and all. Anyway, Cain brought some things he'd grown to the Lord, but the Lord wasn't happy with them. Then, Abel brought the Lord some of his flock and the Lord was very happy, but that made Cain angry. So Cain took Abel out to the field and killed him with a rock."

"Okay and?" Amy asked, shaking her head.

"Well, I just find it interesting in our current world that Cain is still chasing Abel, the shepherd, in a way," Michael tried to explain. "Except he doesn't want to kill him. Maybe, the human race has learned a lesson." Michael looked at them and shrugged. "I mean think about it, Cain technically was the first murderer and Abel was the first victim. The roles are reversed, but the conflict continues."

Amy and Cain were both silent while they thought about Michael's theory but before they could comment, Father Victor, Tony and Katie joined them at the table. Pulling up chairs, they sat down to talk.

"Thank you for asking Willow to talk to her mom," Tony said to Amy.

"Is everything going alright?" Amy asked, as she turned to take a peek.

"They're actually having a little girl talk," Tony said, with a smile. "Willow's telling her mom about her driving lessons and a boy named Charlie from the food market."

Katie laughed and said, "That boy's been in church two weeks in a row now. Last week, he actually offered to deliver some groceries to the church for me."

"Just to see Willow?" Amy asked, with a knowing glance.

"Don't you know it, dearie," Katie grinned.

"She's been so happy since she started helping you in the rectory," Amy pointed out.

"Yes, she's seems much brighter now," Katie agreed.

"It's weird though, the other thing she keeps talking about is the basement of the church since the day you hid down there," Tony chimed in.

Amy turned to Father Michael. "Yes, the basement. We only had candles down there, but it looked very interesting. I saw an old tapestry moving. When I looked behind it, there was a crack in the wall with fresh air blowing through.

"Really?" Cain looked over at Michael with eyebrows raised.

Father Michael smiled. "That old basement of St. Francis has been there for a long time. Lord knows what's down there."

Chapter Sixty Nine

The repast finally broke up and everyone went their separate ways. After driving Katie and Father Victor back to the rectory, Father Michael and Amy walked down to the Divide and sat on their favorite bench. They watched the water flow and relaxed under another gorgeous blue sky. Amy seemed to struggle with something and then finally said, "Michael, I wanted to thank you for walking with me to the St. Francis statue that night. I don't think I could've done it alone."

"You never were alone and I wouldn't have let you go by yourself," Michael said, as he put his arm around her and gave her shoulders a small squeeze. "I'm very proud of you."

"For what?" Amy asked.

"In spite of everything that's happened to you this past year; you faced your fears and did what you thought was right for everyone involved. You had faith," Michael answered, and then quoted a Bible passage.

Be shepherds of God's flock that is under your care, watching over them - not because you must, but because you are willing, as God wants you to be; not pursuing dishonest gain, but eager to serve.

1 Peter 5:2 NIV

"You may have been away from the church for awhile trying to understand your sister's death and all the violence that's happened around you, but deep inside the Lord hasn't been away from you. He's been in your heart even if you're not at church. He's the real Shepherd, protecting, watching, guiding, and tending us. When we stray, he comes back and carries us, but we're never really alone because he's inside us.

Amy smiled up at Michael and looked back toward the Divide. She watched as the refreshing water flowed along with an energy that would always promise renewal and hope.

****

The boy from the nearby college was busily sweeping up around tables on Church Street in Burlington. The summer was ending and college students had started moving back in. The tourists would return when the foliage started to change. It was a good opportunity to clean up from the summer. As he straightened the table and chairs, a napkin fluttered to the ground and got stuck under a nearby potted plant. The boy bent to pick it up and found a flash drive, partially wedged under the pot. It was black, with the letters 'S' and 'F', surrounding a crook, all stamped in gold. Standing up and walking over to the shop owner, he said. "Hey, Mr. Flaherty. I found a fancy flash drive. Do you know whose it is?"

"No, I don't even know what it is," Mr. Flaherty said, looking at it. "You kids and your crazy music and electronic things."

"Is it okay if I keep it?" The boy asked eagerly.

"Keep it, burn it, whatever you want," the owner said, as he turned to go back inside.

The boy smiled and stuffed it in his jeans pocket as he went back to sweeping. "Thanks, Mr. Flaherty. I'll check it out in my multimedia class when the semester begins."

Fini

Made in the USA
Lexington, KY
03 July 2013